Runaway Cara

Therése Welch

First published as an e-book in 2015.

ISBN: 978-0-9943510-1-2
ePub: 978-0-9943510-0-5

All characters in this publication are fictitious. Any resemblance to
real persons living or dead is purely coincidental.

For Dave.

Acknowledgements

I would like to thank my sister, Jacky Baz for encouraging me to take my first shaky steps on this journey; and Dave, my ever-patient husband, for allowing me the time and the means to do this.

Thanks also to Mom, Lisa and Jacky for your feedback when I was done and all the friends, family and colleagues who were my first readers. Your support means the world to me.

To Ray Clarke and my fellow writers at the Sandgate Writers Group, thank you for your invaluable feedback as I wrote and re-wrote. I could not have done this without you.

Chapter 1

On a cobbled street in Dublin worn smooth by the centuries, Cara Sullivan watched her sister disappear into a crowd of Saturday morning shoppers. She shook her head in equal parts sadness and irritation. Today should have been a happy day, one with champagne and sisterly bonding – or at the very least a civil cup of tea. But Bridget just could not help herself. Within an hour they were at each other's throats, with Cara hissing at Bridget to back off and Bridget lamenting it was *nothing but a waste of time, coming all the way up from Waterford for this!*

With Bridget now gone from view Cara stepped in close to the building beside her, seeking shelter in the grubby stone façade as a light drizzle turned heavy. There was no point in ringing Peter. He was off at the football with his mates. The last thing he needed was a grumpy fiancée on the phone.

Not for the first time she wished that her friend Rachel still lived in Dublin. Mind you, in that case Rachel would have been her first choice for bridesmaid instead of Bridget and this morning's fiasco would never have happened. She dialled her brother's number instead. 'Hi Declan. Fancy a coffee?'

'Sure, where are you?'

She looked around for a street name.

'I know it,' said Declan. 'There's a place around the corner called *Ye Olde Coffee Shoppe*. Corny, I know, but they serve a great cappuccino. I'll meet you there in an hour.'

A blast from the heater above the door dissolved the chill that clung to her skin as Cara ducked into the dim interior. Her mouth watered at the sight of a giant slice of cheesecake topped with berries. It conspired with a rich aroma of roasted coffee to tempt her, but she resisted. Not with the wedding coming up.

She ordered a latté from a pasty youth behind the counter and glanced around for a seat. Wooden tables and chairs occupied every inch of space and the far wall was lined with high-backed booths. Being a Saturday morning, the place was jammed. Across the room three women stood wrapping themselves in coats, scarves and gloves. Keeping an eye on them, Cara wiggled her toes inside her shiny leather boots while the youth counted out her change.

'A waitress'll bring it to your table,' he mumbled but Cara was already on the move, for a man had walked in behind her and was headed straight for the newly vacated booth.

Oh no, you don't! Clutching coins in one hand and handbag in the other Cara shoved her way between tightly packed diners. The man saw her coming and picked up his pace. Her elbow connected with somebody's head. She grimaced but pushed on and they reached the table at the same time. His eyes narrowed and he looked her over from head to toe.

Cara sucked in her stomach, glad to be wearing her favourite jeans. Paired with a light knit top that showed off her curves beneath a blue leather jacket, she felt sexy under his appraising gaze. Wait, what was she thinking? In a couple of months she would be marrying Peter. Who cared if a stranger found her attractive?

'This one's taken,' she said and dropped her bag on the seat.

'Fair enough, but if he doesn't show I'll be right there.' He nodded toward a small empty table further along and moved on with a wink and a smile.

As she slid into the booth Cara's phone chirped inside her bag. She fished it out and read Bridget's message:

'Did you get sorted?'

Irritation returned. After her behaviour this morning, Bridget could damn well stew for a while. She stuffed the phone in her pocket and ran a hand through her shoulder-length auburn hair. An hour ago it had been properly long. Wandering into a salon that happened to have a free spot just when she had an hour to kill had been fate, as far as she was concerned. No doubt Bridget would disagree. She would have a fit if she saw how short Cara had cut it. A smug grin tugged at her lips, imagining her sister throwing her hands up in despair, the eternal drama queen. *What were you thinking, hacking it all off with the wedding so close? It's so typical of you, Cara. You never give a second thought to the consequences. Well don't come crying to me . . .*

That was Bridget's favourite punchline. *Don't come crying to me.* As if Cara ever would. Giving her hair one last pat, she scanned the room. What was taking Declan so long? And where was that mythical waitress with her coffee?

All around her cups and spoons rattled amid the hum of conversations and behind her a man laughed. How funny – he sounded just like Peter. The high seatbacks made it hard to eavesdrop between the booths but she caught snatches of a woman's voice and moments later the man laughed again.

Wow, he really did sound like Peter.

The back of Cara's neck prickled. She strained her ears. Around her the coffee-shop clatter seemed extraordinarily loud. Pressing herself back against the vinyl seat she tilted her head, like her father used to do with the TV aerial to try and get a better signal for his Sunday afternoon GAA game, but to no avail. Their voices were lost in the din.

Cara scolded herself for being paranoid. Peter had told her he was going to the football with his mates.

But then she heard it. 'You're gorgeous, you know, but you're a real muppet sometimes.' His familiar laugh followed and now there was no mistake. He had used those words on Cara a thousand times.

Curious, she got to her feet and turned around and sure enough there he was, six feet of blonde, blue-eyed charm folded into the next booth opposite a skinny brunette Cara had never seen before.

'Hello,' she said.

Peter looked up and his face drained.

'Well, Peter Reilly, speechless. That's a first.'

Peter glanced nervously at his companion. 'Uh, I . . .'

Cara forced herself to look at her. She expected to see guilt in her eyes to match Peter's, but the woman just looked confused.

'Peter? Are you going to introduce us?'

He groaned and avoided looking at either of them when he did. 'Simone this is Cara. Cara, Simone.'

Simone eyed her with hostility. 'Is that supposed to mean something to me?'

It seemed Peter had lost the ability to speak. He squirmed in his seat, reached up and rubbed his neck.

'Let me save you the trouble,' said Cara icily and stuck out her hand. 'Cara Sullivan. I am Peter's fiancée.'

Simone looked stunned. She turned to Peter. 'You have a fiancée?'

Cara dropped her unshaken right hand and held up her left, instead. She wiggled her fingers and the large solitaire diamond blinked obediently under the overhead lights. 'Yes, he has a fiancée. And you are?'

'Cara, please.' Peter reached out to lower her hand but Cara snatched it away before he could touch her.

At the same time Simone jumped to her feet so fast she bumped the table, causing cups and teaspoons to bounce and rattle in alarm. She paled before her face turned a deep, mottled red and she rounded on Peter.

'You low-down cheating piece of shite.'

Peter shrank into his chair and for a moment Cara thought the bony cow might strike him.

'Simone, calm down,' he said.

'Calm down?' she shrieked. 'You drop this on me and then have the nerve to tell me to calm down?'

'I—'

'You, nothing! Don't even *try* to justify yourself. You're engaged to another woman. I know, because she's standing right here! So much for this being something special – I cannot believe you had me fooled.'

'Simone—'

'Oh, save it,' she spat. 'I hope you burn in the pits of hell, two-timing scumbag that you are.' She turned her blazing eyes on Cara. 'Good luck with him, lady. You can have him.'

In a fierce motion, she swept up her belongings and stormed

off, bumping into the waitress on her way out. Hot coffee sloshed all over the girl's tray.

'Ah, thanks for that,' said the waitress and returned to the counter to mop it up. Cara wondered if the spilled coffee was hers. How odd that *that* was the thing that made her angry.

'Cara, won't you sit down, love? People are staring at us.'

She glanced around. Everything seemed so far away, like she was looking at the world through a fishbowl. A number of faces turned away rapidly. One did not. Two tables down the would-be table-thief offered a look of compassion that penetrated the fog and spurred her into action.

Her anger exploded and she rounded on Peter. 'Your girlfriend has quite a mouth on her. Or is this the part where you tell me it's not what it looks like?'

He flinched. 'Oh God. Cara, I'm so sorry you had to find out like this.'

'You're sorry I found out? How about being sorry that you cheated on me?'

'Of course, you know that's what I meant.'

'Really.' Her breath came fast and shallow. Tears choked in her throat.

'Cara, I'm sorry.'

'You already said that.'

He took a ragged breath. 'I never meant to hurt you.'

'Well you should have thought of that before you screwed wotshername.'

'Simone. Her name is Simone.'

There was no denial. Up until then Cara had been clinging to a sliver of hope that just maybe it had not gone that far. The truth lodged itself like a knife in her chest.

He looked instantly contrite. 'But it's over, I assure you.'

'Of course it's over,' she yelled. 'She just found out you have a fiancée. You are unbelievable! How stupid do you think I am? How long—' Her hands flew to her mouth as a thought struck her. 'Is this even the first time? Or have there been others?'

His face twisted in anguish. 'Cara—'

A wave of nausea rose in her throat. She shook her head. 'No, I can't do this.' With her right hand, she tried to slip the big, shiny diamond ring off her left hand. It caught at her knuckle. She tugged harder.

'Cara, what are you doing?'

She looked down, twisting and pulling in desperation. Why wouldn't the damn thing come off? The skin at her knuckle turned red, but the ring did not budge.

'Cara, stop it. Let's talk about this,' he pleaded, taking her throbbing hand in his.

She yanked herself free as a ball of uncontrolled rage rose inside her, erupted in a wail of frustration and *crack!* Before she knew it, she had slapped him.

A split-second of silence followed before the coffee-shop hum resumed, embarrassed at having witnessed such an emotional scene.

'No, Peter. Let's *not* talk about this.'

Her hand stung and a purple welt appeared on Peter's cheek. He stared at her in shock. She turned away from him and went to retrieve her bag. The strap got caught up in its tassels and she fumbled, trying to untangle it all.

'Come on, stay. We can work this out.'

'Leave me alone. I can't do this now.'

'Cara, don't be like that – hey man, what the hell?'

She looked back and was surprised to see her table rival blocking Peter's path. He was a good deal beefier than Cara had realised and he placed a restraining hand on Peter's shoulder. 'I think the lady has made it clear that she doesn't want you to follow her.'

'And just who the hell are you?'

'Call me an interested party,' he said and winked at Cara. 'Go ahead, love. I'll take care of this for you.'

Cara did not need a second invitation and with just a moment's hesitation, she fled. Clutching her coat and bag she stumbled out into the cold, her vision cloudy with tears.

Two steps out the door she collided with a bulky figure in a dark coat. She tried to move aside but the figure reached out to steady her.

'Whoa there, where are you going in such a hurry?'

His voice snapped her out of it. 'Declan?'

Her brother's familiar cheeky grin greeted her. 'The one and only. Say, I like what you've done with your hair.' With his stocky build, designer stubble and blue-green eyes so like Cara's own Declan looked every bit the knight-errant, swooping in to save her. Cara's lip quivered and relief washed over her.

'Hey, what's wrong?' he asked, wrapping her in a bear hug.

The instant she felt his arms around her Cara crumpled. She clung to him as if her life depended on it and gulped back a sob.

'Cara, what the hell?' He stepped back, searching her face. 'Man, you look awful. Come over here and sit down, will you?' He motioned to a table and chairs in front of the window of *Ye Olde Coffee Shoppe*, where the ground was littered with cigarette butts.

'No!' she cried, shooting a panicked look at the door.

'Why not?'

Cara grabbed his sleeve. 'Declan, not here. We have to go.'

'Go where?'

'Anywhere but here.'

'Cara, you're starting to freak me out.'

'Declan, come on, we've got to go. Now!'

She took off down the street with Declan in tow. A delivery van roared up behind them and hooted. They leapt out of the way and continued running on the uneven pavement. Her toes cramped up inside the points of her boots but Cara ignored the pain and turned a corner. Buildings passed by in a blur of grey stone, brick and brightly painted store fronts and people moved hurriedly out of the way of her pounding feet. A soft drizzle started up again, wetting her face and cooling her skin. She settled into a rhythm and the words repeated over in her head in time – *gotta go, gotta go, gotta go*. She clutched her bag tightly to stop it banging against her hip while its suede tassels jiggled madly about.

Half a block later Declan pulled her to a halt. A pod of tourists in leprechaun-green trousers stood goggle-eyed, watching to see what drama would unfold. 'Hey, Cara?' he puffed. 'I don't mean to question your authority but do you think you could clue me in on where we're headed and why we're in such a hurry to get there?'

She stopped, her cheeks flushed and her eyeballs stinging from the arctic wind that howled between the old grey buildings. Her breath steamed in the cold air. Shoppers snaked a wide berth around them; it was best to ignore people running through the streets. You never knew what mischief they were up to.

'Sorry,' she gasped as reality set in. She looked around. 'Honestly? I have no idea where we're going. Do you have any suggestions? I could do with a cup of coffee – or even something stronger, for that matter.'

'But we just came from – never mind, you are clearly insane,' declared Declan. 'Okay, I'll play along.' He led her to a traditional Irish pub a block away. It was the kind of place tourists sought out, with its name in gold Celtic letters on the window, dusty artefacts stuffed into nooks and crannies inside and the sour, centuries-old reek of beer spills vying with the smell of cooked food.

After fetching two Irish coffees from the bar he settled them into a couple of wing-backed chairs near the fireplace, away from the general bustle, and raised his glass. '*Sláinte.*'

Cara mirrored the toast but did not drink. Her skin was sticky under her layers of clothing, sweaty from her manic running, and the fire felt too hot for her already flushed cheeks.

'Well I got you your coffee *and* a drink, all in one glass. Are you going to tell me what's got your knickers in a twist?'

'How is it you know all the watering holes around here, Declan?'

'Ah now, a man has to have his secrets,' he said with his trademark cheeky grin.

Cara just stared at him and he shrugged, dropping the levity. 'I go out here. Socialising. You know.'

'You mean womanising.'

'Pot-*ay*-to, pot-*ah*-to.'

'Did you tell Peter about that coffee shop, the one you said we should meet at today?'

'How should I know? I suppose I may have mentioned it. What does that have to do with why you're behaving like a madwoman?'

'He's been having an affair,' she blurted and to her astonishment, nothing happened. No windows shattered. No alarms sounded. The sky did not fall on her head. Around them people chattered away and drank their drinks uninterrupted. Only Declan showed any sort of reaction, his eyes narrowing in anger. 'Why the little—'

'Yeah, I know,' said Cara. She took a sip of her drink at last. Beneath the creamy surface the coffee was hot and bitter. It burned a trail into her stomach and the whiskey bit at the ball of tension gathered there.

Declan shook his head and spoke in a tight voice. 'Do you want to tell me what happened?'

Her lip quivered again. Battling to keep her tears in check she nodded, took a deep breath and recounted the horrible scene in the coffee shop. It came out in disjointed bursts but he got the idea.

'I'll kill him,' he said.

Cara managed a watery smile. 'Thanks pet, but I don't think that'll be necessary.'

'Are you sure?'

'Yeah, I'm sure.'

'Let me know if you change your mind.'

She offered a watery smile and they sat in silence for a moment.

'Do you know what makes it even worse, though? While he was off sneaking around with Slutty Simone, I was out shopping for a wedding gown. With Bridget.'

Declan winced.

'Yeah, I know. But she *is* the sister. I'd have asked you but you'd look terrible in a bridesmaid's frock.'

He chuckled. 'So how did it go? Did you end up chewing the heads off each other?'

Cara rolled her eyes. 'Just about; it was a disaster. She bailed before I even had the last one back on its hanger. In the end, I walked out with nothing. Not that it matters now anyway.' The tears finally spilled down her cheeks and she wiped at them with the back of her hand.

'Ah, you poor thing. Here you go.' He handed her a crumpled serviette.

'Thanks,' she snivelled. 'I'm so glad you're here, Declan.'

'Yeah, just think – you could still have been with Bridget.'

They both laughed at that.

Cara sniffed again. 'I wish I'd never gone there.'

'Gone where?'

'That coffee shop. If I hadn't wimped out on the shopping, I would never have gone there and this whole thing wouldn't have happened.'

'Are you telling me you'd rather just not know? Really?'

She dropped her gaze, dabbing at her eyes with the serviette. 'I suppose not. Maybe. Oh, I don't know. I only know I'd give anything to not feel the way I'm feeling right now.' Her eyes welled up again. 'God, I hate that he's reduced me to this! I feel like one of those silly women in Eastenders.'

'I didn't know you were a fan.'

'I'm not, I'm making a point. Quit giving me a hard time.'

Declan toyed with his drink. 'Do you want to stay at my place tonight?'

Cara thought about the apartment she shared with Peter. It was in a fashionable block in Dublin 4, tastefully and expensively furnished. Peter had lived there since before Cara had even met him. 'I hadn't thought about it. Would you mind? I don't think I can face seeing him again today.'

'You can stay as long as you need to. I even have a spare toothbrush for you.'

She raised her eyebrows and he grinned.

'I always keep a couple around, just in case.'

'You're a man-whore, Declan, that's what you are.'

'Ah no,' he said, grinning, 'I'm more like a boy scout – always prepared.'

Cara chuckled. Trust Declan to lift her spirits. She drained her glass. 'Another drink before we head off?'

'Sure. I'll even spring for it,' he said, jumping up to fetch them from the bar.

In the moment that followed Cara felt more alone than she could ever remember. She shuddered. She'd have to get used to being alone. Thank God for Declan. Ever since childhood, he had always seemed to be protecting her from something – well, mostly from Bridget, really. But here he was, once again offering her refuge today.

And then what?

Cara banished the thought. It was only an hour since her future had disintegrated before her eyes, far too soon to contemplate the details of life after Peter. All she knew was that there would be no more wedding to plan, no honeymoon trip abroad to look forward to. No more Peter. No more happily-ever-after.

A tear trickled down her cheek and this time Cara did not bother to wipe it away.

The rest of the day passed in a blur. Two Irish coffees were followed by three shots of tequila and a quick stumble through Dunnes for a value pack of cotton hipsters and some socks. Declan also picked two tops off the sale rack for her so that she had no immediate need to return home and thus risk bumping into Peter. Their bright colours were not her normal taste but this was by no means a normal day.

Later that evening Cara sat on his sofa with her feet curled beneath her and watched as Declan picked up his keys and patted his pockets. He turned back at the door to look at her. 'Are you sure you'll be okay here by yourself?'

Cara gave a wan smile and lifted a goblet of red wine off the coffee table. 'Of course I will. I have this to keep me company.'

He hesitated.

'Oh, go on.' She shooed him away. 'You can't cancel your hot date just because your little sister's life is in the bog. Go. Have fun. I'll only have one glass, I promise. It'll help me sleep.'

He looked ready to protest but changed his mind. 'Right, well if you get thirsty there's more on the shelf above the microwave. Try not to disturb the neighbours when you start dancing on the furniture, will you?' He raised his hand in a little wave. 'I'll see you later.'

'Yeah, see you later.'

Her smile faded after the door closed behind him. The wine winked at her. What the hell, she thought and gulped a third of it down.

Declan's apartment was comfortable and surprisingly neat. Everything was either brown or beige, but in a neutral, functional way rather than a Seventies throwback way. She spied the TV remote wedged between the cushions on the other sofa. It was too far to reach without getting up so she stared out of the window into the night sky instead. Droplets of rain glistened on the glass from an earlier downpour and traffic noise drifted up from the streets below. She had never noticed it before but now it seemed loud in the empty apartment.

She sighed and swallowed another gulp of Shiraz. *Mm, fruity.* Before meeting Peter, Cara could not tell the difference between a Cabernet and a Riesling. Nor had she cared to. But under his careful guidance she could now pick out just the right bottle for any occasion. Right now though, she did not give a damn what she drank as long as it contained alcohol. To hell with the taboos of drinking alone; an exception could surely be made on the day a girl found out about her fiancé's betrayal.

A sob rose in her throat. She drowned it with another swig of wine and sniffed. Declan kept a box of tissues in the kitchen. She would get one when she fetched more wine. One glass? Like hell.

The opening bars of *The Wedding March* ripped into the silence and Cara jumped in fright. Her wine spilled over the rim of the glass and plopped onto her jeans but she ignored it, ferreting through her jacket until she found her phone. Good God, she *had* to remember to change her ring-tone.

The phone was being secretive: Private Number, it said.

Was it Peter? She pursed her lips. It could be anyone. If it *was* Peter she could always hang up.

'Hello?'

She heard some scratching on the line and then, 'Cara? Are you there?'

'Rachel?' She squeezed her eyes shut to hold back a fresh bout of tears that welled up on hearing her best friend's voice. 'Yes, I'm here. It's so good to hear from you.'

'Likewise. How the hell are you?'

'Me?' Cara swallowed. 'I'm doing okay. What about you? How are things in London these days?'

'Great,' enthused Rachel. 'Really great. The days are getting longer and the daff's are blooming. It looks like winter is over at last.'

'Right,' said Cara. 'And I'm sure you rang to talk about daffodils.' She drained her glass and stood. It was time for a refill.

'Ah, dear Cara. Paranoid as ever, I see. Can't a girl telephone her best friend just to chat?'

'Of course, pet. You can call me any time you feel the need to talk about flowers.'

Rachel's laugh sounded just a little too bright. 'Well there is something I could use your opinion on.'

'Sure, but just hold on one sec, Rachel,' Cara interrupted, 'Let me put you on loudspeaker.' She pressed the button and set the phone down on the kitchen counter.

'What are you doing?' Rachel's tinny voice filled the kitchen.

'Pouring myself something to drink.'

'What are you drinking?'

Cara studied the label for a moment. 'Shiraz. From Chile, apparently.' She yanked out the cork and tossed it in the bin.

'Sounds like a good idea,' said Rachel. 'Wait, is this a bad time? Do you have guests?'

'No,' Cara replied. 'No, in fact I have the place to myself so this is a brilliant time for you to call.' She filled her glass but it was just too small to take the last drops out of the bottle so she emptied them directly into her mouth.

'Cara, please tell me I did not just hear you chugging straight from the bottle.'

Cara licked her lips. 'Rachel, I cannot tell a lie. That is exactly what you just heard.' She picked up the phone again, took it off loudspeaker and carried it through to the living room, the full wine glass in her other hand. 'Want some?' she teased.

All she heard on the line were some scuffling noises.

'Rachel?'

'Yeah, hang on. I'm just pouring myself some Chardonnay. We can't have you drinking alone. You know what they say.'

Cara began to laugh and a moment later Rachel joined it. They laughed so hard that Cara's tummy ached and when their mirth subsided she gasped, 'Thanks, I needed that.'

'You're welcome,' said Rachel as she brought her giggles under control. 'Now, are you going to tell me why you're home alone getting sauced?'

'Strictly speaking I'm not home,' replied Cara. 'I'm at Declan's apartment.'

'Okay, that's even more weird. Why are you alone at Declan's place getting sauced?'

'Because I don't want to go home.'

'Would you care to elaborate?' Rachel pressed

Cara hesitated, fumbling with words in her head. 'Didn't you say you wanted my opinion on something?

'What?'

'I interrupted you earlier, when I was pouring my wine.'

'It was nothing.'

'But—'

'Jayses, Cara. Don't try and change the subject. What's going on?'

Cara's lip trembled and she fought not to lose control again before replying. 'All right, if you insist, I'll tell you.' She stared into the scarlet depths of her wine. 'Do you remember how I used to joke that Peter was too posh and sophisticated for a small-town girl like me?'

'Not that again. Cara, that's rubbish and you know it.'

'Or not, as it turns out.' She stared with unseeing eyes at the rain that had started up again and was now spattering on the window, winking in reflected light against the black night sky.

'What are you talking about?'

This was exhausting. Closing her eyes, Cara took a deep breath and in a rush of words she told Rachel about the terrible events of the day. By the end of the telling her tears flowed unchecked once more and a deep, agonising ache lodged in her chest.

'That bastard! How dare he? And no, Cara, don't you dare put yourself down like that. This is not your fault. Oh my God, I could wring his neck, you poor thing.'

The sympathy was almost too much for Cara to bear. 'Oh Rachel, it hurts s-s-so much,' she sobbed.

'I know sweetie, I know. Nothing hurts like a broken heart.'

Cara cried even harder. 'Oh hell, of course you know – I mean, this is not the same as what you went through, but—'

'It still sucks,' Rachel completed her thought.

Regaining control, Cara sniffed and wiped her cheeks with her sleeve, having clean forgotten to fetch a tissue. Comparing her cheating fiancé with the death of Rachel's husband felt wrong, but since Rachel had brought it up, 'How on earth did you cope when Phil died?'

'You'd be surprised just what you're capable of when you suddenly find yourself in a situation,' said Rachel tersely.

'Sorry, I didn't mean to bring that up. I shouldn't have said anything.'

Rachel's voice softened. 'It's all right and besides, this is about you now, not me. You're stronger than you think, Cara and your circumstances are different to mine. I don't know how you cope. You just do. What choice do you have?'

Cara sniffed again, mulling her words over. 'How's your wine?' she asked.

'Not great, if you must know,' confessed Rachel. 'It's been open a while in the fridge and it sort of tastes quite tart.'

Cara's mouth twitched. 'Remember that awful stuff we had in Ibiza that time?'

'Ugh! How could I forget? I still can't believe you made us stay and drink the whole bottle on top of all that Sangria. It was horrible! And all because of some hot Italian. What was his name again?'

'Nik. He was Greek though, not Italian – from Cyprus.' Cara had not thought of Nik in a while, other than a dream she'd had soon after Peter had proposed. It had lingered for a couple of days after, as if the last traces of him were unwilling to let go. It was funny, the things the mind dredged up when your emotions were all stirred around.

Rachel sighed. 'Sure, we had a great time when we were travelling together, did we not?'

'That we did, Rachel.'

'We should do it again some time.'

Cara snorted. 'How's next week for you?'

Rachel spluttered a laugh. 'I wondered how long it would take.'

'What's that?'

'Ah go on, Cara. You know what you're like. When the going gets tough, Cara gets going.'

'What are you on about?'

'You hate confrontation, my friend, more than anyone I know and you'll do anything to avoid it.'

'You mean like when I walked out on Peter today? Well what the hell was I supposed to do? I felt like someone had punched me in the head.'

'I know and I understand that it's just how you operate – Runaway Cara rides again,' she laughed.

'That's not very nice.'

'Ah, don't be so touchy. Think about it: when we met in College you told me that you couldn't wait to move from Waterford to Dublin because of the way your sister pushed you around.'

'I came to Dublin to study,' Cara said defensively. 'It wasn't because of Bridget.'

'You say that, but that was what, eleven years ago? You still haven't stood up to her and she still treats you like dirt. And then when you came to the end of College and you hadn't found a job and your parents were on your case about it, what did you do? You took off for Europe.'

'You came too, remember? It was our treat to ourselves for all our hard work.'

'Uh-huh, and what about Nik?'

'What's with all the talk about Nik, all of a sudden?'

'Cara, you were crazy about each other, but when things got complicated you ran straight back to Ireland rather than figure out a way around your obstacles.'

'Now you're just making things up,' Cara said crossly. 'Nik was the one who took off for bloody South America.'

'He asked you to go with him.'

'I was twenty-one! I had a life to start, and there were visa issues, and—'

'Yeah, yeah.'

Rachel's words hurt. Was that really what she thought of her?

'Having said all of that, a trip is not a bad idea,' said Rachel.

Still feeling offended, Cara eyed her almost-empty glass and nodded. 'Sure, there's nothing like a bit of booze to make a girl dream.'

A wistful silence fell as they each took a sip of their wine. They might have been in the same room, rather than separated by the Irish Sea.

Rachel spoke first. 'Mind you, we wouldn't have to go for as long as three months this time.'

'Come again?'

'Well, we're entitled to a holiday, aren't we?'

'Rachel, are you serious?'

'Yeah, I think I am. Come on Cara, let's go away somewhere

together.'

'What about work?'

'I'm sure our jobs can manage without us for a week or so. I have some leave days due to me. Now is the perfect time for me to take them. In fact, I just finished wrapping up a case this afternoon.' Rachel seemed to fade out for a moment and then she cleared her throat. 'I may as well take a proper break before they dump the next big one on me. What do you say?'

'I don't know.'

'What don't you know? It'll give you a chance to get away for a bit, to clear your head and figure out your next move.'

'My next move?'

'Jayses, woman, you can be dense sometimes! I don't mean to rain on your pity-party, Cara, but you have some decisions to make. For one thing, you can't expect to stay with Declan indefinitely.'

Cara frowned. She had been avoiding that particular issue all day. Perhaps Rachel had a point. 'Where would we go?'

'I don't know. Where would you like to go?'

'An island. I think it should be an island, don't you?'

'I do. Somewhere sunny.'

'Ooh, like Spain or the Mediterranean.'

'Wait, I have my laptop here. Give me a sec to log in.' Cara heard her tapping on the keyboard. 'Here we go, let's see now – the Canaries? Sicily? Hah! Of course! I've got it!'

'Got what? What did you find?'

'Cyprus, my little flight risk; we should go to Cyprus. According to the Internet it is *The Island for All Seasons.*'

'Nik is from Cyprus.'

'Oh, for goodness' sake – do you remember what part?'

'Not exactly, but I'm sure I'd recognise the name if I heard it.'

More keyboard tapping ensued. 'There's a nice-looking hotel here in a town called Limassol. Does that sound familiar?'

Cara screwed up her face, trying to remember. 'I don't think so.'

'Great. Limassol it is. Besides, it's a big island. Even if Nik *was* from there the chances of running into him must be a million to one. For all we know he's still in the jungles of South America. What do you say?'

Cara drained her glass and peered into the bottom of it, feeling decidedly tipsy. *Runaway Cara* or not, the more distance she could put between herself and Peter, the better.

'It sounds brilliant to me,' she said. 'When do we leave?'

Chapter 2

Twenty minutes later Rachel Jones hung up the phone and swilled the last of the overripe Chardonnay in her glass. It emitted a deceptively pretty glow in the glare from her laptop. The only other light in her living-room came from a small lamp that stood atop her bookshelf, a wonky do-it-yourself thing filled with law books and murder mysteries. A series of muffled thuds indicated that her upstairs neighbours were going to bed and Rachel concluded that it was probably a good idea for her to do the same.

She threw the wine down her throat and screwed up her face. Definitely past its sell-by date, but it did the job. When the table in front of her stopped spinning, she took aim with her mouse and then muttered, 'Bollocks!' at the message that blinked on her screen. The damn thing had been telling her for over a month that the printer was out of ink. She jotted the reference number down on one of the legal pads stacked beside her computer and dropped it into her briefcase. The itinerary would have to keep until she could print it out at work on Monday.

Her stomach knotted at the thought of work on Monday. Normally it was not an issue; Rachel liked her job as a paralegal. It kept her busy and challenged and her colleagues were a friendly bunch. There were the usual office politics, but nothing she could not handle. It was not by accident that she had gone from the blue-collar streets of Dublin's south-side to life in the fast lane at one of London's most prestigious law firms. She worked hard and she worked smart and if there was one thing Rachel prided herself on, it was her ability to remain calm in a crisis.

Today's events, however, had tested her beyond her limits. It was why she had rung Cara in the first place. Flighty though her friend could be, she gave great advice. Just not today. Today Cara had her own stuff to deal with - which did not help Rachel very much at all.

She slumped forward with her head in her hands, her elbows resting on the table either side of the laptop. 'Bollocks,' she said again.

The day had started out like dozens of other Saturdays, with Rachel heading in to the office after lunch to finish up some work. Her desk occupied a great spot beside a window at the far end of a small cubicle farm on the third floor of the building that housed the offices of Davenport Ogden Pike and Davenport. She had been quick to annex it after Mad Marion's sudden departure due to 'stress-related illness' a couple of months ago. Poor Marion; with her anxious hands, shrill voice and paranoid tendencies she'd been a nervous breakdown waiting to happen. There one day and gone the next, she was spoken about now only in hushed tones, as if the mere mention of her name might somehow infect others with a similar affliction. It had worked out well for Rachel, though. Now she even had a small potted plant at her desk – some sort of lily, according to the label. It was thriving in the abundance of natural light.

As expected, today she'd had the office to herself. She enjoyed coming in on the weekends. It was quiet then, allowing her to work uninterrupted. It made her feel a little rebellious, sitting there in jeans and a jumper instead of one of her dark tailored suits, her long blonde hair falling loose over her shoulders rather than neatly tied back. She pulled a fat case file from the cabinet beside her desk, settled her readers firmly on her nose and immersed herself in legalese.

Outside her window daylight faded to dusk. Rachel barely noticed the soft pink glow creep across the sky as the sun set. She may not have known that night had fallen at all if not for the need to switch on the shiny brass lamp that stood beside her lily plant. For a long while she was unaware of anything outside the pool of light at her desk until . . . *bang!*

Her head snapped up. Unmoving, she strained her ears in the silence. A sudden commotion outside brought her to her feet and she peered through the window, her senses on heightened alert. The service road here at the back of the building was deserted, but for three lads messing about with a football in the shadows below. One of them kicked it against a metal roller door and it thundered in protest. Rachel heaved a sigh of relief and laughed at her jitters. That's what came from having a fondness for horror movies! You couldn't even work in your own office at night without imagining all sorts of monsters. She sat down again, her desk an oasis of light in the empty office.

Moments later a loud click echoed across the floor and the overhead fluorescent lights blinked to life. Rachel screamed in fright as her eye caught a blur of movement on the other side of the coffee station and in a frantic display of bravado she snatched up the brass lamp from her desk and jumped to her feet.

'Hello? Is someone there?' She tried to step forward but the lamp's cord pulled taught, holding her back.

There was a scuff and a scrape and a moment where she thought she might die of fright, but then a voice reached her. 'Rachel?'

Its owner stepped into view and Rachel's knees gave way. She closed her eyes and sank to her chair. 'Jesse! You almost scared the life out of me. What are you doing here?'

'Same as you, I imagine,' her colleague replied. 'Uh, I think you can put that down now.'

She looked at the lamp still clutched in her hand and collapsed in a heap of nervous giggles. 'Oh my, I thought you were comin' to get me!'

He winked at her with a boyish grin that perfectly matched his grammar school speech. 'Would that be such a bad thing?'

She squeaked a laugh. *Did he really just say that?* Her head spun in the aftermath of terror. She cleared her throat and set the lamp back on her desk with shaking hands. 'Sure, don't we make a fine pair then? Saturday night and we're in here working.'

'Yes, the joyful life of a paralegal – awful, isn't it?'

Rachel shrugged. The movement felt jerky; her nerves were still zinging. 'I don't mind. I never thought I'd have a proper career, so—' She checked herself. Jesse had only arrived few weeks ago to replace Mad Marion. She hardly knew him well enough to confide in him. It must be fright making her babble on so.

But when Jesse smiled at her it was an open, friendly smile that reached all the way to his gentle brown eyes and made her want to tell him everything and anything. He did have lovely eyes. In fact, Rachel thought Jesse had lots of lovely things, from his black hair cut almost military short to the thin white sweater he wore that complimented his exotic olive skin and left little to the imagination. She wondered how it would feel to run her hands over it and her mouth went dry. *Easy, tiger!*

She swallowed. 'So, what's your story? You've only been here a short while and already you're working overtime?'

It was Jesse's turn to shrug. 'There's a big meeting on Monday. I want to be sure I have all my facts straight. You know how it is when you're the new kid – first impressions, and all that.'

In Rachel's opinion, his making a good first impression would not be a problem.

They stared at each other across an awkward silence which he eventually broke. 'How about I make us some tea? I was going to make myself a cup when you came at me with your lamp.'

'I did not 'come at you' with the lamp! I was only preparing to defend myself.'

'So you say,' said Jesse, laughing. 'Is that a yes to the tea, then?'

'I suppose I could do with a break.' She dropped her specs on her desk and followed him to the coffee station, rubbing her eyes and feeling a little giddy.

He topped up the kettle and switched it on. Rachel watched, mesmerised by the way his sweater rippled as he moved. She could not help herself. It was an awfully long time since she had been with a man. And he seemed like such a *nice* man! He was different to the sort she was usually attracted to – certainly far gentler in demeanour than Phillip had been. That was the trouble with soldiers; they were all such bloody tough guys. A small pang of guilt touched her at the thought of her dead husband. She cast it aside.

'Sugar?' Jesse asked.

'Yes, honey?'

He laughed at her little joke and she smiled back at him. 'Just one, thanks. And milk, if there is.'

He tried pouring some from the dispenser but only a drop emerged. 'It looks like we'll be drinking it black.'

Exaggerating her Irish lilt, she adopted a magical-mystery tone and moved closer. 'Ah but wait, laddie. There's a secret here that only I know.'

'Is that so?'

Rachel unfastened the latch on the side of the dispenser and swung the front panel open. The large milk bag sagged inside, all sucked in on itself now that it was empty. 'Well come on then, lend us a hand.'

'With what, exactly?'

'I'll wiggle the bag around like so, then whatever milk is left will run towards the hole at the bottom. All you need to do is pop a cup underneath and open the tap.'

He manoeuvred himself in next to her and complied gamely. The fresh scent of his aftershave tickled her nostrils and unsettled butterflies in her stomach. Rachel had trouble focussing on the task at hand.

'Wow, not just a pretty face,' he remarked as droplets of milk became a light but steady stream.

They stood so close that his breath warmed her cheek. Her heart raced. She sneaked a quick sideways glance and their eyes met. Oh mercy, he was going to kiss her!

Abandoning the milk, Jesse reached over and gently tucked a lock of blonde hair behind her ear. His hand came to rest at the nape of her neck. They stared at each other for a moment and then he pulled her closer. His soft, warm mouth met hers. He tasted delicious – all man, with just a hint of spearmint. She snaked her hands around him, relishing in the feel of his hard body under the soft fabric of his sweater. This was even better than she had imagined! His kiss grew more demanding. The chafe of his stubble against her cheek stirred up a surge of passion inside her and when at last they separated, it felt like an eternity had passed.

Jesse looked like he wanted to devour her. 'Definitely more than just a pretty face.'

'We shouldn't be doing this,' Rachel managed to whisper. Her knees felt decidedly unstable.

'Probably not. Do you want me to stop?' He traced the outline of her lips with his finger.

She shook her head and he smiled a wicked, irresistible smile, his grammar school manners having left the building. He went to kiss her again but she moved her head away.

'It's against company policy, you know,' she murmured, sliding her hand down his arm in a gentle caress. It was such a lovely arm, all firm and warm and masculine. A small sigh escaped her lips and Jesse groaned.

'Screw company policy,' he growled and pulled her to him again.

The memory of what followed was etched into Rachel's bones. Jesse's gentle nature had a dark, passionate side that had resulted in two broken cups and a handful of stripes on his back from her fingernails. Her eyes flew open, crashing her back to the present where lazy screensaver bubbles popped across her screen. Her heart rate was up and she felt warm and fuzzy in all sorts of places all over again. She groaned. True, it should never have happened but she had not the slightest regret. Her only problem was: what now? For as long as Rachel wanted to remember life had consisted of work, study and the occasional awkward dinner party. There was no time for men or dating, which had not been a problem until now. She shuddered as the memory of Jesse drenched her again.

When she had finally left the office – shaken, elated and just a little bit sore in places – London had been in full Saturday night mode. Traffic crawled through rain-drenched streets where taxis bore their fares about in varying degrees of sobriety while pedestrians huddled into their coats. The daffodils might be blooming but the nights still carried a sharp chill. The pot of instant noodles that Rachel had picked up from the 7-Eleven on her way home stood unopened on the kitchen counter. Her first order of business had been to ring Cara. Who else was she going to confide in? Cara might suck at solving her own problems but she always gave great advice. But then Cara had dropped her own bombshell, making Rachel's conundrum seem petty by comparison. Poor Cara. It wasn't her fault Peter was a tosser.

Rachel eyed the pot of noodles and her stomach growled. She slammed the lid of her laptop shut, carried her empty wine glass to the kitchen and stuck the noodles in the microwave. Perhaps the week away would give her some clarity. She sincerely bloody hoped so, because what had happened today had the potential to take her life to a whole new level of complicated.

The next day was Sunday and around eleven o'clock in the morning Rachel found herself staring in despair at a massive jumble of clothes on her bed. She should never have started this, but reruns of last night's encounter with Jesse had been looping over and over in her head all morning.

In an attempt to escape them, she had started picking through her wardrobe for things to pack for Cyprus. Two hours later every item of clothing she possessed had been hauled out of her cupboard. She had a sort-of system in place. Her obvious favourites had been re-folded and put back. What remained had been sorted into three loose piles on the bed: Cyprus, Goodwill and Undecided. Half of it she had not seen in years. She lifted a faded khaki pullover, standard military issue and stretched so wide it could probably fit two of her. It used to smell like Phillip. Now it smelled like stale cupboard. Time to go, she thought and tossed it into a heavy-duty bin liner at the foot of the bed that was already full enough to stand up on its own. Hangovers brought out her ruthless side.

Her phone hopped on her bedside locker, its shrill ring driving into her skull. Rachel dove across the bed to answer it, wreaking havoc on the already unstable piles. She expected to hear her mother's whiney voice but instead she heard a slightly hesitant, very male, 'Hi there.'

Her heart skipped a beat. 'Jesse? How did you get my number?'

'It's on the Intranet at work. I'm back in the office for a short while and was wondering what you were up to today – if you'd like to get together – you know, maybe eat, drink, talk.'

Rachel's calm-in-a-crisis deserted her. What did he want to talk about? Did he regret what had happened? Was he worried she would say something at work and get him fired? Ugh, did she really need this in her life?

'I thought we might meet somewhere,' said Jesse. 'How about Hyde Park? We could even pick up some snacks and a bottle of wine on the way and have a little picnic, if you like.'

Rachel squinted through the gap in her bedroom curtains to where the light was only slightly less dull than it was indoors. 'You do know it's pouring with rain, right?'

'Ah. No picnic then,' he laughed, 'How about coffee instead? There's no shortage of Starbucks in the city. Or you could have tea, if you prefer.' His tone deepened and softened. 'I know you enjoy a good cup of tea.'

Rachel's insides flipped and a warm flush consumed her from the knees up. 'Ah, play fair!' she said with a nervous giggle. His suggestion to meet was obviously not based on regrets, then.

'Haven't you heard? All's fair in—'

'Yeah, alright, let's not get ahead of ourselves,' she interrupted. Her eye fell upon the discarded khaki sweater. 'Look, I'd love to but today isn't really good for me.'

'I see. I've served my purpose, have I? Just a warm body for a one-night stand – use me up, then toss me aside. I get it.'

'Don't be an arse.'

He chuckled. 'Seriously, I'd love to see you today.'

'Me too, but I have things to do. I'm helping a friend.' She crossed her fingers at the lie.

'Should I be jealous?'

'Not even a little bit.'

After the call ended Rachel lay quietly for a while, phone in hand and her face buried in a scratchy woollen jumper. A one-night stand would have been so much easier. Just a shag, albeit a spectacular one. No complications. A stray fibre tickled her nose and she sneezed. Another one for the bin, she thought and scooped up the jumper as she struggled to her knees. The chaos of clothes mocked her. She could be on her way to meet him for coffee right now. It was a tempting thought, to say the very least.

'Bollocks,' she muttered and sat down heavily on the edge of the bed. She would have loved to have met up with Jesse today. If they lived in a vacuum she would not have hesitated. But they did not live in a vacuum. They lived in a world where both of their livelihoods depended on Davenport Ogden Pike and Davenport. If the firm found out about them she might very well lose her job. Rachel needed her job. Hell, she *liked* her job.

There were other issues, too, but the work thing was enough of a complication on its own. She shook herself and began to fold the clothes in the Cyprus pile with renewed vigour. This trip away could not come soon enough.

She rose early on Monday morning, dropped two stuffed refuse sacks at a clothing bank and reached her desk long before the rest of her colleagues began to trickle in. The cleaner – an older woman who spoke no English – was wiping down the counter at the coffee station. She bobbed her head in greeting and Rachel smiled back and tried not to blush at her memory of what had occurred there over the weekend. Pushing her wanton thoughts aside she retrieved her notepad from her briefcase, navigated to the travel website on her computer and keyed in her reference number. Minutes later the laser printer at the end of her row whirred to life and spat out her itinerary, which she folded and stowed in her bag. Next, she filled in a Leave Request form and left it on her boss's desk.

That done, she busied herself with the work she had intended doing on Saturday before Jesse had distracted her with his rippling biceps. Her sigh morphed into a grin that she hoped nobody saw.

At five past nine, her boss summonsed her to his office.

Dressed immaculately in a pin-stripe suite, the younger Mr Davenport had the sort of face that would do well in politics: clean-cut without being too handsome, with his brown hair slicked back and rimless glasses perched on his nose. His steady gaze inspired confidence and trust and he was a damn good lawyer. Rachel regarded him with a healthy dollop of respect laced with just a teensy bit of fear.

He held up her Leave Request form, tapping at it with his forefinger. 'Going somewhere?'

'That's the plan,' she replied brightly.

'I hope you haven't paid a deposit yet.'

Her heart dropped. 'Is there a problem?'

'This is very short notice, Rachel. I'm not sure we can spare you right now.'

'The Hanson case is just about wrapped up now, Mr Davenport. I'll easily get everything done by the end of the week. I thought I'd use up some of my leave days now while I'm not in the middle of anything.'

'There is a meeting this morning that I'd hoped to get you in on, to do with the Lazenby thing.'

'I thought Jesse was assigned to that.' She said his name without a flinch.

'He is, but as you know he has not been here very long. I thought he might benefit from some assistance.'

In other words, you want me to babysit, thought Rachel. 'I had no idea.'

His eyes narrowed. 'Apparently. Is everything alright with you?'

'Sure, yeah, of course,' she replied. 'Everything's fine.'

He stared at her a moment longer. It was a piercing look, the kind that might make you wonder if he could read your thoughts. Rachel bit her tongue and stood her ground.

He blinked and life resumed. 'I would prefer you to delay for a couple of weeks.'

'I've already paid for the flights,' she said, surprised at how firm her voice sounded.

His eyebrows arched in surprise. 'You seem quite determined about this.'

Rachel maintained eye contact but said nothing.

'I see. And what if I insist?'

'Are you insisting?'

After half a beat, his face crinkled in amusement. 'Well, well, you're turning into quite the ruthless negotiator, Ms Jones.'

'I wasn't—'

'How are your studies going? You are studying Law, aren't you?'

'I – yes – it's going very well, thank you.'

'Good. We'll be lucky to have you once you have your degree.' He plastered her leave form on his desk and signed it with a flourish. 'Enjoy your time off. You can catch up on the Lazenby thing when you get back.'

A little thrown by her boss's sudden change in demeanour, Rachel made her way back to her desk. She passed Jesse along the way, shoulder-to-shoulder with a handful of colleagues, no doubt on their way to the Lazenby meeting. Their eyes met and held for a moment – not long enough for anyone to notice but long enough to unsettle her even further. Her insides clenched and he winked at her. Good Lord, how was she ever going to get through the week?

As it turned out she need not have worried. The Lazenby case kept him tied up in meetings and working well into the evenings. She saw him a few times, but only from a distance and never alone, which suited her fine because she could tell by the way her bits tingled whenever she saw him that time alone with him would only result in one outcome and Rachel was not ready for that. She needed to get her head straight first.

On Thursday evening, she was halfway through a carton of spicy Chicken Tikka Masala at her dining table with her law books open in front of her when her mobile rang. This time she recognised the number and her heart did a flip-flop. She briefly considered not answering, but her tingling bits won out.

'I had hoped we'd at least get to have lunch together this week, but this case has me running around like a crazy person,' said Jesse.

They chatted easily for a while and afterwards she slumped into one hand and poked at the lukewarm remains of her food with her fork. This was so unfair. She really liked him and unless she was reading things completely wrong, he liked her too. That night she dreamed that she and Jesse were running down a beach being chased by stern-looking men in pin-stripe suits. If they could just make it to the aeroplane in the parking garage, they would be safe! She woke up in a cold sweat and afterwards slept in fits and starts until her alarm went off at five forty-five.

By Friday afternoon her desk was clear. She dumped some water in her lily plant, washed her old coffee mug and placed it on top of the pile of notepads that seemed to accumulate around her. She checked her watch – five to four. There was a retirement party downstairs for one of the secretaries and most people had already started packing up and heading down. Some had left already. She had no idea where Jesse was – hopefully in a meeting somewhere. Her nerves were frayed from trying to avoid him. A week had brought her no closer to resolving her concerns about getting involved with him. Every moment spent in his company made it harder for her to think clearly.

She shrugged on her coat, made her way out to the lifts and pressed the button. The mechanism whined and she watched the floor numbers light up.

One. In a few minutes, she would be clear of the building, with a week of breathing space ahead.

Two. She sensed his presence before he spoke, the back of her neck prickling at his proximity.

Three. His voice sounded a little husky when he said, 'If I didn't know better I might think you'd been avoiding me.'

'Not at all.' She had to concentrate to make sure her voice did not squeak.

Ping! The doors slid open to reveal an empty lift. They both stepped inside and their hands went for the panel at the same time. Rachel snatched hers away as if she had been scalded.

Jesse smiled, his composure apparently intact.

'Allow me,' he said and pushed the button for the ground floor. The door hissed closed.

'Alone, at last,' he breathed and reached for her.

Rachel flushed at the physical contact and swept an imaginary strand of hair away from her face.

He frowned. 'Is something the matter?'

'I'm just not sure about all this.'

'This? What, you mean you and me?'

She gulped.

'Look, Rachel, I really hope you don't think I'm in the habit of – uh—'

'Praying on helpless women in the work place?' she offered with an evil grin.

He laughed. 'Hell, no! But listen, this thing with you and me, it is more than that. You know that, right? I know it's complicated, but...'

He stopped talking and edged closer.

Dear God, how was a girl supposed to resist? The man smelled like an ocean breeze, for crying out loud.

Ping!

The ground floor arrived and Rachel turned quickly to face the doors as they opened. Jesse, too, resumed his public face.

The lobby was busy with people. Jesse stepped out first and gestured in the direction of the canteen.

'Can I buy you a drink?'

'It's an open bar.'

'I try not to get hung up on details.'

'Clearly,' she said and laughed. 'I'd love to, but not today.'

'Hot date?'

She shook her head and started to back away.

'I'm sure Jenny would appreciate you making an appearance at her retirement party. Besides, it's Friday. There's always time for a drink on a Friday.'

Rachel laughed again. She seemed to do that a lot around Jesse. 'Her name is Di. And I can't.' She hated lying to him so she bent the timeline on the truth instead. 'I have to help a friend.'

'Same friend or a different one?'

'Same one.'

'Is he tall, dark and handsome? What's his name? I bet I could take him.'

Grinning, she replied, '*Her* name is Cara and I wouldn't bet on it.'

And then she was outside in the crisp London air and walking briskly away towards the Tube station, resisting the urge to turn back to see if Jesse was still watching her.

Chapter 3

After a bumpy flight from a freezing cold morning in Dublin, the sight of Rachel waiting for her in the Arrivals hall at Gatwick Airport brought a fresh flood of tears to Cara's eyes. She was exhausted from too little sleep and too much crying.

'We'll have less of those, you hear?' Rachel scolded as she hugged her hello.

Cara sniffed and laughed. 'They've been ambushing me all week when I least expect it. But these are happy tears, pet.' She held Rachel at arm's length and looked her over. 'You look gorgeous! You've put on a few pounds. It suits you.'

'You're the only person I know who can turn 'you're getting fat' into a compliment.'

'Well it is. Last time I saw you, you were nothing but skin and bone. This is much better – like a twenty-first century Marilyn Monroe. You have a real glow about you.'

Rachel blushed. 'Whatever you say. As for you Cara, you look, um . . .'

Cara rolled her eyes. 'Bloody awful, I know. Don't even bother to pretend otherwise. Between the random tears and getting up at four AM for the flight there's not enough make-up in the world to fix this.' Not that she had tried all that hard.

She sniffed the air. 'Do I smell coffee? Do we have time to drink something before our flight?'

They bought two large cappuccinos and a couple of pastries at a café in the duty-free area. Rachel paid while Cara raced a surprisingly determined pre-teen with pigtails for the only free table. The girl glared at her as Cara flung herself triumphantly into a slippery wooden chair. She thought about the last time she had beaten someone to a table. It was almost exactly a week since her doomed encounter in that coffee shop.

'You always did have a talent for finding a good seat,' said Rachel when she followed a minute later. Squeezing past their luggage to get into a chair, she pointed to Cara's scarlet wheelie bag. 'That's very posh. Is it new?'

Cara nodded. 'Declan gave it to me. It matches the big one I checked in. I think he was going to give them to us as a wedding gift.' She bit into the pastry. Sticky sweet apple and icing sugar knocked back the lump that rose in her throat. She chewed and swallowed, giving her time to compose herself. 'He went to the apartment to collect some of my stuff during the week. When I got home from work these were waiting for me too.'

'That was thoughtful of him.'

'He's been great. I think he's rather enjoying taking care of his little sister. I wasn't sure about leaving him to choose what clothes to bring me but he actually did a pretty good job.'

'Don't tell me he's finally got the hang of co-ordinating colours.'

'To be honest, it wasn't hard. He brought about ninety percent of my wardrobe.' She smiled at the thought of Declan staggering to his car under the weight of her clothes.

'I take it you haven't seen The Bastard, then?'

'Peter?' Cara's heart and her voice hardened at the mention of him. She shook her head. 'I've not spoken with him, either. He called my mobile a few times but I didn't answer. Thank God for caller ID.'

Rachel nodded. 'Did you have any trouble getting time off work?'

'No. I must look pretty awful because my boss hardly said a word and she can be a real bitch about it. How about you?'

She polished off her pastry and set to work on her cappuccino while Rachel spoke.

'Davenport Junior gave me a bit of a hard time, but in the end he said yes. It was kind of a weird conversation. I got the feeling he has plans for me. Did you tell the bitchy boss-lady what's going on?'

'No. There is no reason for her to know what's going on my personal life.'

'I see. So, work is still going well, then?'

Cara grimaced and rubbed her temples with both hands. 'I swear if I did not need the money I'd never go back. It's so good to be getting away this week. I hate working there. There's so much backstabbing in that office, I hardly know which way to turn.'

'Sounds charming. Here, you have icing sugar in your eyebrow.' Rachel leaned across and wiped it off with a paper serviette. 'What do you do when I'm not there? Walk around with food all over your face?'

'Thanks, Ma.'

'You could always change jobs, you know.'

'What, so that I can go do the same old thing in a different office?' She shook her head. 'I know I need a change, but I want to figure out what I actually want to do first. There has to be som—'

The airport announcer's disembodied interrupted her.

'Passengers Jones and Sullivan travelling to Cyprus, please make your way to the boarding gate immediately.'

'Holy moly, is that the time?' squealed Rachel.

Abandoning the last of their cappuccinos they grabbed their bags and pushed their way out of the cramped cafeteria. Cara stumbled on a stray foot and her hip smacked into the corner of a table. She winced and looked up into the spiteful gaze of young Pigtails.

'Cara, come on!' Rachel urged.

With one last scowl at the girl, Cara hurried on. They dashed past the duty-free shops and crowded departure lounges with their wheelie bags in tow. Cara cleared a path while Rachel followed, squinting at her boarding pass as she ran. 'Stop, it's this way!' she yelled and Cara had to backtrack to follow her.

A stern-looking woman in a bland uniform was waiting for them at the boarding gate. Everyone else had gone. She held out her hand. 'Boarding passes.'

Gasping for breath, they handed them over with unsteady

hands.

'Passports,' the woman ordered.

Cara and Rachel exchanged a glance and plastered suitably serious expressions on their faces while the woman scrutinised them. 'She's wondering if that's your natural colour,' Cara murmured and Rachel choked on a giggle.

The woman glared. 'I'll be keeping an eye on you two,' she said and waved them through. 'Go on, you're holding everyone up.'

'She'll keep an eye on us? What the hell does that mean?' Rachel whispered, but Cara withered under the looks of disapproval that followed them down the narrow aisle. She fixed an apologetic half-smile on her face and bumped her way forward. It seemed to take forever to reach their seats near the back of the aeroplane.

'Here we are,' said Rachel at last and shoved her bag into the overhead locker before shimmying into the window seat.

Cara eyed the space in the locker and hoisted her bag over her head, realising too late that she had misjudged her aim and one of the wheels was caught. She shifted her weight, her face flushed with effort, but the seat was in her way and she overbalanced. Her little red suitcase teetered. She had a horrific vision of the bag slamming down onto the little old lady in front of her before a pair of strong arms caught the bag mid-tumble.

'Let me help you with that.' The cabin attendant, dressed in the grey uniform of Cyprus Airways, wiggled the bag into the locker with ease. The little old lady had her nose buried in a magazine and appeared none the wiser.

Cara thanked him with her face flushed. Why was it always the handsome men who caught her in awkward moments? She swung herself into the seat beside Rachel with a bump.

Rachel nudged her. 'Are you blushing?'

'Did you *see* him?'

Rachel leaned across and peeked up the aisle to spy on the attendant's retreating form before replying with a low whistle, 'Nice.'

'Gay,' said the little old lady from behind her magazine and the businessman across from her lowered his newspaper to sneak a glance of his own.

Cara sputtered into giggles just as the loudspeakers crackled to life and a stern voice announced, 'Ladies and gentlemen, thank you for your patience. Now that all our passengers have decided to join us we will close the doors and begin preparing for our departure to Cyprus.'

'Geez, she doesn't hold a grudge at all, does she?' said Rachel and Cara's giggle turned into full-blown laughter. It felt great after the bleakness of the last seven days and as the ground fell away beneath them and the prospect of a week in Cyprus with her best friend beckoned, Cara felt the first thread of hope take hold. An hour in Rachel's company and already the heaviness in her heart had begun to lift. Perhaps she might survive life a without Peter after all.

They touched down at Paphos Airport, in the south-east corner of Cyprus, around sunset. Cara stopped for a moment at the top of the aircraft stairs. She could see over the rooftop of the airport buildings to where the ocean glittered with the light of the sinking sun. It bathed the world in an orange glow and a light breeze tickled her hair. She breathed it in like a tonic.

Rachel prodded her in the back. 'Get a move on, will you?'

Reluctantly Cara descended the stairs and crossed the tarmac to the compact airport terminal, her scarlet wheelie bag bouncing over the rough surface behind her.

'I think I'm in love with this place,' she said as they approached the customs queue.

'Don't be daft. You just got here.'

'Yes, but there's something in the air. I can't explain, it feels so—'

'Warm?'

Cara laughed. 'It has been a long winter.'

After they had reclaimed their luggage, a young man with a clipboard and a name tag that read 'Trevor' directed them to where a number of luxury coaches huddled under palm trees outside. Each coach had its own destination. Following Trevor's directions, they found the one for Limassol.

By the time he had ticked off all the names on his clipboard and joined them on board, twilight had settled on the island and their coach was nearly full. Trevor delivered his welcome-to-Cyprus speech in an appropriately preppy manner but kept it mercifully short and Cara was glad when he switched off his microphone.

As they left Paphos behind, the steady drone of wheels and engine made conversation difficult. Within minutes the coach was hurtling along a motorway and with little to see in the darkness outside and the smooth rocking motion beneath her, Cara had a hard time keeping her eyes open. The four AM wake-up and the change in time zone had her feeling disoriented and exhausted. She slept, waking just in time to see lights of Limassol city twinkling into view.

Rachel grinned at her in the flashes of passing streetlights. 'Welcome back, sleepyhead.'

'How long was I out?'

'About an hour. We're here now. It shouldn't be too much longer to our hotel.'

The coach rumbled through a maze of wide streets past squat, square houses and brightly lit shops with their names emblazoned on signs and walls in bold Greek lettering. The sun-bleached roads looked dusty, the buildings parched and everything washed of colour in the night light. How different to mossy grey Dublin, where the ground never truly dried out even after a rare week of sunshine.

Half an hour later the driver was still working furiously to manoeuvre the bus around tight corners and narrow streets in a part of town populated with hotels and holiday apartments. Every so often he would stop to offload people and luggage. Trevor was one of the first off.

'I thought you said it wouldn't be long,' Cara grumbled. 'Are you sure he hasn't forgotten us?'

'Don't get testy. Our hotel must be on the far side of town. Next time you can pick the accommodation, if you prefer.'

Cara bit her lip. Rachel had a point. She had made all the arrangements – Cara was just along for the ride.

At long last the driver indicated that they had arrived and Cara hauled herself to her feet and stepped off the bus feeling stiff and tired. But that soon evaporated as she gazed up in awe at the grand hotel that reached up into the sky before them, its balconies ablaze with light. Five stars perched proudly over a sleek entrance at the apex of the sweeping driveway.

She gaped. 'Wow, is this us?'

'No, this is the Hotel Somptueux,' replied the driver in a gravelly voice. He pointed behind her. 'That is your hotel over there, next door. We stop here because there is no space to turn around over there.'

He offloaded their luggage with a thud, slammed the hold shut, waved goodbye and drove off into the night.

Rachel had already started walking and Cara discarded a mild sensation of abandonment and hurried to follow her. A trimmed hedge obscured her view of the Lionheart Hotel but she supposed it looked alright, what she could see of the upper storeys anyway although it was less lit up than the Hotel Somptueux and less – well, just less.

They ducked through a gap in the hedge and crossed to where a patch of yellow light spilled out through the glass front doors. These slid open to reveal a haven of huge potted palms, solid square pillars and marble floors the colour of beach sand. Cara nodded her approval. It may not be the Hotel Somptueux, but it held an air of elegance she could definitely get used to.

At the sound of their luggage clacking to a halt on the shiny floor a short, round woman emerged from a small office behind the Reception desk. She had a nest of platinum blonde hair piled high on her head and Cara guessed her age to be somewhere between thirty-five and fifty.

In a sing-song voice reminiscent of an excitable Sybil Fawlty she introduced herself as Sue, barely pausing for breath as she told them, 'You'll need to hurry now because dinner will be finishing up soon.

Leave your bags under there,' she flapped a hand at an ornate hall table bearing piles of brochures and a big blue telephone, 'And head on down those stairs – yes, over there beside the big mirror.

You'll see the dining-room at the bottom by the pool. We'll take care of your keys and what-not once you've eaten something. *Bon appétit!*'

A happy laugh bubbled its way up out of her as she returned to her little office.

Cara stared after her in confusion. 'She didn't even ask our names.'

Rachel shrugged. 'Maybe she's psychic. Come on, I'm famished and you heard the lady.'

Following Sue's instructions, they stowed their luggage and clattered down a marble staircase that sported a beautiful wrought iron bannister fashioned to look like a grapevine.

The dining-room below was entirely devoid of diners aside from a grey-haired foursome who occupied a table near the buffet. Four pairs of bespectacled eyes scrutinised them before returning to their meal in silence.

Cara's mouth twitched and she murmured, 'So this is where the cool kids hang out.'

Rachel grunted at her elbow as they crossed to the buffet, where a man with an impressive moustache stood beneath a deflated chef's hat, ready to serve dinner. The wall behind him was adorned in brightly painted murals of fruit trees, flowers and Greek columns that added a noisy dimension to an otherwise bland room.

The chef looked like he hadn't moved in hours but he sprang to life to ladle rice and a dollop of casserole onto a couple of plates for them before resuming his post. They carried their dinner to a table for two set in a glass corner. On one side, huge sliding doors led to an alfresco bar area that was floodlit and unattended. On the other side floor-to-ceiling windows overlooked an illuminated swimming pool.

After the long day of travel Cara appreciated the peace and civility of it all. As if to reinforce the contrast, no sooner had she flapped her napkin onto her lap than a waiter materialised, wearing a dark green waistcoat over a starched white shirt. His swarthy face was presided over by heavy eyebrows and black hair slicked back to reveal a widow's peak. When he spoke, he pronounced each syllable in a deep baritone laced with a thick accent and accompanied by a slight bow. 'Good e-v-e-ning. I am Stevan. Can I get some wine for the ladies tonight please?'

Cara stared at him. 'Sure, why not? I could do with a drink. What do you recommend, Stevan?'

He thrust a wine list into her hands. 'Yes, you look here, I come back,' he said and disappeared before she could object.

'What a strange little man,' said Rachel.

'I feel like we've fallen into a sitcom. Are these people for real? Do you think they have cameras hidden somewhere?' Cara looked around with suspicion.

Rachel responded with a snort of laughter that drew disapproving looks from the grey-haired foursome.

'Oh, get a life,' mumbled Cara and tucked into her food, which turned out to be a spicy chicken dish with a hint of nutmeg that washed down well with a glass of the house white that Stevan eventually brought for them.

Afterwards, stuffed from dinner and mellowed by wine, they made their way back up to Reception. Cara was relieved to find their luggage exactly where they left it, although quite what ill fate might have befallen it in her absence she could not say. Sue materialised to breeze through the check-in process with practised efficiency and within minutes they each had an electronic key card. At last! Cara could hardly wait to flop down on a bed, or maybe soak in a bubble-bath.

Rachel had other ideas, though. 'Where would we go to have a couple of drinks around here?' she asked Sue.

Cara hid her dismay while Sue pondered the question. After a moment, she pointed over her shoulder. 'Well there's the hotel bar, just there.'

Cara poked her head around the corner to take a look. The lobby opened up into a spacious lounge area where a number of sofas, chairs and coffee tables were artfully arranged under bright but soft lighting between large columns and leafy plants. On the far side, she spied a polished bar and pool table in the shadows and beyond that, a smaller lounge area. The lights had been dimmed and both were deserted.

She looked back at Rachel with a subtle shake of her head, hoping that would be the end of it, but Rachel smiled at Sue and tried again. 'We were thinking we'd like to go out somewhere. It is Saturday night, after all.'

'Ah.' Sue nodded slowly and winked in understanding. 'Well in that case—'

A loud crash from somewhere down the passage behind them startled them all. Sue stalled, her eyes wide. A moment later

Stevan appeared. He bobbed his head in greeting but scurried past unchecked and vanished down the corridor past the lifts.

Sue cleared her throat. 'Drinks, yes, let me see. There are a few places around Old Town. That's near the port, although you're probably better off going there in during the day.' She tapped her finger thoughtfully against her chin. 'Or you could go into the Tourist Area, where most of the night clubs and bars are. It's straight down this main road that we're on. But it's too far to walk. You'd probably want to take a taxi.'

Stevan scuttled past again, this time with a woman in tow, dressed in a grey pinafore and carrying a mop. They both bobbed their heads at Cara and Rachel as they passed.

Sue went on, unperturbed. 'There is also the Irish bar in that direction and it's a bit closer than the Tourist Area, maybe a couple of kilometres. That's quite popular. You do not want to go to the place next door,' she said, lowering her voice. 'I've heard they spike the drinks there. You need to be careful, two girls alone.'

Cara wondered which place she was referring to – presumably not the Hotel Somptueux.

She sighed. This all sounded far too complicated after her long day. She stole a glance at Rachel. Maybe she would change her mind and Cara would get that bubble-bath after all.

'Or,' Sue paused with her head tilted, 'You could go to Harry's Bar. You might like that, actually. It's just over the road and one block up.' She leaned over the counter and pointed through the sliding glass doors. 'Just past those red and blue lights you can see there. It's owned and run by an Englishman.'

'Harry?' Cara asked.

'No, actually his name is Martin.'

'Of course it is.'

The mop lady came sidling past again, muttering to herself. Cara avoided looking at Rachel, knowing that to do so would make them both start giggling again.

Sue continued, unperturbed. 'Yes, that's a good idea; they'll look after you girls all right, over at Harry's.'

She beamed at them and they thanked her, grabbed their gear and hastened to the lifts. There were no more crashes and no more mop ladies but Cara had been right about the giggles, which erupted as soon as they were safely in the lift. Cara contemplated putting her bubble-bath theory out there, but changed her mind. She had been moping around Declan's flat all week. A night out might do her some good.

Though probably not as plush as the ones next door at the Hotel Somptueux, their room on the fourth floor had everything they might need: comfortable twin beds, a television, desk, armchair and a large marble en-suite bathroom that gleamed in hues of blue and grey. Best of all was the small private balcony that overlooked the sea, even though Cara could not see much beyond the lights of the hotel right now. A burst of chilly air gusted in as she slid the door open. The balcony was just wide enough for a couple of plastic chairs and a small table. Perfect for sundowners but perhaps not for after-dark loitering. She quickly banged the door shut again to kill the draught.

Rachel claimed the bed near the window by hoisting her suitcase onto it. After a bit of rummaging she asked, 'Is it warm enough for this?'

Cara studied the flimsy sleeveless top that she held up for inspection and a short debate on the weather ensued. They both settled on sparkly jeans and high heels. After showering off the travel grime it felt good to dress up. Before long a jumble of cosmetics had exploded across the bathroom as the women elbowed each other for mirror-space. By the time they were ready it was almost nine-thirty.

'To Harry's Bar?' Rachel enquired.

'To Harry's Bar,' echoed Cara, revived after her shower. The bubble-bath could wait until morning. But a few minutes later, shivering in a puddle of light beside the busy road outside their hotel, she had a moment of regret. 'Summer holiday, my arse! I should have worn my coat.'

Spotting a gap in the traffic she dashed across the road as fast as her high heels would allow, with Rachel right beside her. The icy night air sliced through her chiffon top and snatched at her bare arms. But thankfully, Harry's Bar was as close as Sue had said and they found it after only a short walk. Nonetheless, they were both a little breathless and rosy-cheeked by the time they reached it. Inside the pub was warm and cosy, if somewhat dim. Pockets of people huddled around a televised football match that flickered on a cloud of cigarette smoke and the place erupted as someone scored a goal.

Cara hated football. She had never been a fan, but since learning that Peter had taken advantage of that to meet his mistress, her disinterest had turned into loathing. 'Great,' she muttered.

'Do you want to go somewhere else?' asked Rachel without enthusiasm.

Cara shook her head and pointed to an empty table near the window, far away from the televisions. It hardly seemed worth it to go back out into the cold in search of another pub. A young waitress approached and they ordered two local beers.

'I'll get this,' said Cara and fished in her purse for Cyprus Pounds. 'Oh hell, I really should take my Euros out of here so I don't get mixed up with the money—' She stopped suddenly and stared.

'Did you find a monster in there?' Rachel joked.

Cara's attention was riveted on the ring that winked up at her. Slowly she withdrew it from the folds of her purse and held it up for Rachel to see.

Rachel's smile faded. 'Oh.'

'I forgot I put it in there. It wouldn't come off at first but then it did, later. I didn't want to leave it lying around Declan's place so I dropped it in here for safe-keeping.' She turned it around, mesmerised by the way it threw out rainbow stars as it moved. 'I wanted a smaller one, you know, but he insisted on this one. Bigger is better, as far as Peter bloody Reilly is concerned.' She gave a hollow laugh.

'Are you okay?' Rachel asked.

Cara cleared her throat and nodded, dropping the ring back where she found it. It would just have to stay there for now. In a superb act of perfect timing the waitress returned with two bottles and a couple of frosted glasses, set them down on the table and flashed them a toothy smile.

'Enjoy,' she said as Cara paid her. 'The game will be over soon.'

Cara started to pour her beer into a glass. 'There you go, that sounds promising. Meanwhile we'll have a quiet drink, just us girls. It'll be like old times. Oh crap!' Her beer frothed up in excitement and she brought it to her mouth and quickly slurped the overflowing foam.

'You're such a dope,' laughed Rachel. Having poured her own beer slowly, her glass was now full without a drop spilt. 'And when did we ever manage to have 'just a quiet drink', you and I?'

'A poor choice of words perhaps,' said Cara with a grin. 'But we're older now. More mature.'

'Jayses, you make us sound like grannies. I'm only just thirty myself and you're not even there for a few more months. Don't write us off yet, Cara. The night is still young.' She raised her beer and they clinked glasses.

'What are we toasting?'

'Good friends and far-off places.'

The beer was ice cold, strong and bitter. Cara took another sip. She watched Rachel lean back in her chair and do the same. They sat in silence for a few moments and without warning an image of Peter popped into Cara's head. With it came a stab to her heart, for in that image he was with Simone the Slut and they were hugging and kissing and laughing about her behind her back. Shakily, she washed the vision away with a large gulp of lager. No need for that now. Besides, Simone had obviously been blindsided too, so the image was nothing more than Cara's own battered ego torturing itself.

'What do you reckon we should do while we're here in Cyprus?' she asked, determined to shake off the dark mood that lurked.

Rachel looked as if she were a million miles away. 'What? Oh. Good question. I read about some day trips in the in-flight magazine.'

They chatted and drank their beers and Rachel seemed as pleased with the small-talk as Cara did. Cara wondered what was on her friend's mind – probably work, knowing Rachel. Somewhere in the midst of a colourful discussion about the likelihood of their getting lost in the Troodos Mountains, the soccer game came to an end. The televisions blinked off and a gentle glow replaced the dimness as someone turned up the lights. A familiar rock song began to play and Cara tapped her fingers against her beer glass in time with the music. That was more like it.

Their drinks were almost finished when the waitress reappeared with a tray bearing more.

'Thanks, but we didn't order anything.'

'No, no,' smiled the waitress, 'This is from those guys at the bar.' She gestured over her shoulder with one of the beer bottles.

Cara and Rachel exchanged an uncertain glance.

'It is okay,' the waitress reassured them. She smiled again and walked away.

Cara squinted at the bar but all she could see were bobbing silhouettes.

'Bloody hell,' muttered Rachel. 'That's all we need.'

Cara thought about it for a moment, then shrugged and nodded a general thank-you in that direction. 'Free drinks?' she said. 'Sure, why not?' The beer had begun to drive her tension away and it felt good.

'You know they're going to come over.'

'There's no harm in being friendly,' Cara replied with a reckless toss of her head. 'It doesn't mean anything. It's not like they proposed marriage. We're under no obligations. Besides, it's Saturday night, right?'

'What's that got to do with it?'

'Well I didn't come all the way here just to hide in a corner. Who knows? It could be fun.'

Rachel fidgeted in her seat.

'Something wrong, Rachel?'

'Not at all,' she replied defensively and then confessed, 'Only, I'm a bit out of practise. It has been a while since I was part of this whole scene.'

'What, the being-single-and-having-some-fun scene? You and me, both! But we have to start somewhere and this seems as good a place as any. We're on holiday, my friend. Live a little. What's the worst that can happen?'

Rachel's eyes widened. 'Seriously? Oh, I don't know – we could be abducted and sold to gypsies and end up working as slaves to a sultan in the desert somewhere.'

'You'd best brush up on your belly-dancing, then.'

A light touch on Cara's shoulder interrupted her laugh and she looked up to find two men standing beside them. One had a

45

pleasant round face and smiled shyly as he asked, 'Do you mind if we join you?'

Still grinning at the image of Rachel as a belly-dancer, Cara opened her mouth to politely decline, but when she looked at the second man – the one who had touched her shoulder – her breath caught and her grin dissolved. The words that fell out of her mouth betrayed her. 'Sure, why not? Make yourselves comfortable.'

While Sex-On-Legs pulled up a chair beside her a deep flush spread from her core and she silently gave thanks for soft lighting.

'I am Yiannis,' he said and indicated his friend with a dip of his head. 'This is Ari.'

Yiannis smiled at Cara as if she were the only person in the room. His teeth were perfectly straight and white and his dark hair curled a bit around the sides of his neck in a way that made her want to wrap her fingers in it. The glint in his olive eyes set her hormones abuzz like they had snorted a dozen espressos and alarm bells sounded in her head, loud ones with flashing red lights and sirens.

She ignored them. Shifting in her seat, she crossed one sparkly foot over the other and flashed him a coy smile. 'I am Cara and this is my friend, Rachel.'

Yiannis smiled briefly at Rachel before turning his attention back to Cara. 'Have you been in Cyprus long?'

Even over the music his voice sounded deep and sexy. Cara shook her head, afraid that her reply would come out as a squeak. By contrast, Yiannis looked completely at ease. A dark T-shirt hugged his broad chest and Cara found herself fighting the urge to reach out and touch it. Talk about lust at first sight! She tore her gaze away to glance across the table at Rachel and Ari, who were also exchanging greetings. They looked as awkward as each other but with surprise, it occurred to Cara that she did not care. In fact, it occurred to her that she did not care about anything at all, other than this gorgeous stranger beside her. When last did she have a man like this take any interest in her? *About eight years ago,* replied a small voice in her head, *and look how that turned out.* She shut the voice off in irritation. Taking a deep breath, she met and matched his unwavering gaze with an audacity that surprised her. She had always had a weakness for Mediterranean types, and as for that accent . . .

To hell with the consequences, thought Cara. After what Peter had just put her through, her ego deserved a bit of indulgence.

Chapter 4

Yiannis and Ari spoke reasonably fluent English heavily laced with the thick accent of Greek Cypriots. Yiannis explained that they had spent a year in New York City in the late Nineties.

'Did you like it?' Cara asked. 'I always wanted to go but never quite got there.'

Yiannis shrugged. 'It was okay.'

Ari chuckled. 'Yiannis was – how do you call it? Homesick. There we were on our big life adventure and he missed his mama's cooking.'

Yiannis threw up his hands and let loose a torrent of abuse in Greek while Ari roared with laughter.

'You must excuse Ari. He has the manners of a monkey.' He shook his head. 'It was not so bad over there, but to be honest it was too noisy, too busy. People are always rushing here, rushing there, all the time. They never stop. This is not a way to live. Even Ari was glad to be home, in the end.'

'I understand,' said Rachel. 'Big cities can be overwhelming. London is the same.'

'You are from London?' Ari asked.

Rachel nodded.

'Not me,' said Cara. 'I'm from Dublin.'

'Ah, you are Irish,' exclaimed Yiannis.

'We both are, but Rachel ran away to London years ago.'

'Ran away?'

'She's only joking,' Rachel laughed, shooting a murderous look at Cara. 'I'm not the one with running-away issues.'

Cara narrowed her eyes. *Touché.*

'You two ladies are friends for a long time,' observed Ari.

'Like me and Ari,' said Yiannis.

'Yes. We were in college together, but we don't get to see each other very often,' replied Cara.

Yiannis grinned. 'Not like me and Ari. Sometimes I think we see each other too much.'

Ari adopted a weary expression and nodded. He had a gentle humour about him that Cara found disarming. She hoped Rachel would warm to him, too.

Yiannis touched her arm. 'But you ladies, you miss each other, yes?'

Cara nodded. His touch was a little disconcerting.

'And so, you decide to come to Cyprus for a holiday together. Are you are here for one week, or two?'

'One.'

'One week is okay.' He smiled a smile that knocked the breath from her body. 'But two would be better. There is much to see in Cyprus. You are staying nearby – at the Hotel Somptueux, perhaps? I hear it is very nice there. You will like it, I think.'

'Not quite. We're just next door.'

Ari laughed. 'Ah, the Lionheart; it is the little hotel with the big personality, eh?'

'I see you know it.'

'The locals call it Fawlty Towers.'

Laughter erupted all around and the ice was well and truly broken. Yiannis had a round of drinks delivered with a single nod of his head and this time the beers were accompanied by four shot glasses filled with a clear liquid.

'Zivania,' said the waitress as she deposited the drinks on their table.

Cara eyed it sceptically.

'It is a local drink,' said Yiannis.

'Like tequila,' volunteered Ari.

The waitress flashed her toothy smile and left them to it.

Rachel lifted a shot glass, sniffed at it and recoiled. Yiannis and Ari grinned and raised theirs in challenge.

'I don't know,' began Rachel.

'Ah, go on,' Cara clucked with impatience and raised a glass. 'One . . . two. . .' On three she, Yiannis and Ari knocked back their shots. Instantly Cara's eyes filled and she screwed up her face. 'Ugh, that's horrible!'

Yiannis and Ari cracked up and grabbed their beers.

'Well, if you can't beat 'em, join 'em,' sighed Rachel and swallowed hers. 'My God, that'll strip paint,' she spluttered, slamming the glass back on the table.

'You can use it for toothache, also,' said Ari seriously.

Cara swigged at her beer, trying to rid her mouth of the vile taste and cool the flames that burned a trail to her stomach. It certainly warmed her up from the inside out and mind you, once she had the gag reflex under control it felt pretty good. Before long the alcohol started to do its thing and a floaty sensation enveloped her. On the other side of the table a goofy grin spread across Rachel's face too. Ari looked pleasantly relaxed and Yiannis . . .

She gulped. Yiannis looked back at her with a wicked smile and fire in his eyes. *Oh hell.* Cara excused herself and stumbled to the ladies' room. She locked herself in a cubicle, leaned against the wall and squeezed her eyes shut. She felt confused, disoriented. What was she doing here, exchanging *that* sort of look with a dark, handsome Cypriot instead of her blonde, blue-eyed Peter?

No, not her Peter, not anymore. She opened her eyes and breathed deeply, then wrinkled her nose. *Eeuw!* It smelled of toilet in here.

Hastily she finished up and vacated the stall, resuming her contemplation while she washed her hands. What was it that drew her to Yiannis? How was it even possible for her to feel this way when just one week ago she had been planning her wedding to someone else? She squinted at her fractured reflection in a tiny mirror above the hand basin. And how did she go from Cinderella into Rumpelstiltskin within the space of just two drinks, or was it three?

Taking a deep breath, she smoothed her hair, reapplied her

lipstick and smacked her lips together. They felt decidedly numb – not a good sign – so on her way back to the table she stopped to have a word with the barman. 'Are you Harry?' No, that was wrong. What was it Sue had said? 'I mean, are you Martin?'

He smiled. 'At your service.'

'This may sound a little shtrange, but Sue from the Lionheart Hotel mentioned this place. She recommended it as somewhere we might be . . . um . . . the thing is, those lads have bought us drinks but we only met them tonight. I was hoping you might just keep an eye out for us. You know, just so they don't shling us over their shoulders and carry us away.' Her smile felt like it was slurring a little too.

Martin leaned forward on the counter to get a good view of their table. 'Those two over there?'

She nodded.

'Yeh, that's okay luv. I know those chaps. They're harmless. You'll be fine with them. Ari is a good bloke. You go and have fun.'

Relieved, she thanked him and wobbled back to the group. It was all very well to live a little, but Cara really didn't think that belly-dancing was her thing.

Yiannis greeted her return by extending his hand to guide her back to the chair beside his. Martin's words rang in her ears. *Ari is a good bloke*, he had said. What about Yiannis? Was he also a good bloke? Because frankly, the glint in his eye said otherwise. She giggled. In fact, it made him look delectably naughty.

Before settling into her seat, Cara leaned over and quietly relayed her brief conversation with Martin the Barman to Rachel.

'Just be careful, Cara,' was Rachel's response.

Cara drew back and stared at her. What did she think was going to happen? It was not as if Cara had any intention of going off somewhere with Yiannis. How much trouble could she possibly get into inside a pub full of people? She ended the exchange with a dismissive toss of her head.

Flattered by Yiannis's relentless attention, she ignored a lingering sense of unease. Rachel was just being over-protective. She looked over and caught Yiannis watching her intently. His lips moved but his words were lost in the loud music. She shook her head – *I didn't get that.* He spoke again and she dropped her gaze to his mouth. Her breathing quickened and she was swallowed by a powerful urge to kiss him. She looked up as he leaned in and her senses screamed in anticipation but at the last moment he turned his head.

His breath was hot in her ear as he said 'Is everything okay?'

Then he was gone again and the air around her felt cold. His hand brushed her forearm as he withdrew, scorching a trail of delicious goosebumps. They locked eyes and there was no hiding what she was feeling.

Mercifully, she was saved from complete meltdown by the intrusion of an odd noise, a wailing sound that originated up near the bar. She and Yiannis frowned simultaneously and peered into the smoky gloom. Cara started to giggle. 'Karaoke,' she said. 'Very, very bad Karaoke.'

A diva with ironed hair, squished into a slinky dress two sizes too small, bellowed into a microphone.

Yiannis looked amused. 'Do you like to sing?'

'Me? You must be joking,' Cara laughed and shoved his leg playfully, unprepared for her body's reaction to the feel of his muscular thigh beneath her hand. She felt a stirring deep inside and her heart beat wildly in her chest. She swallowed.

Yiannis watched. His eyes darkened and he reached for her hand. 'Do you want to go for a walk with me?'

Hell yes! screamed her inner harlot, but she shook her head. Even through her alcoholic haze she knew it would be a bad idea.

He studied her for a moment and then shrugged. 'Okay,' he said, leaning back in his chair.

Relief mingled with disappointment. The thrill of wanting and being wanted was like a drug and Cara wanted more. Had she made a wrong move? How could he give up so easily? Did she really want Yiannis to respect her refusal? Part of her desperately wanted him to persist and make her change her mind. Damn it to hell! After seven years with Peter she had forgotten how to play this game.

A third man joined their table, distracting her from the whirlwind in her head. He looked younger than Yiannis, perhaps twenty-one or twenty-two at most, a burly lad with a stony expression like Marlon Brando in *The Godfather*. Yiannis introduced him as Kostas.

Kostas dipped his head in greeting but did not smile. He wore a long black trench coat over black shirt and black trousers. Cara fully expected him to pull a cigar from his pocket at any moment. He exchanged some subtle nods and grunts with Yiannis and Ari, then sat back in his chair and folded his arms. Within moments the waitress brought over a tray and set it down in front of him. It bore a small teapot, a teacup and a bowl of sugar cubes.

'No Zivania for you?' asked Cara.

Kostas threw her a withering look. Yiannis leaned forward to tell her, 'No, only tea for Kostas.'

Cara hadn't the nerve to ask why. He might be an alcoholic, or perhaps he was on some sort of medication. There was a slim chance that he simply liked tea, but it seemed rude to ask.

As drinks and conversation continued to flow, Cara discovered that Yiannis possessed a dry wit that had her and Rachel in stitches. Kostas said little, and never directly to either of the girls. Cara concluded that of all the characters they had yet encountered on Cyprus he was the strangest by far. He sat and watched and drank his tea, while the other four got to know each other.

Yiannis had little to say about his job. 'I am just a boring computer programmer. Ari is the one with the glamorous life. He works as a game ranger.' Cara pictured Ari tramping through the wilderness in khaki shorts and hiking boots. Where was the glamour in that? But Yiannis had already moved on, wanting to know what their plans were for their week in Cyprus.

'I'm embarrassed to say we have not decided yet.'

'It was sort of a sudden decision to come,' added Rachel.

'You should go to Kourion,' said Ari. 'There is a theatre there.'

'I'm not sure we want to spend our holidays watching movies,' said Cara with a small frown.

Yiannis and Ari roared with laughter. Even Kostas cracked a smile and his teacup rattled in its saucer as he set it down, the noise unexpectedly loud in a brief lull between songs.

The music started up again and Yiannis explained, 'It is not a movie theatre. It is an ancient stone theatre up in the hills, from the time of the gladiators. You should go there. It is beautiful.'

Ari agreed and advised them to bring a camera.

'But if you want to see beautiful places, Cara, I would love to show you the beach of Aphrodite,' said Yiannis. He held her gaze and brushed his fingertips across her knee. 'It is very romantic. We could bring some wine, some food. We could go tomorrow.'

'It sounds tempting,' Cara said with a coy smile. Her knee tingled where he had touched her and she tried not to get too excited that he was still interested.

'So, you will come with me?'

'How can I say no?'

He smiled. 'I will be at your hotel at nine o'clock.'

'Goodness, Ari, and how do you feel about having your services volunteered as a tour guide tomorrow?' Rachel laughed. Both Cara and Yiannis looked up in surprise.

'It will be my pleasure, of course,' Ari stammered.

Cara frowned. So much for a romantic date on the beach. No wonder Rachel's boss thought she'd make a great lawyer, the sneaky cow.

Another round of drinks arrived, along with a fresh pot of tea for Kostas. As the night wore on the room spun a little faster and faces grew fuzzy around her. Yiannis bombarded her mercilessly with intense, seductive looks and light touches, sending Cara's libido into frenzy. It was torture and ecstasy at the same time. Loud music and laughter coursed through her and she lost all sense of time and place. But after the fourth – or was it the fifth? – round of Zivania, Rachel clunked her glass down on the table and announced, 'Right, that's it. I'm shattered. I'm going to bed.'

Reluctantly, Cara reached for her bag.

Yiannis caught her wrist. 'You do not have to go. There is a place we can go, a party with friends of mine.'

Cara tried to focus on his face. Through a slight blur his olive-green eyes pulled her in. They crinkled at the corners as he turned a lazy smile on her, reminding her of another Cypriot who had seduced her years ago.

'Or you could come home with me,' he suggested. 'My place is not far from here.'

Her insides melted. It must be a Cypriot thing; Nik had been just as persuasive.

Cara sighed wistfully. 'Oh Yiannis, you are lovely and I'd love

54

nothing more than to spend the night with you. But I'm really quite drunk and I just don't think it would be wise, my pet.'

'That is a great pity, Cara.'

Her name sounded like foreplay from his lips. Warmth stole through her and she looked down to find her fingers entwined with his. With her free hand, she traced a tender line up his smooth, dark forearm. Her fingers stopped where his shirt sleeve bunched in the crook of his elbow. She wanted to go further. Quite frankly she wanted to rip the shirt right off him, feel the warmth of his skin under her hands, taste his lips on hers and feel him inside her. She shuddered slightly and when she raised her eyes she knew, again, that he knew.

'Cara, are you coming?' Rachel bumped her chair as she stood to leave.

'Um, yes,' Cara croaked and grabbed her bag before Yiannis could stop her again. He pushed his chair back and walked with them to the exit. The cold air was like a slap in her face as they stepped outside.

'You will be okay to get back to your hotel?' Yiannis asked.

'We'll be fine,' called Rachel over her shoulder as she began to teeter off down the road. 'C'mon, Cara. It's freezing out here.'

Cara fidgeted with the tassels on her bag. 'I'll see you in the morning – for the beach trip thing.'

He said nothing so she turned to go, but he suddenly pulled her back and without warning took from her a deep kiss that briefly stopped time. It tasted of man and beer and left her shaken and breathless.

'Sweet dreams, Cara,' he breathed in her ear and vanished back inside the pub.

Cara stood swaying on the pavement for a moment.

'Cara, are you comin' or not?' Rachel had stopped at the corner to look for her.

Cara snapped her mouth shut and started after her. Her ears rang from the noise inside the pub, her breath steamed on the air and her pulse raced from the devastating kiss. Consequences be damned, she thought. That was completely worth it.

A pounding headache ripped her from a state of bliss. One

moment she writhed in ecstasy in a tangle of bronzed limbs and olive eyes and the next it was but a throbbing memory. She groaned, flipped onto her stomach and buried her head in her elbow. If she could sleep for just one more hour – two, tops – the headache would surely go away. But sleep had gone and with it the shadow of Yiannis. Heaving a big sigh, she rolled over and opened her eyes. The room spun a bit, tilted and finally swam into focus. The lump in the bed beside the window groaned.

'You awake?'

She tried to swallow. Her mouth was parched and coated with the sour aftertaste of alcohol. A ray of bright sunshine sneaked through a chink in the curtains and stabbed at her eye. 'What time is it?'

An arm reached out of the other bed, fumbled on the nightstand and held up a wristwatch. 'Eight o'clock.'

'Damn!'

'What?'

'They'll be here in an hour.'

Rachel groaned again. 'Do we have to?'

But Cara was already out of bed, spurred into action by the first flutters of excitement. Never mind her dream – the real thing was on his way and she had to get ready!

Fifteen minutes later she emerged from the bathroom refreshed and smelling faintly of lavender-scented soap. While Rachel showered she packed her beach towel, sunscreen and old compact camera into her tote bag, boiled the little kettle on the tray beside the television and poured them each a cup of instant coffee that she hoped would drive away the cobwebs in her head.

'Nice bag,' remarked Rachel, coming out of the bathroom. 'It suits you.'

'Thanks,' said Cara. Her tote was big and purple, with a bright yellow flower on one side. 'I found it on Henry Street.

I thought it looked about right for a spontaneous trip to Cyprus.'

With twenty minutes to go they tumbled downstairs to the dining room dressed in shorts and flip-flops. Chef seemed quite perky this morning but his smile drooped when they declined his offer of eggs, bacon and sausage, opting instead for fresh croissants with sweet strawberry jam. The thought of a fry-up turned Cara's stomach. Meanwhile Stevan scuttled about with a pitcher of fresh orange juice, looking harassed. Heaven knew why, for they were his only customers.

Cara and Rachel exchanged few words beyond *pass the butter*. Rachel looked tired and hungry enough to bite someone's head off at the slightest provocation, which was a pity because while Cara looked forward to seeing Yiannis, she had doubts too. She was dying to talk it out with her best friend but Rachel's warning from last night stopped her.

Be careful, she had said.

Cara did not think Rachel would classify her kissing Yiannis as being careful, even though technically *he* had kissed *her*. Perhaps after a good breakfast and some fresh air Rachel would come around. Cara hoped so, otherwise it could make for an uncomfortable day. Right now, though, she was suffering from an explosive case of nervous excitement she could barely contain.

At three minutes past nine they headed up to the lobby and stepped outside into the sunshine, sunglasses firmly in place. The world looked different in daylight. A stiff breeze tugged at tall palm trees up and down the road, beneath an endless pale blue sky that somehow looked bigger than it did back home in Dublin.

'Look, no clouds!' Cara grinned and inhaled a deep breath of warm, sunny air.

'Yeah. Amazing.'

Cara pulled a face. She refused to let Rachel's grumpiness get her down.

A faded silver sedan pulled up into the small parking lot in front of them and Cara's heart flipped at the sight of Yiannis's lazy smile. He was even sexier in daylight, with his eyes hidden behind dark aviator glasses.

'Jayses, he looks like something out of Top Gun,' muttered Rachel.

Cara thought he looked good enough to eat.

Ari stayed in the driver's seat while Yiannis hopped out to greet them, hugging Cara and kissing both girls on the cheek. Cara looked inside the car and waved at Ari.

'No Kostas?'

'No Kostas. You have only me and Ari today.' Yiannis's accent sounded even more exotic than Cara remembered. 'Are you ready for a wonderful day? We have many beautiful places to go.'

'Just a moment, I forgot something,' said Rachel and dashed back inside the hotel.

While they waited Ari popped the boot and Cara stowed her tote bag beside a rucksack, a rolled-up sweater and a couple of beach towels that were already there. Rachel returned within minutes, dropped her own bag in beside Cara's and opened the rear door.

'No, no, you take the front,' insisted Yiannis. 'Cara and I will sit in the back, today.'

Rachel's smile was polite, if not filled with enthusiasm. Cara was relieved. Rachel could be pretty cranky with a hangover. She might be more polite with Ari beside her.

Yiannis had to fold his long legs sideways to fit in behind the passenger seat and Cara was acutely aware of his knee rubbing against hers as they headed west. Did he notice it too? She thought about how she had felt the night before with his teasing touches, flirting and finally that devastating kiss. Would he kiss her again today? It was a great kiss. Just thinking about it set her heart racing. She glanced at him and the corner of his mouth twitched into an almost-smile. What was she thinking? Of course he noticed!

It took far less time to make their way out of Limassol City than it had taken coming in on the coach the evening before. Ari drove along the shorefront past high-rise buildings, palm trees and parklands as far as the old port, allowing them to glimpse some of the places they might want to explore over the next week. After that, they headed out of town and were soon surrounded by farmland. The countryside was a palette of dusty beige and olive green, stark contrast to the bright emerald greens of Ireland. The only thing brighter was the blue of the sky, although it was now marked by banks of puffy clouds that seemed to be growing at a surprising rate.

They were headed to a medieval site located about twenty kilometres out of Limassol city. Instead of taking the motorway, Ari followed the coastal route towards Paphos. Upon reaching the little town of Kolossi, he skirted the ruins of an old sugar mill until the tyres of the sedan crunched onto the gravel parking area outside Kolossi Castle.

Three storeys high and built of stone, it reminded Cara a little of Blarney Castle down in County Cork: big, square and impenetrable-looking. However, while Blarney was stony grey and surrounded by lush green countryside, this one towered over a dry, dusty landscape, it massive walls bleached blonde by hundreds of years in the sun.

'Well would you look at that. It's a castle,' said Rachel and a large raindrop splatted into the dust next to her foot.

'Come, quickly,' urged Yiannis.

Taking Cara's elbow he hurried her forwards. A moment later a heavy black cloud obliterated the day and as they crossed the paved courtyard and dashed over a wooden drawbridge, a torrential downpour engulfed them.

They burst into the castle, laughing and shaking droplets from their hair and clothes, their voices lost in the drum of rain. Inside, beneath the ancient roof, the castle remained warm and dry.

'The rain comes quickly, this time of year,' said Yiannis. 'It will not last long.'

He took Cara's hand and led her to a wall painting of the Crucifixion, faded by centuries and worn away in places.

'It's beautiful.'

'Yes,' he replied. He wasn't looking at the painting.

Cara blushed and he smiled. It was a great smile. Peter never smiled at her like that anymore. Peter called her a muppet. Then again, it seemed Peter called lots of people 'muppet'.

Bastard.

'You look angry.'

'It's nothing.'

'A man?'

'I don't really want to talk about it.'

He lifted her hands for inspection. 'You are not married.'

'Would it make a difference?'

'To me? No. But to you? I think so.'

'Well we don't have to worry about that. There is no husband and as of a week ago, no fiancé either.'

Yiannis was still holding both her hands. He nodded and

lifted them to his lips, landing a gentle kiss on each in turn. 'I understand.'

Behind them Rachel squealed with laughter at something Ari said, her earlier grumpiness apparently forgotten. Yiannis squeezed Cara's hands and they joined them in exploring while the storm raged outside. While the two men discussed the logistics of battling enemies with swords in the spiral stairwell, Rachel pulled Cara aside.

'I told Sue where we are, in case you're wondering,' she said in a low voice.

'You did what?'

'When I ducked back inside the hotel earlier I told Sue at Reception that we were going out for the day with these lads, and I gave her the car's registration number. I thought someone should know where we are. Just in case.'

Cara stared at her in disbelief. 'Are you serious?'

'Yeah, I am. I figured *one* of us should be sensible before being whisked off to God-knows-where by two men we only just met.'

Cara rolled her eyes. 'Paranoid, much?'

'Jayses, Cara. Don't get all judgemental. It's no worse than you talking to the barman last night.'

Even though she knew it made sense Cara couldn't help feeling annoyed. Last night the two men were strangers. Today they felt like friends.

Upon reaching the top of the stairs she found Yiannis waiting for her. Had he heard the echo of their conversation? If so, he made no mention of it. Instead, he beckoned her over to one of the windows that allowed daylight to penetrate the thick castle walls. Cara tried to brush off her irritation with Rachel, taking some time to appreciate the view of a countryside bathed in eerie half-light as the sun tried to break through.

The rain had begun to ease and as daylight returned a bus pulled up beside their silver sedan. Within minutes Kolossi Castle would be invaded by a horde of tourists.

'I think it is time to go,' Ari's voice bounced off the stone around them and Yiannis nodded.

They descended the staircase, skirted a gaggle of tourists gathered around the wall mural on the ground floor and escaped back across the drawbridge. Puddles dried in the sun and the rich smell of wet earth surrounded them.

Cara exchanged polite smiles with a couple of stragglers who hung around in the gardens below, admiring bright red and yellow roses that lined the pathway. They were German, by the sound of it. Yiannis explained that there were more tourists than normal for this time of year. 'Many Cypriots live in other countries now, but they return because they want to vote next weekend. There is a – how you call it? Election . . . no, a referendum on Saturday. You did not know this?'

Cara shook her head. 'I've been kind of distracted lately.'

'I understand.'

His smile turned her knees to jelly. Of course he understood. He was perfect.

Continuing on their journey, as they sped along quiet roads between fields and villages, Yiannis gave a brief account of the history of Cyprus since the Turkish invasion of 1974. He explained what it had to do with next week's referendum. His eyes danced as he spoke and his hands waved about for emphasis.

Cara heard about half of what he said. Mostly she concentrated on controlling the impulse to ravish him right there in the back seat. She could think of a far better use for those expressive hands of his. If he displayed this much passion when talking about his country, imagine what he was like in bed!

Ari interrupted the history lesson – and Cara's fantasy – to point out a sign on the side of the road. She frowned as it whizzed past. 'Did that say what I thought it said?'

'Yes,' said Yiannis. 'We are now inside the perimeter of the British Air Force base.'

'And why is that, exactly?'

He laughed. 'We have to go this way to get to Kourion.'

A small booth in a patch of dirt in the middle of nowhere marked the entrance to the site at Kourion. They paid 75c each to enter and Ari navigated a bumpy gravel road to a parking lot on top of a hill. This was the only apparent sign of civilization in an isolated place with nothing but rolling foothills and valleys all around. From here the world looked green and crisp, freshly washed from a recent rain shower – probably the same one that had swamped them at Kolossi, thought Cara. But the huge grey clouds responsible for it had moved off to cause trouble over a distant mountain, leaving this one hot and steamy for now.

'We walk from here.'

Yiannis led them over the crest of the hillside to a wooden walkway that meandered around an archaeological site on the other side. It was difficult to imagine that the crumbling mounds before them had ever been a city. To Cara's untrained eye it appeared little more than a haphazard maze of bumps and gullies where once there had been walls and alleyways. Only the mosaic floors dotted around here and there stood out as distinctive. A huge awning supported on massive wooden trusses protected them from the weather. It looked out of place amid the ancient ruins but Cara stopped gratefully in its shadow. With the rain clouds gone, the heat from the sun pounded at her temples and she wished she had brought a bottle of water along.

She glanced at her three companions. They stood in a row leaning on walkway's wooden hand rail, staring blankly at the mosaic before them. Cara grinned to herself, sidled backwards and snapped a photograph from behind. *Hangover, in Triplicate*, she thought with a smile. Nik would have appreciated that. He used to love taking unexpected snapshots.

At the click of the shutter Yiannis shifted his weight and checked her out over his shoulder, smiling. She could not help thinking that Peter would have rolled his eyes and said she was wasting film. He might even have made her pose in front of the mosaics for a 'proper' picture – assuming she could have talked him into visiting Cyprus in the first place.

Peter did not travel well.

'Come on, you lot. We can't stay here all day,' she said. 'What's next on the itinerary?'

'Come this way,' said Yiannis. 'You have not yet seen the best part.'

They rounded a bend to a view that stopped Cara in her tracks. To her left, the hillside dipped steeply to a valley made up of a patchwork of green and yellow fields that eventually met up with the deep blue ocean in the distance. The bleached stone tiers of Kourion amphitheatre rose in a semi-circle to her right, overlooking a stage perched on the edge of a precipice. The simple railing at the very edge hardly seemed adequate but anything more would have spoiled the grandeur.

Cara laughed in delight. 'Oh, it's *that* sort of theatre! Can you imagine what sort of shows they must have put on here? It's huge!'

Yiannis grinned as if he had built it himself, just for her. 'They still do, Cara.'

'So much for movies, eh?' observed Rachel and Cara felt a swell of resentment at her intrusion.

'No movies,' said Yiannis with a chuckle. 'Once upon a time, the gladiators came here to play. Now, they use it for music and shows.'

They climbed all the way to the top and sat, feeling hot and lazy under the sun. There was no sign of the earlier rain clouds and Cara leaned back on her hands, enjoying the peace of the moment. It did not last long. She squinted behind her sunglasses, searching the skies to find the source of a faint buzzing noise, which grew to a steady drone and finally erupted in a thunderous roar behind them.

Cara screamed and ducked, covering her ears with her hands as a bright red aeroplane swooped overhead so low it stirred up the dust around her and rattled her bones. Just as suddenly it was gone, reduced to one of nine small aircraft flying in formation out over the sea, trailing red and blue smoke behind them.

Yiannis laughed at her. 'Do not look so worried, Cara. You are lucky – today we have the best seats in the house.

Those are England's Red Arrows. They come here in the winter to the air force base. See? They must be out for a practise today.'

Cara watched in awe as the famous RAF aerobatics team danced their aerial ballet over the fields and beaches of Cyprus. With hardly a breath of wind to contend with their colourful trails painted the sky and when the squadron buzzed the amphitheatre a second time she squealed with delight.

Rachel was just as captivated and Ari sported a broad grin.

Yiannis sank backwards until he was lying flat on the stony ground beside her, soaking up the sunshine. Cara could not tell if his eyes were open or shut behind his sunglasses. In a subtle movement, his hand crept along the ground and gently prodded her hip. He smiled and she turned back to watch the show. Boy, would that busload of tourists back at Kolossi Castle have loved to have seen this!

When at last the planes flew out of sight, Ari suggested it was time to move on. In an attempt to deal with the heat, Cara bought ice-creams for everyone from a van that had arrived in the car park. She scratched around for change and her engagement ring blinked accusingly up at her from the depths of her purse. What would Peter say if he saw her now? *You know all that sugar will only go straight to your hips, love. And what are you thinking, throwing yourself at a bloody Greek? You know he just wants to get into your knickers.*

She snapped the purse firmly shut. Peter had given up his right to have an opinion the day he decided to bang Simone and whatever other tarts she did not know about. Cara would eat her ice-cream guilt-free. As for Yiannis, it was barely noon – who knew what might happen by the end of the day? Regardless, she would be damned if the ghost of Peter would ruin it for her.

Fresh air whipped in through their open windows, chasing away the stuffy heat that had built up inside the car. Ari turned up the radio. It played mostly Greek ballads – beautiful but unfamiliar to Cara – with the occasional classic rock song thrown in for variety. She hummed along to *Pretty Woman* and Yiannis drummed his fingers on his knee in time to the music while absently watching the countryside roll by.

Cara stole a look at him, allowing herself the delicious pleasure of examining every visible inch of him, from the kinks in his hair to the trace of stubble on his cheek and the little mole just below his ear. When he turned his face to hers she did not look away. Sunshine fell through the window over his shoulder, lighting him up from behind and allowing her to see past his sunglasses. He winked and lifted her hand to his lips, brushing little kisses on each fingertip before lowering it possessively onto his denim-clad leg.

He cleared his throat but his voice rasped when he spoke. 'This place where we are going, they say it is the birthplace of the goddess Aphrodite.'

Rachel chimed in from the front seat. 'Wait, I remember reading something about that.'

She retrieved a small guide booklet from her handbag and rifled through the pages. 'Yes, here you go; according to legend this is the place where the Titans hurled the severed genitalia of Uranus into the sea and Aphrodite emerged.'

Cara winced. 'That sounds painful.'

Yiannis and Ari nodded their agreement.

'Nothin' like a legend for a touch of dramatics, what?' Rachel chuckled, twisting in her seat to look at Cara. Her smile dissolved at the sight of her hand entwined with Yiannis's and she faced forward again without another word.

Cara frowned as it occurred to her for the first time that Rachel's cranky mood might be the result of more than a hangover. She cast her mind back over the day to search for clues, but aside from her brief caution the night before, she came up empty. Cara had assumed Rachel had meant it literally when she had warned her to be careful – don't wander off into the night with a strange man, and make sure someone knows where you are and who you're with – that sort of thing. Now she wondered if Rachel's words held a deeper meaning.

But that made no sense. Surely, she understood that this was just a fling? Cara would have thought Rachel would be cheering her on, not warning her off. *Attagirl Cara! Give 'em hell! Show the lousy bastard you don't need him – indulge yourself!*

Not, *Be Careful.*

Ari pulled over at the side of the road and the car skidded to a halt on gravel, cutting Cara's speculations short. They had stopped at a viewing point overlooking the coastline where turquoise waves crashed and frothed onto the rocky shore far below endless folds of tall limestone cliffs. The glare on their rough white surface was so bright it hurt Cara's eyes when she tried to admire the scene without her sunglasses.

'This is a good place to take your photographs,' said Yiannis. 'See over there? That is where we are going: *Petra Tou Romiou.*' He pointed to a large rock stack some miles away. It looked like a giant dumpling in the water beside a small beach. 'They say that if you swim around that rock you will remain forever beautiful.'

'Sure you will,' Cara laughed and crept over to the cliff's edge to get a good picture.

'Be careful,' Rachel warned.

Yeah, yeah, thought Cara.

'Do not worry,' said Yiannis, staying close. 'I will watch out for her.'

'I don't need a nanny,' Cara retorted, but her words were barely out when her foot slipped, sending a shower of stones onto the rocks far below. She gasped in fright and a pair of strong hands grabbed her from behind.

'Not a nanny, but perhaps a guardian angel?' Yiannis murmured in her ear and a shiver coursed down her spine.

'Cara! Are you okay?' Rachel cried.

'I am fine,' stammered Cara, more disturbed by Yiannis's touch than by her misstep. Distracted by the warmth of his hands on her waist, she snapped a hurried photograph and backed up nervously. Yiannis watched her like a cat toying with a mouse. When they returned to the car he held the door for her, positioning himself so that her breast brushed his arm as she got in. *Jammy bastard*, she thought and a swarm of butterflies danced a jig in her stomach. He knew exactly what he was doing.

A few kilometres further down the road Ari pulled in at a dingy-looking roadhouse and Yiannis announced, 'We are here.'

Cara thought it looked about as romantic as the Bates Motel. 'Do they serve coffee?'

'You would not like it,' advised Yiannis. He hoisted the rucksack out of the car's boot. 'I have some cold drinks in here. We can drink them on the beach.'

'No wine?' she asked.

'I thought cola might be better today after the Zivania last night, no?'

'Good point,' said Cara. 'I don't suppose you have water in there?'

'That, you can get from the shop.'

Cara went to do just that and Rachel joined her. It was time for a bathroom break. Cara waited until they were both washing their hands before trying to broach the subject foremost on her mind. 'Are you enjoying yourself, pet?'

'Sure. I'm having a grand old time.' Rachel's answer reeked of sarcasm.

'Is there a problem?'

'What gave you that idea?'

'You have a face like a sack of lemons, if you must know.'

'Thanks,' said Rachel, wiping her hands dry on the back of her shorts and walking back out into the dusty shop.

Cara followed her and they scoured the place for bottled water.

'Rachel, please don't be like that,' she said, trying to keep her voice low.

'Like what?' She handed two small bottles to Cara, picked up another two and went to pay for them.

'Like you're a disapproving mother and I'm the naughty child who just let you down.'

The scruffy young girl behind the counter avoided eye contact as she slipped Rachel her change, and quickly went back to unpacking a box of chocolate bars. You did not have to speak English to understand the two were having a squabble.

'You're exaggerating,' said Rachel.

'Well that's what it feels like,' Cara replied as they stepped back outside into the sunshine. 'I don't understand why you're judging me. I thought you'd be happy I'm not huddled in a corner somewhere, moping. Isn't this much better – being out in the fresh air, seeing the world again?'

'It might be better if you and Romeo weren't playing house in the back seat.'

'What exactly is it you have a problem with?' Cara slowed as they neared the car. She really wanted to finish the conversation.

But Rachel kept walking, handing Ari a bottle of water and switching on her pleasant-lawyer face. 'So where is this beach you've been bragging about?'

Cara had no choice but to let it go. She gave Yiannis the fourth bottle and he thanked her with a light kiss on the cheek. Rachel's glare bored into her from three feet away but she ignored it. They would sort it out later, when they had some privacy.

A musty underpass led from the parking lot to the beach on the other side of the road. When they emerged on the other side

Cara felt like she had stepped onto the page of a tourist brochure. Small waves curled and rattled over the pebble beach and the water glowed as if lit from below.

'Wow, I don't think I've ever seen water that colour,' she said.

'It matches your eyes,' murmured Yiannis and she giggled.

'I bet you say that to all the girls.'

'No. Most of the women in Cyprus have eyes the colour of mud. It does not work so well as the ocean,' he teased and she punched at his arm. He ducked sideways, laughing.

The giant rock dumpling was far bigger than it had looked from a distance. Cara thought you'd have to be mad to swim around that. She would probably start to drown halfway there and then Yiannis would have to dive in to save her – not an entirely unpleasant thought, although he had already saved her once today when he stopped her plummeting off the cliff. She would hate for him to think she was one of those women who always needed rescuing.

'Come this way,' called Yiannis. His voice whipped away on the breeze to join a seagull's cry. Apart from two solitary figures wandering the shoreline, the secluded cove was deserted. Cara followed him, picking her way over the pebbles to a flat rock surrounded on three sides by water further down the beach, from where they could look back and admire the mythical dumpling. She made slow progress, for the smooth stones poked painfully at her feet through her flip-flops. When she finally reached the platform Yiannis offered a hand to help her up. Was there no end to his charm? Peter would have left her to fend for herself. *No – Peter would not have brought her here in the first place. Peter would be curled up on a couch somewhere, watching football, or screwing a skinny brunette called Simone.*

Yiannis's rucksack turned out to be a picnic cooler and it yielded a feast of crunchy bread, dips, olives, tomatoes and cheese, plus some Cypriot pastries that tasted of honey and walnuts. True to his word there was also small selection of cold drinks to refresh and revitalise.

After eating their fill, they spread out on their rock ledge in the sun. Cara dangled her feet in the icy swell of the Mediterranean Sea while Yiannis stretched out on the rough, warm rock beside her, propped up on one elbow. He spoke in a voice low enough so that only she could hear. 'You look happy, Cara.'

She looked down into his handsome face and smiled. 'Right now, I am happy.'

It was true. How easy it was in this peaceful place of myths and legends, so far removed from reality.

He reached up and traced her smile with his fingertips. Cara thought her insides might explode. Damn Rachel for inviting herself and Ari along! All she wanted to do was lose herself in Yiannis – his touch, his scent, his taste; to discard the darkness that had plagued her all week and satisfy the randy harlot that he had woken inside her. Instead she had to make do with stolen glances and hand-holding while the other two chattered away behind them. The romance of this wild, beautiful place was completely wasted.

Yiannis seemed to understand her mood, for he inched closer and planted a kiss on her thigh before resting his head in her lap. They stayed like that for a while, not talking. Cara gradually brought her emotions under control and peace returned. But it was still early in the season and when the afternoon breeze grew too chilly for comfort they packed up and started back to the car over the stony beach. Halfway to the underpass Cara stepped awkwardly and crumpled to the ground with a cry of pain.

Yiannis reached her in an instant, dropping to one knee and dumping the rucksack beside her. 'Cara, are you alright?' The concern in his eyes made her laugh.

'I'm fine, just twisted my ankle.' She rubbed it furiously, feeling foolish.

'Can you walk?'

'I think so. Help me up, would you?'

He circled his arms around her and rose, bringing her to her feet with him. With her eyes closed she took a deep breath to steady herself. Yiannis smelled like sunshine. The warmth of his lips on hers took her by surprise and her eyes flew open. Inches away his face crinkled into a smile.

'Can you walk?' he asked again and she giggled.

'After that, I'm not so sure.' Her ankle throbbed as she tested it. 'Yes, I'll be fine.'

He grinned, hefted the rucksack and held out an arm to support her as she hobbled back to the car. Aside from her ego there appeared to be no serious damage and by the time they reached Paphos forty minutes later, only a mild ache remained, although the taste of his kiss continued to linger.

The town teemed with people and they joined the throngs strolling along the harbour, past dozens of yachts moored in the grey-green water of the marina and towards the old fort at the end. Bathed in late afternoon sunshine, quayside restaurants and taverns tempted them with the aroma of fried seafood and a love song rang out over some hidden loudspeaker. The singer had a voice like liquid velvet.

'I don't know what he's saying, but whatever it is, the answer is yes,' Cara laughed.

'He is singing to his lover,' said Yiannis. 'He is saying that he cannot wait to be alone with her.'

'I am sure the feeling is mutual,' she responded before she could catch herself. She picked up the pace and hoped he did not see her blush. Perhaps she was not as rusty at the flirting game as she had thought.

At the end of the pier, Cara thought that the best part about Paphos Castle was the moat. She remarked that she could not remember the last time she'd had to cross one with actual water in it. Mostly they were dry, nowadays. She wanted to know if she should be concerned about crocodiles. Yiannis played along, suggesting there might be more danger from sharks, since the moat was filled from the ocean. Ari shook his head in despair and Rachel smiled her pleasant-lawyer smile.

But despite her bravado, Cara's enthusiasm for exploring had deserted her. She was tired and cranky from her sore ankle and annoyed with the tension between her and Rachel, so after a cursory investigation of the fort she retreated to a bench outside, overlooking the water. Less than twenty-four hours ago she had marvelled at the sunset as she stepped off the plane from London. It seemed a lifetime ago.

Yiannis joined her on the bench. He sat close so that the warmth from his thigh spread to hers. It was almost too much. Worn out from the sights and sounds of the day and her rollercoaster emotions, she leaned her head on his shoulder. He snaked his arm around her, pulled her closer and dropped a kiss on the top of her head. She looked up. He had pushed his sunglasses up on top of his head and she noticed that his olive-green eyes were flecked with amber in the orange light of late afternoon.

With excruciating slowness, he lowered his lips to hers. Her eyes closed in sheer delight. She had been waiting for this all day. His kiss was surprising gentle and Cara lost herself in the soft heat of his mouth, the spicy scent on his skin and the locks of hair at the nape of his neck that tangled themselves around her fingers, which seemed to have found their way there of their own accord.

When they eventually came up for air Yiannis leaned back, lay her head once more on his shoulder and stared out over the water.

'Where are Rachel and Ari?' she asked.

'Hush,' he soothed, stroking her hair. 'Ari is showing her the fort. They will be here soon enough.'

They stared out at the yachts, whose long shadows shimmered on the water like ink blots. Music and laughter echoed across the marina from the dockside where the restaurants and tavernas were beginning to light up for the evening. She shivered and snuggled closer to Yiannis, drawing comfort from his closeness. She had gotten what she wanted. That kiss had lived up to its promise, and then some.

The trouble was that now she wanted more. What would he be like as a lover? The thought shocked her. How had she reached this point in the space of only one day?

Behind her she heard Rachel call out, 'Ari, they're over here!' A moment later she stood before them. 'Where the hell have you been? We've been looking all over for you.'

Ari followed a few feet behind. Cara could have sworn he winked as he said, 'It is true. We searched everywhere inside the fortress but all the time you were out here.'

Yiannis smiled and he and Cara rose from their bench. Their sightseeing was done. It was time to return to Limassol.

In the shadows of the back seat of Ari's car Yiannis held Cara close. He murmured in her ear with hot breath and light kisses that made her giddy and made little white stars dance before her eyes. 'I want to take you home with me,' he said. 'I want to have you for myself so that I can kiss you properly – the way you want to be kissed, the way you should be kissed.

I want to kiss you here,' he touched his fingers to the base of her throat, 'And here,' he trailed them along her neckline, 'And especially here.' It was all Cara could do not to groan out loud, but she dared not for Rachel's angry eyes were only two feet away. Thankfully, they were focussed on the road ahead and the old car made enough noise on the road to cover the sound of her laboured breathing. Still, she wasn't going to push it.

Yiannis had no such qualms. He nibbled her earlobe. 'What do you say, Cara? Will you come home with me?'

She shuddered with longing. 'I'd love to, but no.'

He dropped a line of skilful kisses from behind her ear down her neck. 'Are you sure?'

She squeezed her eyes shut. Her body responded of its own accord, her head tilting to further expose the flesh he was so intent on arousing with his gentle lips and darting tongue. This must be what heaven is like, she thought, delighting in the sensation but at the same time terrified that Rachel would turn around. The fear only heightened her pleasure. But she finally gathered the strength to push him away, and groaned 'I'm afraid so.'

He stopped the kissing and raised his head to meet her gaze. His hand came to rest on her side. His eyes bored into hers. His face was so close she could still feel the heat of his breath.

'You do not want this?'

'I do, but . . .'

He finally showed mercy. A brief smile doused the fire in his eyes and he withdrew his hand.

'I understand,' he said. 'It is too soon for you.'

Cara smoothed her hair. 'It's not just that.' Her eyes darted to Rachel in the front seat.

'It is okay, Cara.' He settled back in the seat but left his arm draped behind her, maintaining only light contact. 'So, tell me, what plans do you have for tomorrow?'

She cleared her throat. 'None, yet. We might take a look around town and do some shopping, I suppose.'

'Maybe I will see you around Old Town tomorrow.'

'Do you not have a job to go to?'

He laughed. 'Old Town is good for shopping. I think you ladies will enjoy it and if you happen to be at the castle around lunch time, there are many places to eat nearby. Also, it is not too far from where I work.'

'We do like shopping. And castles. That is a good suggestion, Yiannis,' she grinned and heard him chuckle in the dark.

Upon their return from Paphos, Sue spotted the two women over a sea of newly-arrived heads.

'Good, you're back, all safe and sound,' she called in her sing-song voice. 'I do hope you will join us all in the lounge later. We have some top-notch entertainment lined up this evening.'

The entertainment consisted of an ageing singer with a frizz of over-dyed black hair and a scrawny keyboard player with dark circles around his eyes. One side of the lounge had been cleared to make way for their performance and the tables and chairs arranged to face them. The two older couples that Cara recognised from the dining room the previous night looked like they had been there for hours.

After the worst rendition of *Girls Just Wanna Have Fun* that Cara had ever endured, the singing duo launched into *It's Raining Men*. Cara could stand it no longer and they fled to the relative peace of the adjacent bar. Here the noise was somewhat muted, at least enough so that the woman's plaintive voice no longer drilled into Cara's skull.

The gin was Rachel's idea. Hair of the dog, she called it. Cara was still working up the courage to drink it.

Perched on a chrome-and-leather stool at bar, watching tiny bubbles fizz to the surface of her drink, Cara glowed at the memory of Yiannis's smile. Rivers of condensation ran down the outside of the glass and pooled on the polished black counter, where they glinted like crystals under the glow of recessed spotlights.

'Oh, good heavens,' Rachel's exasperated voice cut in. 'Can you not go for five minutes without drifting off like some teenager into a daydream?'

Cara flushed in anger. 'There's no need for you to talk to me like that!'

'Well forgive me for being so inconsiderate as to wish for some attention from my friend, who I've not seen in years. You're so preoccupied with your little holiday romance I may as well be here by myself.'

'Is that what this is about? You're jealous because you want attention?'

'No, that is not what this is about. I'm not a spoilt child.'

'Well you're acting like one.'

'I am not!'

'Are too!' Cara sniggered. 'Sure, that didn't sound childish at all.'

Rachel sucked a big gulp of her gin and set the glass back on its coaster with care.

'Okay, so maybe I do feel a little left out. Can you blame me? You and I came here together, but you've been wrapped up in Yiannis from the moment you laid eyes on him. I thought you were here to work things out about Peter. I don't see how diving straight into another relationship is going to help you.'

'Well, that's a matter of opinion,' drawled Cara. She sipped her drink and pulled a face. 'Bloody hell, that's strong!'

Rachel grunted. 'Yeah, the barman is a little heavy-handed.'

The young man in question sat about five feet away on a shiny barstool identical to theirs. He had strong Slavic features, jet-black hair and a bored expression on his face while he watched the guests over in the lounge area watching the 'entertainment'. Cara guessed him to be in his late twenties.

'With looks like that, I imagine he can get away with making less-than-perfect drinks,' she said drily. 'What is it with this place? I've never seen so many hot men just walking around.'

Rachel rolled her eyes.

'You don't agree?'

'I hadn't really noticed.'

'How could you not? They're everywhere, and I'm not just talking about Yiannis. Even Ari is quite handsome, don't you think?'

'Or maybe it's just your frenzied libido that's making them look more attractive to you. Honestly Cara, I don't know what's got into you. And what's the deal with your man Yiannis, anyway?'

'Are you joking? He's gorgeous!'

Rachel shrugged. 'He's not *that* hot.'

Cara mulled it over for a moment. She sipped at the cold, bitter gin. It warmed as it slid into her stomach.

'I don't know,' she sighed. 'It's like I know him, even though we only just met. He seems familiar, somehow. It's hard to explain.'

'He probably reminds you of Nik. What is it with you and the dark Mediterranean types? Maybe coming to Cyprus was not such a good idea, after all.'

Cara stayed silent. She had a point. It was annoying how Nik's name kept cropping up.

'Regardless, I don't think it's a good idea, you getting involved with Yiannis,' said Rachel.

'Well that's not your call to make,' snapped Cara.

'Maybe not, but how are you ever going to sort yourself out if you don't give yourself time to work through things?'

'Breaking up with my fiancé isn't just 'things', Rachel. It's pretty much the end of my life as I know it.'

'You don't have to tell me what it's like to lose your partner, but it's not the end of your life, for God's sake. Besides, from what you've told me you haven't *officially* broken it off with Peter. You had a fight and you stormed out. That's not exactly final, is it?'

Cara bubbled with anger at the insinuation.

'Rachel, Peter cheated on *me*, remember? I'm not the one being unfaithful here. And don't compare this to what you went through with Phillip. He didn't *choose* to leave you. Peter, on the other hand, chose to be someone else. The ugly truth is that I was not enough for him. He didn't want me anymore, plain and simple. He wanted some leggy bitch called Simone instead. It's not nearly the same thing, so don't try and tell me you know how I feel because you don't.'

Rachel looked away.

'Oh hell, I'm sorry.' Cara's head drooped and she rubbed her eyes. They felt gritty and tired. 'That was a horrible thing to say.'

'No, you're right,' Rachel's face was grim. 'It's not the same thing. I wasn't saying it was. All I meant was that I know it feels like it's the end of the world, but it's not. You'll get through it and you'll move on. But Cara, you have to get through it, and hiding in a romantic fantasy is not the way to do it.'

'Again, that's a matter of opinion,' she sulked. 'Look, I'm not going to fight with you about this. I understand what you're saying but you have to let me deal with this in my own way, without judging. Do you think you can do that for me?'

Rachel stared at her and at last, capitulated. 'Okay. I'll try and do that for you. But please be careful, Cara. It's nothing personal against Yiannis. Just take it easy, alright?'

There she went with the warnings again. Cara bit her tongue. She knew it came from a place of concern. They called the truce with a clink of their glasses, but as soon as her drink was finished Rachel went to bed, claiming fatigue.

Cara stayed behind. The day with Yiannis had been full-on and after having it out with Rachel, she needed some space. The barman sauntered over to clear away Rachel's empty glass.

'Another gin for you?' he asked.

'Sure, why not,' she replied and watched him pour the drink in silence.

'Is your friend coming back?'

'Rachel? No. I'm afraid I hurt her feelings.'

His expression was unreadable.

Cara sighed. 'You must hear all sorts of things from people, in your job.'

He smiled. It was a beautiful smile that lit him up from the inside and Cara could not help thinking that if only Rachel could have seen it she might have seen what Cara was talking about.

'This job is new to me,' said the barman. 'Ask me again two months from now.'

'I'll be long gone by then,' she chuckled. 'Two months from now this will all be but a distant memory.'

She sipped at her gin and tried not to flinch.

'The drink is okay?'

'It's a little strong,' she admitted with an embarrassed smile.

'That is okay.'

He hovered and Cara realised he must be bored to pieces, hanging out in the bar all by himself. In the hour that she had been there only three other customers had come over to buy drinks.

'My name is Cara,' she offered. 'My friend is Rachel, although I believe we've already established she won't be back tonight.'

He folded his arms and leaned against the bar counter. 'I am Zoran, and your friend will feel better in the morning.'

'How can you be so sure?'

'I have five sisters. They fight, but they always feel better in the morning.'

She gave a short laugh but then shook her head. 'I don't know, Zoran. I said something pretty mean to her.'

'It was not so bad.'

'You heard?'

'A little.'

She toyed with the straw in her drink and watched the bubbles rise to the surface and pop, an endless stream of them. *Pop, pop, pop!*

'So, what do you think?'

He raised his eyebrows. 'Me? I do not think anything. It does not matter what I think. It does not matter what anybody thinks.'

'Next time you see Rachel, you be sure and tell her that,' she said in a wry voice.

He laughed and moved away to serve a customer. One of the bespectacled foursome required more beer. Maybe Zoran was right. Maybe it did not matter what anyone else thought. But if that were true, why did Rachel's resistance bother her so much?

A veil of melancholy settled on Cara and she concentrated on the cold, dewy glass in her hand and the sharp tang of her drink, using her physical senses to distract her from her emotions. The truth was that it bothered her because beneath the excitement of new romance and behind her belligerence dwelt fear; fear that without Yiannis to distract her, the darkness of the last week would return to consume her; fear that without Rachel to lean on she might spin out of control; and most of all, fear that the two of them could not coexist.

Chapter 5

Peter shook the rain off his black wool coat and took the stairs two at a time. The smell of Sunday night dinner filled the building – roast beef and cabbage mixed with stale cigarette smoke. He hoped Declan was not home. Peter wanted to talk to Cara alone.

It had been just over a week since the whole debacle with Simone in the coffee shop. She must have calmed down by now, surely. Cara never stayed angry for long. It was one of the things Peter appreciated about her. So what, if Declan had come to fetch some of her things from their apartment. All that meant was that Cara needed her stuff. Women could not go without their stuff for very long. Upset or not, she still had a job to go to and her brother was hardly in a position to loan her clothes for work. He had passed him in the driveway on the way home, a couple of nights ago. That was how Peter knew where to find her.

Besides, where else would she go?

He knocked on Declan's door and waited. Footsteps approached. He heard the lock tumble, his mouth went dry and he steeled himself for confrontation. When the door swung open he found himself faced with familiar blue-green eyes, but unfortunately this pair belonged to Declan, not Cara.

'Hey, Declan. How are you?'

Declan's gaze was hard and unfriendly. 'What do you want?'

At six foot one, Peter stood at least three inches taller than his almost-brother-in-law. He tried to peer round him into the apartment but Declan stood like a rock, blocking him.

'Is Cara here?'

'No.'

'Really? I thought for sure she'd be here, being Sunday night.'

'Well, she's not.'

'I see. She is staying with you though, right?'

Declan eyeballed him and Peter took it for a 'yes'. Silence hung between them like a stone wall.

'Right. Any idea when she'll be back?'

'You have some bloody nerve.'

'Come on, Declan. Let's be civilised.'

He heard a sharp intake of breath and Peter braced himself but instead of hitting him, Declan responded in a steely voice. 'You're right. It's nothing to do with me that you ripped my sister's heart out and ate it for breakfast. Or was it brunch?'

Jesus. Peter tried a gentler approach.

'Look, I'm sorry. This is really awkward for me. I don't want to fight with you. I just want to talk to Cara. I've heard nothing from her all week.'

Declan stared at him a moment longer and Peter thought he saw his jaw relax slightly.

'Fair enough. But she's still not here. I'll tell her you were looking for her.'

He started to close the door. Peter stopped it with his hand.

'Wait!'

Declan raised an eyebrow at the hand and Peter dropped it at once.

'What I mean is, it's too easy for her to ignore a message – and I can't say I blame her,' he said with a pained expression. 'I've been a right prick.'

Declan watched him, his face unreadable. 'Go on.'

'My only chance is to see her face to face,' explained Peter.

'Chance for what?'

This was harder than he'd imagined. 'To apologise.'

'Are you serious?'

Peter shrugged. 'It's a start. What happens after that, well I can only hope.'

Declan laughed, a harsh, mocking sound. 'You actually think you can talk her into forgiving you and taking you back, don't you?' He shook his head. 'I don't know, man. I think you've a better chance of seeing England winning a world cup.'

Peter gave a wry smile. 'I have to try. I want to marry her, Declan.'

'Good luck with that,' Declan smirked.

'Are you going to tell me where she is, or at least when she'll be back?'

'She has gone away for a week on a girl's holiday. Never mind where – if she wanted you to know, she'd have told you. She'll be back after next weekend. I guess you can try again then, if you're still interested.'

He shut the door without waiting for a reply.

'Thanks a lot,' muttered Peter and turned to leave. A girl's holiday? With who? Cara did not have many close friends. One of the lads would have said something if she was holed up with any of their wives and it surely wasn't her sister. Cara couldn't stand Bridget.

He plodded through the puddles to his car, deep in thought and oblivious to the icy rain. His windows fogged up as soon as he started the engine and it took all his concentration to peer through the wet darkness and get home without sliding his BMW into a gutter.

Upstairs in his apartment he headed to the bedroom to change out of his damp clothes. It was no wonder Cara complained about the weather. He did not mind the rain so much but Cara hated it. How often had he been subjected to her stories about the time she had spent in – where was it? Spain? He could never remember. It was before he had met her. She and that friend of hers in London had done some travelling in Europe one summer.

He sat on the bed and pulled off one soggy sock. He was in the midst of removing the other one when a thought occurred to him.

Cara still kept in touch with that friend. She was the one whose husband had died. Cara had flown over to London for the funeral. Could that be where she was now? He closed his eyes and screwed up his forehead. What the hell was her name?

In a fit of frustration, he balled up his socks and lobbed them into the corner where they hit the wall with a splat. Why did he not pay more attention to her stories?

Scanning the room, his glance fell on the little table next to her side of the king-size bed. The only thing on it now was a small lamp. Had Declan emptied out the contents of the drawer too? He clambered over the bed, yanked it open and started to go through the jumble of hair bands, cosmetic bottles and bits of paper. Why on earth did she keep this rubbish? There were clothing receipts galore, an old airline ticket and a card from Valentine's Day, from him: *Yours, forever ... P.*

Well he'd gone and screwed that up now, hadn't he? Idiot! He should have been more careful. He rubbed his brow. There was no point in self-recrimination.

He continued snooping until he found a bundle of postcards from her travels tucked away at the back of the drawer. *Bingo!*

But they were unused. She must have bought them for herself. There was nothing from her friend and no return addresses. *Damn!*

He spread them out like a fan and something caught his eye. Right near the bottom a photograph peeked out. In it stood a young, tanned-looking Cara and her mystery friend. Peter's face clouded over. There was a third person with them; a dark, olive-skinned young man had his arm draped around Cara's shoulder and he was looking at her with an expression that made Peter want to punch him. He flipped the picture over in irritation. Three names were scrawled on the back, along with the date: *Rachel, Cara & Nik.*

Rachel! That was her friend's name. All sorts of details about her started to filter back to him. Rachel Jones. She worked at a law firm in London. Smiling now, he congratulated himself as he shoved the photograph and the pile of postcards back into Cara's drawer.

He pulled on his slippers and went through to his study. Their paperwork lived in a small file cabinet there and it did not take long to locate her latest mobile phone statement. He cursed when he saw it. Of course! He remembered now the fuss she had made because they wanted to charge her extra for the itemised billing. The silly woman was always trying to save a buck. Wait, if she were concerned about costs, she would not call an overseas number from her mobile.

Peter smiled to himself. The bill for their landline definitely *was* itemised. He pulled it out and ran his finger down the page. Two UK numbers showed up a couple of times. Within minutes he had the last six statements out. One of the numbers showed up at least once on all of them and the other was missing from only one. Peter certainly had not made those calls and he could not think of anyone Cara might have called over there except her old friend, Rachel.

Confident that at least one of the numbers belonged to Rachel – probably both in fact, perhaps one for work and one for home – Peter packed away the paperwork and got comfortable at his desk. As he lifted the phone his mouth went dry. Assuming that Cara was there and assuming she would talk to him, he was not entirely sure what he was going to say. He had imagined having this conversation in person. His odds were far greater if she were unable to simply hang up on him.

'Ah, just get on with it,' he muttered to himself and punched in the first of the numbers. It rang and rang and eventually cut over to a long beep.

Maybe that was the work number.

He tried the second number but it also rang out.

Disappointment mingled with relief. He would try again tomorrow. That would give him time to think about what he could say to keep her on the line long enough to hear him out.

As he switched off the light in his study and padded through to the lounge room to watch *Top Gear*, he allowed himself a smug little smile. Screw Declan. He may not be willing to tell Peter where to find Cara, but if you wanted something badly enough there was always a way.

'Yiannis!'

He looked up upon hearing his name, slowed his pace and scoured the faces around him.

Being Monday, most of the shops in this area had already closed for lunch. They would reopen at four, as was customary in the summer months, but there were few people about, only a couple of shopkeepers and a handful of tourists strolling in the sunshine.

In this old part of Limassol most of the buildings were low-set and looked in need of a coat of paint. However, unlike those in the Tourist Area that were crammed with gaudy ceramic ashtrays, beach towels and bottles of Ouzo, Old Town housed some great little shops where visitors to the island might find trinkets of value hidden behind a dusty window in a crooked street.

A scooter zoomed past, the beep of its horn echoing off the shop-fronts. He heard his name again and stared with surprise as his brother stepped out of a shadow and hurried towards him. 'Nikolaos!'

They gave each other a hug and simultaneously started babbling in excitement.

'It is good to see you.'

'It has been too long!'

Yiannis held his brother at arm's length and studied him. A few fine lines had appeared at the corners of his eyes. 'You are getting old,' he teased.

'You are only two years behind me, little brother,' Nikolaos shot back. 'Soon, you too will be losing your boyish charm.'

Yiannis threw his head back and laughed. 'Still the same old Nikolaos, eh? It's good to have you back for a while. How long are you staying this time?'

Nikolaos shrugged as he swung his rucksack gently to the ground. 'Maybe a week, maybe a month – I have not decided yet. On Saturday, I will cast my vote. After that maybe I will stay a while and take a holiday here at home.'

Yiannis clapped his hand on his shoulder. 'That is good to hear. We can spend some time together.'

Nikolaos nodded. A wicked grin stole across his face. 'Your girlfriend won't mind?'

'Girlfriend? No, there is no girlfriend.' He shook his head vigorously as an image popped into his mind of Cara with her auburn hair and curvy little figure.

'That is not what I heard.'

'Who has been spreading lies about me?' Yiannis chuckled to hide his discomfort.

'A little bird,' said Nikolaos. 'One who drinks too much Zivania and then likes to tell stories to our mother so that she will feed him her special home-made *kataifi*.'

'Ari,' breathed Yiannis with dramatic effect, 'The traitor. I shall have his head.'

'So, it is true? There is a woman in your life?'

Yiannis shook his head. 'Ari exaggerates. We were at a bar in Amathus on Saturday night and we met two Irish girls. Yesterday we took them on a road trip. It was just a bit of fun.'

'Ari says you show a lot of interest in this girl. Are you going to see her again?'

He shrugged. 'I don't know. Maybe. We made no plans, although …'

Nikolaos poked him playfully. 'Yes? Go on. What were you going to say?'

Yiannis grinned. 'I suggested she come here to Old Town today. Maybe I will see her here. Maybe I will not. It is up to the Gods.'

Nikolaos nodded and studied him with a thoughtful expression. 'You like this girl. Our mother will not be pleased she is not one of us.'

'It is a little soon to worry about that, Nikolaos.'

'Perhaps,' he replied. His jovial expression returned. 'I also hear there is going to be a party tomorrow.'

'There is,' exclaimed Yiannis. 'My long-lost brother has returned from his travels so tomorrow, we celebrate!'

'This is good news. But your long-lost brother has to go home to his mother now.' Nikolaos picked up his backpack. 'I have bought her some fresh pastries and I should get them to her while they are still warm.'

'Ah, that is why you're in this part of town,' Yiannis said. 'I was surprised to see you.'

'And I was surprised to see you,' said Nikolaos meaningfully.

'My office is not too far away. I decided to go for a walk during my break.'

'And if you ran into your little Irish lady at the same time it would be a happy coincidence.' Nikolaos winked at him and started to walk away. 'It is okay, little brother. I understand,' he called over his shoulder. 'If you see her, make sure you invite her to the party tomorrow. Tell her your big brother would like to meet her.'

Yiannis waved him off. 'Yes, yes. See you later.'

The smile did not leave his face as he continued on his walk. Unexpected though it was, it would be good to have Nikolaos home.

Jesse Shaw dropped his pen onto his desk in frustration, unable to concentrate on the report in front of him. He folded his arms and stared across the office. From his desk, he could normally see the top of Rachel's head through the leaves of the large ficus next to the coffee station. Not today, though.

By eleven o'clock he had grown curious. She was never this late. A few discreet enquiries revealed little. No-one had seen her since Friday, although one of the secretaries – a nosy little thing with eyes like a hawk – told him that she had glimpsed a Leave Request form on Davenport Junior's desk. Why, where and for how long she had gone remained a mystery. The secretary smiled coquettishly at Jesse. Did he want her to see what else she could find out? He told her it could wait. It would not do to alert the office grapevine.

But Jesse was curious. He would have expected Rachel to at least have mentioned to him if she was going away. There had been every opportunity to do so on Friday after work. Why hide it? Had he only imagined there was something more between them than a quick shag, just that one time? Jesse considered himself pretty good at reading people and situations and it irked him that he might have gotten this one so wrong.

He scanned the room. By now most of his colleagues were out to lunch. Only Mary Johnson remained, tucked away in her secluded corner with her head down. The desks surrounding Rachel's were all empty.

Jesse hesitated for a moment and then muttered, 'To hell with it.'

Assuming a nonchalant air he made his way over to her cubicle, glancing around one last time as he approached. Mary Johnson looked up and he assumed the position of a man lost in thought, staring out of the window. He waited until Mary's reflection put its head down again, then with one hand in his pocket he cast his eyes over Rachel's work area. His free hand he ran idly across the desktop.

A yellow legal pad lay off to one side underneath an old coffee mug with a faded print of the Eiffel Tower on it. He wondered when she had been to Paris and with whom and snuffed an unexpected pang of jealousy. Keeping casual, he shuffled closer to the desk. After a quick check over his shoulder he moved the coffee mug and slid the pad closer to get a better look. It was covered in scribbles, doodles and random words that he could imagine Rachel scrawling absently while lost in thought. He looked closer. Some letters and numbers were grouped together in the top right-hand corner of the page. She had circled them and gone over the circle a few times with a black pen so that the line was thick and dark. Was that a flight number?

Behind him, Mary Johnson coughed. He jumped and checked her reflection but Mary was paying no attention to him. He looked down at the pad again. The phone on the desk rang and he answered it without thinking.

'Jesse Shaw.' Damn it! He should have let it ring.

'Hello,' said a man's voice.

'Can I help you?'

'Maybe,' the voice replied. 'I'm looking for Rachel Jones.'

'This is her number, but she's out,' said Jesse. Perhaps it was a client. 'Can I help you with something?'

There was a pause. The man cleared his throat. 'Right. Any idea where I can reach her?'

Jesse identified the accent as Irish. 'Who is this?'

'My name is Peter. Who is this?'

'My name is Jesse. I'm a colleague of Rachel's.'

'Right,' the Irishman said again. 'So, when will Rachel be back?'

Something set off his bullshit sensor. 'Uh, she's – I'm not sure, exactly. What is this in connection with? Perhaps I can help?'

'I doubt it. It's a personal matter.'

'Oh?' Who the hell was this guy? Brother? Ex? Boyfriend? Jesse's jaw clenched at the thought. Surely not. 'Why don't you tell me what this is about and—'

'Yeah,' Peter cleared his throat again. 'Okay look, Jesse. I'm going to go out on a limb here and tell you what's happened and yeah, maybe you *can* help. The thing is, I'm pretty sure Rachel has gone away with my fiancée, Cara. Now I've gone and lost the bloody flight details and forgotten the name of the place where they're staying and I need to find them again because if Cara gets back and I'm not there to meet her at the airport I'll be sleeping on the sofa until I'm eighty, do you know what I mean?'

Jesse listened with interest. Cara; he recognised the name. She was the friend Rachel was supposedly 'helping out'. Had they taken a trip somewhere? Was that where Rachel had gone? It sounded plausible. The only thing that did *not* make sense was why Rachel wouldn't have said anything to him. He tapped his finger on the legal pad in front of him. 'Cara's fiancé, you said?'

'That's right.'

'Why don't you just ring her and find out?'

Peter laughed. 'I wish it were that easy. Her phone is off. Maybe they're out of range, who knows? But listen, if you can help me it would be great not to get a bollocking for not paying enough attention to what she was saying, you know what I mean?'

Jesse frowned. 'Sure, but why would you ring Rachel's number if you knew she wouldn't be here?'

'I took a flyer, mate. I thought maybe they hadn't left yet – to be honest I thought this was her home number. It took me by surprise when you answered.'

Jesse pursed his lips. All he knew was that Rachel was not where she was supposed to be and the longer he stared at them, the more the scribbles on her legal pad looked like they could be flight details. Other than those, this Peter actually seemed to know more than he himself did. Maybe he could even shed some light on things for Jesse. Curiosity won out.

'Yeah, well, Peter, you may be in luck because I happen to be looking at a piece of paper with some flight details on it.'

'That's great, man. You'll save my hide, I swear.'

'No problem,' said Jesse but he hesitated, buying time while he weighed up the pros and cons. If he gave him the details there was a good chance Peter would open up and share something with him. But what if Peter was not who he said he was? He decided on a compromise. He would give him the flight details but then Jesse would go to the airport himself when the time came, just to be on the safe side.

'So, the flight details?' Peter prompted.

'Right, um, well from what I can make out here the flight lands at Gatwick on Saturday afternoon.' He read out the flight number and arrival time.

'Is that it?'

'Were you hoping for more?'

'No, that's great. Although I was hoping to find out about Cara's flight back to Dublin, or at least which hotel they're in so I can phone her and check.'

'Dublin?' Jesse relaxed. Peter's story seemed more and more genuine. 'Sorry, there's nothing here about that. The only other thing that I can make out is part of a word – it looks like 'Lion'-something. She's scribbled over it so I can't see the rest of it.' He squinted at the paper but whatever else she had written was obliterated by the scraggly circle Rachel had drawn around the details. 'Does that mean anything to you?'

'It sure does,' Peter laughed as if he was enjoying an inside joke.

Jesse gritted his teeth. He was coming off second best in this encounter. 'Well that's it. The rest is a mess. Sorry. '

'No problem, you've been a great help Jesse.'

'Sure.' He cast a glance back to Mary Johnson's desk. She looked up, caught his eye, blinked and looked back down again. Jesse turned his back to her, unsure how to proceed. He was frustrated at being unable to wheedle any further information out of Peter and already beginning to regret telling him what he had.

'Hey, Jesse?'

'Yes?'

'Are you Rachel's boyfriend or something?'

'Or something. Why do you ask?'

'A hunch,' said Peter. 'I was just curious about if she has started dating again.'

What the hell did that mean? On one hand, it was a relief that Peter sounded as if he really did know Rachel. On the other hand, what the devil was he talking about? This conversation was raising more questions than it had answered. But Peter did not give him the chance to ask any of them.

'Great, well listen man, thanks again. I owe you one. I'll buy you a pint some time, yeah?'

'Sure, that sounds good,' said Jesse as people began to trickle back into the office. He was out of time. 'Look, I have to go. Good luck, Peter. I hope you don't get into trouble with your fiancée.'

'Yeah, me too,' he said with a stilted chuckle and ended the call.

Jesse stared for a moment at the page in front of him, committing the flight numbers to memory. He took care to replace the legal pad exactly as he had found it, with the scuffed old Paris mug back on top. Lost in thought, he made his way back to his own desk. He felt uncomfortable about having given Rachel's flight number out on blind faith and he would make damn sure he was there himself when she landed. Just in case. He leaned forward with his elbows on his desk and pressed his fingertips together in front of his face. It would be simple enough to find out where the flight was coming from. All he had to do was type the numbers into a search engine.

That was the easy part.

What concerned him more was why Rachel had taken off like that in the first place. Why had she not mentioned it to him on Friday after work? And what the hell did Peter mean when he said that about her dating again?

Jesse Shaw was beginning to wonder just how much he still had to learn about the lovely Ms Jones.

Over in Dublin, Peter hung up and let go with a gleeful, 'Hah!' He could hardly believe his luck that Jesse had answered Rachel's phone.

Peter had been dialling the two London-based numbers all morning. None of Rachel's other colleagues had bothered to pick up, but Jesse obviously had a vested interest. Based on his initial caginess Peter had taken a gamble and it had paid off. Peter had assumed Cara was hiding out with her old friend in a dingy London flat, talking trash about him. He had been prepared to beg and plead to be able to talk to her. Now, with the information Jesse had given him, he could find out exactly where Cara was. He had yet to decide what he would do about it, but his focus now was on finding her.

He opened the browser on his computer. The flight number

started with the letters 'CY'. He entered the full string and within a few clicks of the mouse, he determined that Rachel's return flight originated in Paphos.

Cyprus? He frowned. That was random. What the hell was in Cyprus? Here he was, all strung out and worried about her and she was off gallivanting on an island in the Med. Nice!

But then his conscience prickled. He could just imagine the poor girl, heartbroken, spending her days on the verge of tears, trying to distract herself with all sorts of lame touristy crap. Oh well, she was always going on about wanting to go abroad again. Maybe this was good thing. Perhaps this little trip would satisfy her wanderlust for a while.

Peter, himself, was not so keen to travel the world. He had everything he needed right here in Dublin. When she saw how tedious it was to poke through musty old museums and listen to the fake enthusiasm of half-arsed tour guides it might make Cara realise just how good she had it here with him. That would make things a lot easier when it came time for him to carry out his mission to win her back. With any luck, his parents would never even know there had been a split.

He returned his attention to his computer. The next part was a bit trickier. The most obvious guess was that 'Lion' had something to do with their hotel, so he typed it into the search box and stuck 'Cyprus' on the end for good measure. Was it too much to ask of Fortune that his search would find it on his first attempt?

It was. All sorts of links to do with Richard the bloody Lionheart came up. What the hell did *he* have to do with Cyprus? He drummed his fingers on his desk and stared out of the window at the grey drizzle outside. Bloody rain. His fingers stilled and an idea began to form. Smiling to himself, his mission took on a new dimension. He *had* to find out where Cara was.

Trying a different tactic, he typed 'Cyprus Hotels' into the search box and scanned the list of suggested sites. The third link took him to a page that listed establishments by location and star rating. He scrolled down, scanning the list for anything with 'Lion' in its name.

'Bingo,' he murmured. He used an online map to check distances and nodded with satisfaction. Paphos was the closest airport alright, and the hotel looked reasonably small. Cara had never gone in for the full five-star treatment, although God alone knew why. Yes, this must be it: The Lionheart Hotel in Limassol, Cyprus.

Peter leaned back in his chair and laced his fingers behind his head. Basking in the glow of his own brilliance he started making his plans.

What woman could resist a man who would travel clear across Europe just to sweep her off her feet? Hah! Cara would have no choice but to take him back.

Chapter 6

After a slow breakfast in the hotel dining room Cara and Rachel spent a lazy Monday morning wandering the streets of Old Town. Thankfully, there was barely a twinge from her twisted ankle and she was able to do the tourist thing unhindered.

Rachel seemed to have set her opinions aside and they were back to the easy companionship they had always shared. They chatted and laughed through breakfast and the short taxi ride to Old Town and spent imaginary Lotto winnings while they window-shopped in its winding streets, before heading to the medieval museum inside Limassol castle. This was an imposing fortress nestled in well-kept gardens of tall trees, sweet oleander blooms and pale displays of ancient pedestals. Its thick stone walls reminded Cara of the sandy yellow ones at Kolossi Castle.

They started in the basement. Cara had always thought of dungeons as dark, damp places but daylight seemed to seep into this one making it bone dry and somehow less scary, although she was sure the prisoners it had once held would have had a different opinion. The tombstones on display went a long way to keeping things sombre, too. Upstairs they admired displays of jewellery, pottery, weaponry and even a full suit of armour. Also, Richard the Lionheart was said to have married there in the year 1191. That explained the name of their hotel, then.

Between the Byzantines, earthquakes, Knights, Venetians and

Turks, the building had been captured, destroyed and rebuilt so many times that Cara was amazed it was still standing. There was far more to Cyprus than beaches and olive groves and Cara was beginning to understand Yiannis's fierce passion about his country and his heritage.

Looking down from the battlements at the very top of the castle, she concluded that Old Town certainly lived up to its name. Terracotta rooftops that looked nearly as old as the castle itself spread out in a haphazard pattern at her feet. Further away, the more modern parts of the city crept out towards the mountains but below the steep castle walls, centuries-old streets darted this way and that like a disorganised spider's web. Some of the buildings were so far beyond repair they looked ready to be condemned, but overall it looked like exactly what it was: an old port town that had survived for centuries and was being regenerated into a tourist centre.

A flimsy plastic bag rustled against her leg. It came from a tiny shop, tucked away in a paved alley covered over with bright pink bougainvillea, and it held a dainty linen tablecloth she had bought for her mother. She might make the trip down to Waterford to see her when she got back. It had been a while. A sense of dread took hold. She had yet to break the news to her parents that the wedding was off. How would they take it? Would they blame her? Her mother adored Peter and her father – well, he only wanted to see Cara safely married to a good man. *Hah, shows how much we knew, Dad.*

A stab of anger spurred her to action and she crossed the rooftop quickly as if to distance herself from the thought. She fixed her gaze on the queue of cargo ships that waited their turn at sea to enter the big new harbour that took care of business now. All around the world life went on and Cara knew she had to do the same.

Her thoughts turned to Yiannis. He seemed a good place to start. She glanced down to the streets below, her gaze scanning the crowds. People looked different from this angle. Would she recognise him from up here if she saw him? Her heart skipped a beat as a man in dark clothes emerged from a side street with a rucksack slung over his shoulder. She squinted and tried to get a better look but he turned a corner and was lost from view. Was it Yiannis? She laughed at herself. More like wishful thinking, no doubt, although there had been something about the way he moved . . . She shook her head reproachfully. How the mind could play tricks when you wanted something badly enough!

Rachel ambled over, having finished her own tour of the rooftop. 'Are you ready to go?'

Cara threw one last glance over the edge and nodded. 'Yes. I think I've seen enough.'

They ate lunch in the shade of an umbrella at one of the cafés beside the castle square. While she munched her way through a seafood salad and their shared portion of fries, Cara kept an eye out for Yiannis, searching the faces of passing pedestrians as casually as possible. People looked so much happier here than in Dublin. They were less rushed, and the locals stopped to greet each other as they passed. It must be nice.

But there was no sign of Yiannis and she began to wonder if she had misunderstood him. She couldn't eat another prawn if she tried and Rachel looked as if she would be ready to finish up soon.

'Wouldn't it be great to live here?' she mused aloud.

'Do you really think so?' said Rachel. 'I mean, it's fine for a holiday but I don't think I could *live* here. I would miss London too much. It has a real vibe about it, like it's the very heart of civilization, you know?'

Pushing her sunglasses to the end of her nose, Cara peered at her over the top of them. 'If you say so.'

Rachel smiled and Cara pushed the glasses back into place. She resumed her speculations with a sigh. 'Well I would love to live in a place like this. London would be way too busy and noisy for me. Even Dublin overwhelms me sometimes and don't even get me started on the weather. If I never saw another raindrop it would be too soon.'

'Mm,' said Rachel, munching on a crabstick. 'But what would you do here?'

Cara shifted in her chair and tilted her chin back in thought. Her heart flipped as she thought she caught a glimpse of Yiannis behind a pair of young mothers with strollers. They stopped and the man stepped into view, dashing her hopes. It was just a man, a stranger. He saw her looking and sent her a lascivious wink. She looked away without acknowledgment and thought about Rachel's question.

'I'm sure I could find something. With so many tourists around there must be loads of jobs here for people who speak English. Maybe I'd get something at one of the hotels. I don't have to work in HR. It's not like it's a calling, or anything.'

Rachel set down her cutlery, pushed her plate aside and wiped her fingers on a paper napkin.

'Cara, you'd hate to work those long hotel hours – and what about all the people you'd leave behind? You couldn't just nip down to Waterford to visit your folks any time you like, the way you can now.'

Cara flicked her eyes around once more. *Where was he?*

'I hardly ever go to Waterford, except maybe for Christmas and Easter.'

'But you could, if you wanted to,' argued Rachel. 'And what about Declan? You see a lot of him, don't you? Who would you go drinking with on those nights when Peter—' She slapped her hand over her mouth, her eyes large. 'Oops, sorry.'

Cara gave a weak smile. 'That's okay. I've decided I'm not going to break down every time someone says his name.'

'Well, that's progress.'

'Yes, and that's sort of my point, too. Without Peter in my life there is nothing holding it together. It really doesn't matter if I'm there or if I'm here. At least here I could be *warm* and miserable.'

Cara's smile wavered and she looked down. No, that was no good. Sadness and anger welled up inside her again so she cast her gaze outwards, towards the castle instead.

And there he was.

The sight of him created an instant tug-of-war amongst her emotions. Lust won, sending heartbreak into hiding. Yiannis stood on the other side of the road, his shirt brilliant white in the sunshine. With skin the colour of caramel, he resembled a Calvin Klein model in his aviator glasses. He smiled and started towards her just as a car came roaring around the corner. Her hands flew to her face in fright and she gasped, watching in horror as, by some miracle, the car missed Yiannis by inches as he sprinted across the road.

Rachel looked up in time to see him make it safely to the pavement.

'Oh. Of course,' she said sarcastically.

'What a maniac,' Cara exclaimed.

'Do not worry,' said Yiannis, approaching their table. 'Everybody drives like this here. It is normal.'

'Not him – you!' she scolded. 'I almost had heart failure! Would you not wait until after he'd gone?'

Yiannis laughed heartily. 'I could not wait any longer to get to you, Cara.'

'Oh, for heaven's sake,' muttered Rachel.

'*Yassou*, ladies. I hope you are enjoying your day?'

To Cara's ears, his accent made this polite greeting sound like a proposition.

'We've had a great morning, haven't we Rachel?'

Through her giddy swirl she remembered to make the effort to include her friend. She did not want a repeat of yesterday.

'Sure, great,' said Rachel minus enthusiasm. 'Boy, what are the chances we'd bump into you here?'

Yiannis pulled up a chair without waiting for an invitation. 'On sunny days like this one I like to go for a walk. The place where I work is not too far from here.'

Rachel nodded but her eyes conveyed suspicion. Tension knotted Cara's stomach, like when she was a child and her mother had caught her out in a lie. Perhaps this was not such a good idea after all.

Yiannis must have reached the same conclusion, for he glanced at Cara and his lips twitched in a tiny smile. 'Sadly, I cannot stay.'

'That's okay, neither can we,' said Rachel.

'We can't?' said Cara.

'We have to get back to the hotel to meet up with our travel rep, remember?'

Cara remembered no such thing.

'It was in the information pack that we got when we arrived,' Rachel prompted.

'The . . . information pack? I'm afraid I didn't actually look inside it.' Cara turned to Yiannis. 'Do you have to leave already?'

'Yes, but before I go—'

'Well, of course you didn't,' Rachel cut in.

Cara blinked. 'Excuse me?'

'The information pack; the itinerary; the reservations. You didn't do any of it. I did, just like I always do. I organise things and take care of the details while you run around having the time of your life like a spoiled princess.'

Cara and Yiannis both stared at her. Her cheeks had turned pink and she had tight lines around her mouth.

'Forget it,' she said. 'I'm going in to pay for lunch. When I get back, we have to go, Cara, alright?'

'Sure,' mumbled Cara but she was already gone.

Yiannis stared after her. 'I think it is better if I leave you two ladies alone for the day, yes?'

'Maybe. I don't know what's got into her.'

'Do you think she will be better by tonight?'

'I hope so. Why?'

'I would like you to have dinner with me. Just us, this time.'

Her spirits soared. To hell with Rachel's little temper tantrum, there was no way she was turning down this invitation. 'I would like that, too.'

His face split into a smile. He leaned forward, kissed her lightly on the lips and stood. 'Good. I will fetch you at eight o'clock at your hotel. Tell Rachel there is a party tomorrow night. My brother has returned from his travels and we will have some drinks at a bar in the Tourist Area. One of our friends is the manager there. You should both come along. It will be fun and your friend looks like she needs some fun.'

Cara laughed. 'I'll mention it to her later – give her some time to warm up to the idea.'

He nodded and moved away, raising his hand in a farewell wave to Rachel as she returned from paying the bill. 'See you later,' he called and dashed across the road, dodging a scooter and disappearing into the crowds.

'Later?' Rachel enquired.

Cara picked up her shoulder bag and the plastic bag containing her mother's gift. 'Yes. I hope you didn't have anything special planned for tonight because I,' she said, pausing for dramatic effect, 'have a date.'

It was already dark when Yiannis arrived to fetch her. 'I thought it was Ari's,' she said, surprised to see him driving the silver sedan they had taken to Paphos the day before.

'It is. I borrowed it for tonight. I thought it would be more comfortable than my motorcycle.'

She looked down at her pointy designer boots and the short green dress she wore beneath her blue jacket and nodded. 'Good call.'

He hooked an arm around her neck, drawing her into a hug that ended with a kiss.

Cara glowed with pleasure. 'Where are we going?'

'To the finest restaurant in *Lemesos*.'

'*Lemesos*?'

'Limassol, *Lemesos* – it is the same.'

Lemesos. Something pinged in her memory but it was lost before she could catch it. She shook her head. Cyprus was as bad as Ireland, the way they had two names for everything.

'Does this restaurant have a name?'

He threw her a secretive smile and opened the car door for her. 'It is a surprise.'

They turned off the main road that would have taken them towards Old Town and headed away from the coast and into the part of the city where the locals lived. Traffic snarled and pavements were crowded. Here Cypriot life existed without the glamour and coloured lights of the Tourist Area. Four boisterous young men strutted out of a café, laughing loudly and drawing furtive looks from a couple of old men who sat at a rickety table outside. What the hell was she doing here, alone with a man she had known only two days, at night, in a city she did not know? Cara chewed on her lip as she stared out at the busy streets flashing past her window. You read stories about this sort of thing in the newspapers. Innocent tourists taken in by con-men, robbed and murdered, their mutilated corpses discovered days later in deserted fields. She sneaked a glance at Yiannis as he skilfully manoeuvred the car through a busy intersection. *Get a grip*, she told herself. *He's a horny programmer, not an axe-murderer.*

Two corners later he pulled over and announced, 'We are here.'

She got out and looked around but all she could see were apartment blocks. 'Where .. ?'

He locked the car and gestured upwards. 'This is my place.'

She looked up at a small block fronted with patchy white balconies. 'I thought we were going to a restaurant.'

He took her hand and smiled. 'Did I mention I can cook?'

Cara hesitated, suddenly afraid. She had imagined a romantic dinner, perhaps followed by a little heavy petting. In fact, she had rather looked forward to it. After dinner, he would have invited her to go back to his place, like he had on Saturday. After dinner, she would have decided if she wanted to go.

After dinner.

'Cara? Are you okay?' His voice was gentle. 'We can go somewhere else, if you like. I wanted to cook for you, but if you would like, we can rather go somewhere else?'

They locked eyes. Who was she kidding? She took a deep breath and jumped in. 'What sort of girl would turn down a man who wants to cook for her?'

His apartment was on the third floor. It consisted of an open-plan living area, one bedroom and a bathroom. There were two beige sofas in the living area and a desk loaded with computer equipment where most people would have a dining table. A nest of cables gathered around a plug board beneath it. Functional and minimalistic, this reminded her very much of Declan's place, apart from the computer stuff. Declan had only a laptop that he took out once a week to check his email.

The tiled balcony looked onto similar ones across a wide street. Most had their doors closed and curtains drawn. His was just big enough to fit a small outdoor dining set and a gas barbeque, above which a dim light glowed. After turning on the oven in the kitchen, Yiannis lit the barbeque and within minutes had eight small lamb cutlets sizzling on the grill. A white linen cloth covered the plastic table which held a blue storm lantern and two place settings. The smell of cooking smoke and baking potatoes soon filled the air and Cara's stomach growled in anticipation. Yiannis poured her a glass of wine and opened a beer for himself while he tended the barbeque. Cara settled into one of the plastic chairs, her ankles crossed and her jacket wrapped tightly around her. It smelled of leather and creaked a bit as she moved.

'Did you have any trouble with Rachel about tonight?' he asked.

'No. She wasn't exactly thrilled at first but she was okay by the time I left.' She shook her head, annoyed. 'I still don't understand what her problem is. I find it hard to believe she's simply jealous over the time I'm spending with you. It is very unlike her.'

'Maybe there is something else.' He shrugged. 'But I do not know her as well as you do.'

Cara thought about it while she sipped the cool, sweet wine. Yiannis had a point. Was there more to Rachel's pouting than petty jealousy and misplaced concern for Cara's well-being? Was she hiding something? It was unlikely. They told each other everything. She remembered Rachel's hysterical phone call the day that Philip died, and shivered at the terrible memory.

'Are you cold?' Yiannis asked and she started as he placed his hand on her shoulder.

'Not at all,' she said with a quick smile. 'I'm from Dublin, remember?'

'Of course,' he chuckled and stroked her cheek lightly with his thumb before turning back to the barbeque, flipping the cutlets with practised ease.

Her senses tingled as she watched him. He was not as tall as Peter but he was broader across the shoulders, which tapered to slim hips. His long legs were clad in a pair of snug, faded denims and his back rippled beneath his light khaki sweater when he moved. No, he was definitely not Peter. Yiannis was infinitely more exciting. The thought took her by surprise.

'Tell me about your life in Dublin,' he invited.

She sipped her wine to clear her head. 'It's probably not that different from yours, only with more crap weather.'

'So you keep telling me. You do not like it there?'

'It's okay.' Cara had no desire to admit to Yiannis that she hated her job, was sick of the rain and had nothing to look forward to since her fiancé had ripped her life apart. It seemed a little heavy for their second date. 'Did I tell you we met with our travel rep earlier?'

'That was real? I thought perhaps Rachel made it up to get you away from me at lunch time,' he laughed.

'Maybe you know her better than you think,' she said with a chuckle. 'But no, there really was a meeting. We were supposed to see her on Sunday but as you know we were too busy looking at castles and deserted beaches with you and Ari.'

'And what did you learn from your travel rep?'

'That there are lovely castles and deserted beaches to visit in Cyprus.' Yiannis laughed and Cara grinned. 'To be fair, the meeting wasn't a total waste of time. I had no idea Egypt was so close to here. Did you know they run day-trips to Cairo? Well, they do, so we decided that since neither of us has seen the Pyramids we should go while we have the chance.'

'To Cairo?'

'Yes. We're going on Thursday. I'm quite excited about it. Even Rachel cheered up at the idea.'

He nodded in approval. 'It sounds nice. Stay clear of the camels. They are smelly beasts, and they bite.'

'Sound advice, I'll keep that in mind.'

In flickering candlelight from the storm lantern, they dined on flame-grilled lamb, a salad of fresh tomatoes, cucumber, feta and olives, crisp bread with tzatziki, and Greek-style potatoes baked in cream with a hint of aniseed. Yiannis had not exaggerated his skills in the kitchen. Cara had eaten worse meals in some posh Dublin restaurants.

He wanted to know all about her, so she told him about Declan, Bridget and their parents who still lived in the house in Waterford in which she grew up. She avoided the subject of Peter and he did not ask. At one point, he observed, 'You are right, it is not so different from my life. I think perhaps people are the same all over the world, yes? We have parents, brothers, sisters, friends – jobs, if we are lucky. The places, they may be different but people are basically the same no matter where they are.'

'In a way,' said Cara. 'But at the same time every place has something that marks it as special. Even in Ireland you have people from Dublin and people from the country. In some ways, they could be from different planets. It's more than just big city versus rural tradition. Even while the people are all Irish, they are different because of where they come from. Each place is different and those differences make the people unique. It's what makes travel so interesting. Different places, different people. I'd hate to think we were all the same. That would be so boring, don't you think?'

She pushed her plate aside. It was bare now, save for the stripped bones and olive pips.

He laughed. 'Now you sound like my brother. I can see you like to travel. That is good news for me, otherwise I may not have had the good luck to meet you. Now come, let us go inside for some coffee and dessert.'

'Dessert?'

'Of course.' He stood and began to clear the dishes. 'Every restaurant has dessert and I have something special for you.'

'I'm counting on it,' she replied cheekily and instantly regretted it.

He stopped what he was doing and raised his eyes with a look that froze her breath. 'Comments like that will get you in trouble.'

She let out a nervous giggle. 'Here, let me help you with those.' She grabbed the casserole dish with leftover potatoes in it and hurried off to the kitchen. He followed after a minute, and ordered her out while he brewed coffee and prepared dessert.

Unable to sit still, Cara went to freshen up. In the sanctity of the bathroom she combed her auburn locks with her fingers, alternately smoothing and tousling until she was satisfied that it looked both shiny and natural in the mirror. She touched up her face with a few dabs of powder and ran a finger past her lashes to remove imaginary smudges of mascara. She washed her hands with soap that smelled like oranges and afterwards she dried them on a course beige hand towel.

And then she panicked. Why had she agreed to this? Her knuckles turned white as she gripped the basin. She should have insisted they go somewhere public. Sure, Yiannis had behaved like a perfect gentleman up to now, but what came next? And what the hell was she thinking, dropping that suggestive comment? If she turned him down now he would accuse her of being a tease for sure, and he would be right. Okay, so she had dreamed about sleeping with him and even fantasised about it during her waking hours, but in some deep corner of herself she still felt like Peter's fiancée and this . . . this was overstepping. Cara retrieved the engagement ring that was still buried in her purse, pushed it onto her finger and waited for her conscience to tell her what to do.

The large diamond blinked up at her, but the wave of guilt that she anticipated did not come. Instead, a perfectly calm inner voice told her to take off the ring, go out there and drink her coffee. *You know damn well that you're here because you want to be, not because Yiannis tricked you into it. You want him, pure and simple. So, go get him. Or don't. Either way it's your decision – not Peter's, not Yiannis's. You're a grown woman. Act like one.*

The voice made sense. It also sounded remarkably like her sister, but this was not the time to examine that particular detail. She looked up at her reflection and noddd. *Well okay, then.*

Feeling strangely calm, she replaced the ring in her purse, adjusted the neckline of her dress and went to join Yiannis in the lounge.

Two red mugs steamed on the coffee table. Yiannis approached from the direction of the kitchen, bearing two bowls with dessert spoons. He handed one to her and lowered himself onto the sofa beside her.

She looked down into the bowl and her lips twitched in amusement. 'Ice cream?'

'Not just ice cream – Rocky Road ice cream, the best in the world.'

He smiled, and his eyes crinkled in the corners and suddenly she knew that everything would be alright. So, when he took her empty bowl and placed it beside his on the table, reached over and took her in his arms, Cara responded without a second thought.

They were horizontal on the couch and Cara's jacket and boots were in a heap on the floor next to them when his phone rang.

'Ignore it,' she urged.

'I wish I could,' he groaned through breathless kisses. He tore himself away and she giggled watching him fumble in the pocket of his jeans. Running a hand through his tousled hair, he answered curtly.

Cara's breathing slowly returned to normal as she manoeuvred herself up into a sitting position. She wondered if her eyes were as glazed as his. She did not understand Greek but she could tell he was trying to keep the conversation brief. Through smiling replies his tone was filled with impatience and the call lasted less than a minute. Cara was pretty sure he was telling the caller – Ari, perhaps – that she was there.

'I am sorry about that,' he said, tossing the phone onto the table with a clatter. 'My brother has bad timing.'

'Your brother – the one who was away?'

He nodded. 'He wanted to know something about tomorrow night.'

'Oh right, the party.'

'You are coming, yes?' His look of sudden consternation made her laugh.

'Yes. I even got Rachel to agree. I sprang it on her while she was still in a good mood after booking our trip to Cairo.'

'Ah, so you are clever as well as beautiful.' He licked his lips and reached for her again. 'Now, where was I?'

His lips found hers and she sank back against the sofa under the glorious weight of his body. She wrapped her leg around his, pressing him closer. He pushed himself up on one elbow and gazed at her. Her lips ached for more but he held back, teasing her. His olive eyes were bright with tiny golden flecks and Cara's chest heaved with deep, quick breaths. Tracing her hairline with his fingertips, the touch of his fingers was divine torture. He watched them trail down her neck and across her shoulder, devouring her with his eyes until he broke the contact so suddenly she nearly cried out. He smiled a smile she had not seen before. This one was dark; he was the master and her body was his slave. She twitched as his fingers resumed their contact, this time with her thigh just below the hemline of her dress. A small moan escaped her lips and his smile deepened. He traced tiny patterns on her skin and it puckered under his touch. Slowly, tortuously, he slid his hand up under the stretchy fabric of her dress. She moaned again and her thighs parted of their own accord. His hand moved higher and her eyelids fluttered closed. Higher, and her eyes opened again in surprise and in a sudden, horrid moment of confusion they filled with tears and a wracking sob burst out of her. 'Oh God, I can't!'

He froze immediately. 'Cara, are you okay?'

Her hands had flown up to her mouth to stifle the sob and though no more followed, tears spilled down her cheeks.

'Cara, what is the matter?'

How could she explain the shock seeing his face instead of someone else's when she opened her eyes? She could hardly grasp it herself that for one oblivious moment she had been with another man. What kind of cruel trick was her mind playing on her?

'Oh Yiannis, I'm so sorry.' She tried to laugh but it sounded strangled. 'I don't know what happened. This is all happening so fast. I guess I got a bit spooked.'

He shifted sideways so that he lay beside her, giving her space. 'No, I am sorry. I have rushed you. We can stop, if you like.'

'No! I mean – oh God,' Her cheeks flamed with embarrassment and she covered them with her hands.

He gave her a quizzical look and ran a hand through his hair, the way he had when he'd answered his phone. The gesture betrayed his unease and yet strangely, she felt comforted by it. A cool imprint remained where the hand in question no longer rested on her thigh.

His voice rasped as he spoke and she could tell that he was struggling to bring himself under control. 'You need not worry, Cara. We will not do anything you do not want to do.'

'You are a good man, Yiannis.'

He gave a harsh chuckle that was laced with a trace of the darkness that had stirred up her passion before. It had the same effect again and Cara felt her disorientation bleed away the way it did when she awoke from a bad dream. Reality resumed; the heat of Yiannis's leg along the length of hers, the rise and fall of his chest against her side and the musky scent of desire that hung between them.

She reached up and smoothed the frown from his forehead. 'I really am sorry. I had a moment, but I am okay now, I promise.'

His eyes searched hers, clouded once more with longing. 'I do not want you to regret anything.'

'I won't.'

She pulled his head closer and brushed her lips against his as she pushed aside the ghost of the image that had haunted her.

He responded with a primal groan that rumbled through him as he wrapped her once more in his embrace.

Chapter 7

Rachel flicked through the channels for the fourth time, puffing her cheeks with a bored sigh. So many channels, so much crap, she thought and switched the television off. The radio on the wall between her and Cara's beds played nothing but static. Silence pressed in and she turned the television back on, leaving it on the news channel with the volume way down. Resisting the temptation to check her phone she picked up her novel instead, a three-for-two detective story that would join dozens of others gathering dust in her aged bookshelf when she got home.

She and Cara had made a pact to keep their phones off the whole week, declaring that the world would just have to cope without them for a while. But after reading the same sentence three times over Rachel dropped the book face down on the bed beside her and stared blankly at the television. The pact had been made when this was still a girls-only holiday. Now Cara was off on a hot date and Rachel questioned whether the rules still applied.

Oh, what the hell.

She dug her phone out of her suitcase. It took a minute or two to power up and work out that it was no longer in London, and then it beeped, announcing that she had four voicemail messages. It then went *freep* to let her know the battery was low.

Four messages; had something come up at work? Did she really want to know? Probably not, but she'd come this far so there hardly seemed much point in stopping now.

With the first message, her mother's broad lilt filled the room. 'Rachel, it's Mammy. Where in the world are you? Would you ring me to let me know you're still alive, please?'

She rolled her eyes and deleted the message.

Freep, said the phone.

The other three messages were nothing but hang-ups. How disappointing. Rachel sat on the bed and looked at it. A second later it sprang to life, making her jump as it erupted in a shrill ring.

'Hello?'

'Rachel? It's Jesse.'

She sat bolt upright at the sound of his voice. 'Jesse? How did you find me?'

'You're joking, right? We've been through this before. Your number is on the company Intranet, remember?'

She gave a nervous laugh. 'Oh right. This is my mobile.'

'That is correct. Are you okay?'

'Sure, of course. Why wouldn't I be?' She frowned with sudden concern. 'Are you?'

'Me? I'm fine.'

'Great. That's great.'

'Actually, that's not entirely true,' he said.

Her heart stopped. 'Oh?'

'You see I came into work this morning expecting to see this girl that I work with. I have a bit of a crush on her, as it happens and I thought the feeling was mutual. Only she wasn't here and I haven't seen her all day. You can see how I might have grown a little worried, right?'

Rachel's shoulders drooped. 'I see.'

'So anyway, I did a bit of asking around and I found out that she's taken a week off, which surprised me a little because when I spoke to her on Friday she didn't mention she was going anywhere. In fact, I'm almost sure she said she would see me next week, which is today, of course. Only, she's not here. She's somewhere else, although nobody seems to know where.'

'She sounds like a real bitch, this girl.'

'Well I didn't think she was. I'm just a little confused about why she lied.'

'Lied? That's a little strong, isn't it? I mean, is it written somewhere that this girl is required to tell you her every move?' Rachel squeezed her eyes shut and smacked herself on the forehead, lightly, with the phone. She had not meant to antagonise him. 'I'm sorry, I didn't mean—'

'No, that's okay,' he said, his voice hardening. 'You're right. You don't owe me any explanations. My concerns were obviously misplaced. Sorry I disturbed you. I won't bother you again.'

'Jesse, wait!'

Silence.

'Are you still there?'

'Yes, I'm here.'

Oh God, what to tell him? This phone call had caught her completely off-guard.

Freep!

'Bollocks, my battery is going to die. Look, I'm sorry I didn't say anything to you on Friday. Honestly, it seemed too complicated to go into. This thing with us, whatever it is – God, I don't even know what it is! I don't know what the rules are, here or even if there are any.'

'Rules? Why do there have to be rules? Can't we just take it easy and see how things play out?'

'I wish it were that simple. This is all happening so fast. I need some time.'

'Time for what?'

'Time to think. Things are not always as straightforward as they seem, Jesse.' Her voice almost broke as she said his name. Used to being in control of herself and her life, Rachel had no idea how to deal with this uncertainty. She hated feeling like this.

'That's your argument – 'it's complicated'? I would expect more from someone of your talents.'

Rachel took a breath and when she spoke again it was in a gentler tone. 'I suppose I deserve that. For what it's worth, I apologise for not being upfront with you, but I don't want to get into it on the phone. Look, I'm in Cyprus with a friend of mine. She's going through a bit of a rough time right now and we came here so she could to get away for a bit. I'll be away for the rest of the week but we'll talk when I get back, okay?'

'Cyprus. Right. Um, this friend, is it anyone I know?'

She smiled to herself. Was that jealousy she heard?

Freep!

'No, you haven't met her. It's my old friend from Dublin, Cara. She caught her fiancé screwing around so we're here trying to mend her broken heart.'

'Christ,' breathed Jesse.

'Yeah, I know. It's horrible. So anyway, that's the story; that's why I'm here. But I'm not going to lie to you,' she babbled. 'I need the break, myself. There are some things I need to sort out in my own head, too. God, I sound desperate! And here we've hardly even begun. I wouldn't blame you for walking away right now. I sound like a bloody crackpot. Oh dear, I'm rambling, aren't I? Look, I promise I'll tell you what this is all about but now is not the time. Not on the phone. I know it's a lot to ask, but do you think you can hang in there until the end of the week?'

'Your friend has broken up with her fiancé? Rachel, I—'

'Yes, but look, I'll be back on the weekend and we can talk about it—'

Freep-freep-freep!

'Jesse? Hello? Damn it!' She stared at the now dead mobile phone in her hand. Her charger, if she remembered correctly, was still plugged in beside the table in her flat in London. She would have to check if Cara had one she could use. She considered looking for it herself but she did not feel comfortable going through Cara's things uninvited. With the way things were between them it might look like she was snooping. She dropped the phone back into her suitcase with a groan.

Had she just messed things up with Jesse? Damn it, why hadn't she given more thought to how he might react to her taking off unannounced? Until now Rachel had not realised just how much she missed him. It was half the reason she was so cranky with Cara. She had sacrificed time with Jesse to help her friend and instead of appreciating her attention, Cara was off having an affair with a handsome local.

Not that missing Jesse made things any less complicated. She rubbed her eyes and lay back on the bed for another attempt at reading her novel, but got no further than before. The television still flickered on a continual news loop in the corner. Bored and unsettled, she got up and paced around the room. No doubt Cara would be out for a while. Why should she sit around by herself, stewing?

Making a sudden decision she slipped on a pair of heels with her jeans, brushed her hair, dabbed some perfume on her wrists and headed out the door.

The polished chrome and leather hotel bar area hummed with quiet. A handful of aged guests played cards in the lounge next door, where muzak piped in from somewhere softened the silence. A fresh breeze sneaked in through an open window, doing its best to dispel traces of cigarette smoke and dinner smells. Rachel planted her behind on a bar stool with more confidence than she felt and crossed one leg over the other. She hated going out alone, but anything had to be better than sitting by herself in her room. Besides, it was not like this was a *bar* bar. She thought it unlikely that any of the geriatric card players would try to hit on her.

'Gin and tonic?' the barman asked with a polite but friendly smile.

She smiled and shook her head. 'Not tonight. Can I get a glass of chardonnay instead?'

'Of course.' He splashed some into a glass and it glinted, pale under the recessed spotlights. 'You are not going out tonight?'

'No. I thought I'd come down and see if there was any more of that world-class entertainment to be seen.'

He jerked his head in the direction of the lounge. 'They had Bingo in there earlier, but it is over now. Now the old people just play cards until bed-time.'

Rachel almost choked on her first sip of wine. 'Bingo? What, are we staying in a retirement home?'

He grinned. 'There is a big group here from Germany – ex-Cypriots who have come back so they can vote on Saturday.'

'Vote? Oh, of course, the referendum. I heard about that.'

Still smiling, he looked down and idly wiped the bar counter in front of him with a grey cloth. Rachel took a more successful sip of wine and wondered what Cara was up to. God, she hoped she wouldn't do anything stupid.

'Is the wine okay?'

'It's great, thanks.'

He nodded. 'You are Cara's friend, yes?'

'I am,' she said, startled that he remembered her.

'We talked for a bit last night, Cara and I, after you went upstairs,' he said by way of explanation. 'She kept me company for a while. My name is Zoran.'

'Rachel,' she said.

'Cara is not with you tonight?'

'No. She has a date.' She did her best to keep the hard edge from her voice. Cara must have made an impression with those blue-green eyes of hers.

'Ah,' he said with a knowing nod of the head.

'Ah?'

He chuckled and went back to wiping the bar counter.

'You can't 'ah' like that and then say nothing more,' she objected. 'What do you know that I don't know?'

'Probably nothing,' he said, but when he looked up there was a twinkle in his dark eyes.

'What the hell did you two talk about last night?'

'This and that.'

'Men?'

'A little. She did not say much.'

'Well what *did* she say?'

'I believe that conversation is between Cara and her barman,' he said, with a barely concealed smile.

'Right, the sacred bond between barman and barfly,' Rachel laughed. 'Fair enough. I wouldn't want to compromise your principles.' She sipped her chardonnay and added, almost to herself, 'I just hope she's being careful.'

'You are worried about her.' It was a statement, not a question.

'I am. I don't think she should be getting involved with one man when she hasn't resolved things with the other.'

Zoran said nothing.

'I'm not going to get you to talk about this, am I?'

'I do not like to talk about other people,' he said and Rachel

112

blushed.

'I wasn't—'

He raised his hand to quiet her. 'No, no, that is not what I meant. All I say is that I do not know you or Cara very well, so I do not want to interfere.'

Rachel studied Zoran with curiosity as a sip of wine slid down her throat, cool and crisp. Cara was right. He was rather good-looking in that dark Mediterranean way and his eyes wore a gentle expression that was neutral and disarming. Did they teach them that in barman school? Swallowing her wine, she muttered, 'Well *someone* should interfere.'

Zoran raised his eyebrows.

'Fine, you don't have to say anything. But you can't blame me for worrying about my friend. A week ago, she was planning her wedding. Now she's off with a complete stranger, doing God-knows-what. I don't know what's got into her. Today she was even talking about *living* here! What next? She's lost the plot, I tell you.'

One of the card players chose that moment to march up to the bar. He barked his order in the manner of a man used to getting his own way. Zoran winked at her and held up one finger to indicate he would be back. He filled the order with an unrushed indifference that visibly irritated the man, who stood drumming his fingers impatiently on the polished counter.

Rachel smothered a smile. This lad was more than just a pretty face.

When his customer had been dispensed with Zoran returned, casually leaned one hip against the bar counter and continued the conversation as if there had been no interruption.

'People sometimes do crazy things when terrible things happen to them.'

Rachel's stomach dropped and the words were out before she could check herself. 'Not everybody.'

His eyes interrogated hers through narrowed lids and she looked away.

'Do you want to talk about it?'

He was teasing her, the cheeky bastard! She tossed her head defiantly and met his gaze but her ire was short-lived. There was no malevolence there, only kindness.

113

'You're a strange one, you are.' She took another swig of wine, set the glass back down and fingered the smooth stem.

'May I ask you a question?' he asked.

She shrugged. 'Sure. Knock yourself out.'

'Why do you sit here with me tonight instead of going out?'

'I thought that was obvious. My travel buddy is out on a hot date.'

'I find it hard to believe you could not get a date also.'

'That is very flattering, Zoran, but who says I want one?'

'Ah.'

'Ah?'

He smiled.

'You see, there you go again, with the 'Ah'. You can't say that to a girl and then leave it hanging!'

'Okay, okay,' he laughed. 'In this case 'Ah' means that I understand; you have a boyfriend.'

Rachel dropped her gaze. 'Not exactly.'

'A girlfriend?'

She giggled. 'No, no girlfriend either.'

He squinted at her hands, checking for rings. 'Husband?'

Rachel sighed. 'Not anymore.'

Zoran gave her a questioning look.

'He died,' she said. God, she hated telling people that. They always looked at her with such pity and said useless things like, 'I'm sorry.' As if it was their fault.

But Zoran did not. 'That is sad,' he said. There was no sympathy; it was a statement of fact. 'Was it a long time ago?'

'About a year and a half,' she replied, relieved and also a little intrigued.

'Ah, and you are not sure if it is too quick, with this new man,' he observed.

'Wait, I never said there was a new man.'

'You did not need to.'

She rolled her eyes. 'What, do you have some sort of superpowers or something?'

He laughed and ruffled his hair with his hands, embarrassed. 'Your friend Cara, what does she say about it?'

Rachel avoided his eyes. 'I haven't told her yet.'

'Ah.'

Rachel shot him a look of warning.

'My apologies,' he smiled. 'I just thought girls, they tell each other everything.'

'No, you're right. I should be having this conversation with Cara. I wanted to but she was so upset, it just didn't feel right when she had just had her heart ripped out. I just haven't found the right time and now, with her so preoccupied with bloody Yiannis . . . I don't know. Maybe I'll say nothing. Maybe I'll wait until we're both back home before I bring it up. Or maybe it will just blow over and then it won't matter anyway.'

Zoran frowned. 'What do you mean, 'blow over'?'

'I don't know,' Rachel sighed, thinking about the abrupt end to Jesse's phone call. 'I've been acting so nuts, it's entirely possible Jesse might have changed his mind by the time I get back and it will all be over before it began.'

'Do you really believe that?'

Rachel's met his dark, gentle gaze. Her spirit rallied a little and she believed it when she said, 'No, actually, I don't. Wow. How did you get to be such a good listener, Zoran?'

He shrugged and grinned. 'I have five sisters. They talk a lot.'

Rachel laughed. As an only child, she could not imagine growing up in a large family. Cara was the closest thing she had to a sister. They had been inseparable in their college years, and the months spent travelling Europe afterwards had only served to cement their bond so that afterwards, even when Rachel had abandoned Dublin for the promise of London, they had not lost touch. The thought sobered her. She must not let this tension between them escalate. Jesse, Yiannis, Peter – no man was worth losing her best friend over.

Cara crept into their darkened room well past midnight, so quietly that Rachel barely registered it through her gin-assisted sleep. When she awoke the sun was already high overhead and they had missed breakfast. She suggested they try the Italian place across the road.

'Good idea,' Cara mumbled on her way to the bathroom. 'I saw a sign outside yesterday advertising a Hot English Breakfast for

115

five pounds.'

They ate on the wooden deck of the pizzeria overlooking the hotel, at a table clothed in red and white checks. Hats and sunglasses shielded Rachel's eyes from the bright morning but there was nothing to be done about the traffic noise. Only aspirin would fix that. She tried to block it out and focus instead on the palm trees, seagulls and clear blue sky.

Breakfast came with sweet, freshly squeezed orange juice and strong filter coffee and was served with enthusiasm and a sleazy smile by the greying proprietor.

Determined to ensure things were right between them, Rachel waited until he had finished delivering the juice before asking Cara, 'How was the hot date?'

'It was good,' Cara replied with a smile that gave away absolutely nothing.

Rachel fidgeted with the sachets of salt on the table. 'I had a couple of drinks in the hotel bar, myself. The barman kept me company. He's an interesting lad, your man Zoran.'

Cara smiled again. 'That he is. I'm glad you had a nice time. Did the two of you . . ?'

'No, we did not! Hell, Cara, it was just a couple of drinks.'

Cara shrugged. 'I was only asking. You're both young and pretty. It's a natural question.'

'Yes, well I'm not in the habit of hopping into bed with every handsome man I run into,' Rachel said crossly, and there ended her plan to talk to Cara about Jesse, for was that not exactly what had happened with him in London?

Cara obviously saw the comment as a cheap shot at her, because she retreated back behind her mask of serenity. Fortunately, a plate each of fat, juicy sausages, eggs, bacon and fried tomatoes went a long way to restoring the humour in both of them. By the time they were done, they were back on speaking terms.

After breakfast, they strolled along the busy roadside – in the opposite direction to the city this time, towards a couple of curio shops behind a bright blue exterior, where they spent some time browsing quiet rows of beach-themed knick-knacks and decorative bottles of *Ouzo*.

'How about these for Declan?' Rachel held up a pair of shiny ornamental duelling pistols made of polished wood and shining brass.

Cara laughed. 'Yeah, he'd get a kick out of them all right, although I don't fancy my chances getting them through Customs. Perhaps I'll grab him a shot glass instead?'

'Sure, or you could always get him a hand-made candle,' she teased. 'There's a heap of them over here with sparkles in them.'

But Cara had something else in her hands and was no longer listening.

'What do you have there?'

'A photo album. Isn't it lovely?'

Rachel reached over and ran her fingers over the cover, which was made of a curious mixture of fabric, pressed reeds and vine leaves. The pages were thick and rough, with protective gossamer sheets between. It smelled like dried wildflowers.

'Wouldn't it make a lovely wedding album?' Cara's voice sounded like it came from far away.

'Oh dear,' sighed Rachel. Her heart broke for her friend and she rubbed Cara lightly on the shoulder, but Cara shook her off, snapped the album shut and dropped it back on the shelf.

'Moving on. What else is there to look at?'

'Cara?'

But Cara had pushed past her and was already holding up a carved wooden box inlaid with mother-of-pearl. 'Here, I might get one of these for Bridget. Or maybe I'll keep it for myself. What do you think?'

'I think you deserve it more than Bridget does.'

With a brittle laugh Cara went to pay for it. It dawned on Rachel that she would have to choose her moment carefully if she wanted her friend to respond to what she had to say without an emotional flare-up, no matter how much better she insisted she was doing.

Back outside in the glare of late morning, past the end of the row of small shops they were delighted to discover a site of excavated ruins on the side of the road. Beyond stretched endless miles of open scrubland, indicating that they had suddenly reached the very outskirts of Limassol.

Since there were no signs telling them to keep out – none that they could read, anyway – they spent an hour crunching over the broken ground of what must once have been a Greek temple, and took turns photographing each other leaning against the remains of Grecian pillars. A couple of times Rachel took a breath to talk to Cara about Jesse, or to probe her about Yiannis, but each time she chickened out. Cara looked happy there, absorbed in her exploration. Why spoil it for her?

Despite a steady breeze that swirled the dust at their feet, they were soon parched by the baking sun. Crossing back over the road they followed a rough path through the dunes to the beach. There, they discovered a bistro at the end of a promenade, where an old grapevine twisted itself around fat wooden beams to provide shade over the tables.

Rachel contemplated the menu. 'I can't believe I'm saying this after that massive breakfast, but I'm famished.'

Cara pointed to a blackboard advertising fresh *Kalamari*. 'I could eat.'

'*Kalamari*. That's like octopus, isn't it?' Rachel pulled a face. 'I can't say I've ever tried it.'

'It's squid,' replied Cara. 'I am surprised you've not eaten it before. It's quite good. You'd never know it was squid, really. They normally serve it battered and cut up so it looks like those onion rings they serve at Eddie Rocket's.' She paused. 'I had it at a restaurant in Dublin once. I wanted to order the fish but Peter ordered that for me instead.' She grimaced at the memory.

'Arsehole,' offered Rachel kindly.

'Thanks. But occasionally he was right. It was bloody delicious.'

'*Kalamari* it is then,' said Rachel and the waiter nodded his approval when he took their order. 'What are you grinning at?' she asked Cara.

'Not grinning, just smiling. I like it here. It's peaceful.'

Rachel surveyed their surroundings. The restaurant was about half filled with customers, many of them women out for afternoon tea. She heard no English spoken in the buzz of conversation around them. Here on the foreshore the pleasant breeze had grown into a gusting wind, the way it seemed to do in this part of the world. It slashed the sea into choppy white peaks and forced people off the beach. Those out walking stayed on the promenade, skirting a wide berth around a large pelican that stood sentinel on the steps of the restaurant like a big white mascot with black-tipped wings and a long orange bill.

'Peaceful, yes.' She sighed.

'Something on your mind?' asked Cara.

It was the perfect opening but it took Rachel by surprise, rendering her silent while she tried to decide where to start. She was still pondering when Cara spoke up again. 'It's just that we haven't had much chance to talk properly since we arrived.'

Rachel resisted the urge to ask whose fault that was.

Cara continued. 'But we're here now, so I have to ask: how are you, really? I mean, since Phillip . . . with Phillip gone.'

Rachel felt a flash of irritation that Cara couldn't even say the words. 'You want to know how widowed life is treating me?'

Cara's expression tightened. 'I would not have put it like that but yes, I suppose I do. It's been what, two years now?'

'Not quite,' said Rachel, glad that her eyes were hidden behind dark glasses.

'Well, if you don't mind me saying so, to look at you I would guess the worst is over.'

'What the hell is that supposed to mean?'

Damn it, this was not going at all as she'd hoped.

'Nothing! I just want to know how you're doing. You don't say much about what's going on with you anymore, in your emails and when we talk on the phone. All you talk about is work – which is great,' she added quickly. 'I'm really glad that's going well for you, but what about *outside* of work? There is more to life, you know.'

Rachel studied her across the table. Cara's sunglasses were pushed up on top of her head to reveal those startling blue-green eyes now filled with gentle concern. Her hair had fluffed out like an auburn halo in the sea air and shadows from the overhanging vine leaves played across her face.

'You're looking pretty hot yourself these days, broken heart or otherwise,' she said and mentally slapped herself. Cara was obviously trying to patch things up with her. Why could she not just come out and talk to her? A gust of wind flapped through the restaurant and a yellowed leaf plopped onto the table in front of her from the vine overhead. She picked it up and twiddled it between her thumb and forefinger.

She looked up to find Cara staring at her with her you're-not-getting-off-that-easy face.

'Yeah okay, I know and yes, I *am* doing all right. If I talk about work a lot it's because after Phillip died, I threw myself into it. I needed the distraction. Somewhere along the way I developed this desire to become a lawyer and so now I have this goal to achieve. Plus, I enjoy it.'

Some part of her was urging her to just get on with it, to tell her everything, but she balked.

'That's fair enough,' said Cara. 'But you need a social life too.'

'I know.' Rachel's focus was set firmly on the dying vine leaf. She had kept these emotions under control for so long she wasn't sure how to let them out. It was as if all of this lived behind a door and she had lost the key to open it. Perhaps she should start with some easy stuff.

'I do go out, you know. I still see the friends we had when Phillip was alive. They still invite me to the monthly dinner parties. Hell, I even hosted one myself in February.' She laughed at the memory. 'I made pasta and they were all very polite about it.'

'Still a genius in the kitchen, are you?'

'Thank God for Marks & Sparks,' she replied, rolling her eyes. Her smile faded. 'But it's not the same as before. Sometimes I think they only invite me out of some sort of obligation. It's like they're not sure how to treat the grieving widow. Even worse, every now and then one of them brings along one of their single male friends. Supposedly, it's to even out the numbers, but it just feels like a really awkward set-up.' She looked at Cara fondly and her next words were heartfelt. 'I do miss having you around, Cara. It would be great to be able to just drop in for a visit whenever I felt like a chat.'

Cara nodded and blinked rapidly. 'I know what you mean.'

Rachel tossed the yellowed leaf and took a breath. 'But hey, I guess I'm about as happy as I could be, all things considered. I don't know what is normal for a woman when her husband dies. It's not like they give out a handbook at the funeral parlour. But I am okay and thank you for asking.'

Talking about it left Rachel more frazzled than expected and she could not face bringing up the whole Jesse situation now. The emotional turmoil that always accompanied memories of Phillip was enough. *One thing at a time,* she told herself and instead she fixed her gaze on her friend across the table. 'Now, never mind my old ancient history drama. What about yours, Cara? What are you going to do about Peter?'

Chapter 8

Cara let the question go unanswered, for the waiter returned at that moment bearing two plates of food. He set them down with a flourish. 'Enjoy!'

She stared at the food in front of her in surprise. Her food stared back at her. Well not really, she thought, because it was deep fried and therefore dead, but still the dozen or so golden-brown itsy-bitsy and fully intact little squids on her plate appeared for all the world as if they were looking up at her. She turned her eyes to Rachel, who was staring at her plate in horror.

'Oh. My. God.'

'There is a problem?' asked the waiter.

'The rings. Where are the rings?' Cara stammered.

The waiter shook his head, confused. 'This is not what you ordered?'

'No – yes – I mean it is, only we were expecting something different. The rings, you know?' She drew circles in the air above her plate for emphasis.

He nodded slowly, like someone trying to placate a crazy person. 'Ah yes, but no. It is baby *kalamaris*. This is how we cook them here.'

Cara looked up at a speechless Rachel.

'It is OK?' The waiter asked. He clearly thought they were a little mad.

'Yes, it is fine,' she sighed. How bad could it be?

He was gone before she even drew her next breath.

Rachel prodded a squidlet with her fork and eyeballed Cara. Resignation slowly replaced her horror on her face. 'Onion rings, eh?'

'Well that's how they do them in Dublin,' said Cara defensively. 'How was I to know they'd feed us baby ones here, complete with their beady little eyes and all.' She slapped her hand over her mouth to stifle a squeak. She looked down at her plate again and sniffed. 'It doesn't smell bad – just like fried seafood, which, I suppose, is what it is. Oh, to hell with it, Rachel. I'm so hungry I'll eat anything.'

She wrung every last drop from the wedge of lemon on the side of her plate, popped one of the critters in her mouth and crunched down. If she forced herself to ignore the squishiness of its rubbery little tentacles . . .

'It's not so bad,' she said with a brave face. 'It's just like crumbed mushrooms. Herby and spicy.'

'Sure. Just like mushrooms, only with legs.'

'Tentacles,' corrected Cara. 'Go on, try one. I promise it's not so bad.'

Rachel speared one with her fork and lifted it, her nose wrinkled.

'Don't look at it, just eat it.'

She closed her eyes and obeyed. The look of distaste that followed had Cara in stitches.

'You lying cow, you said it was good!'

'I said it wasn't that bad,' said Cara between giggles. 'I didn't say compared to what!'

In the end, she managed to eat nearly half the *kalamari* on her plate while leaving not a trace of chips or salad behind, all the while thinking longingly of the juicy chops that Yiannis had cooked for her last night. She would definitely stick to more normal food from now on. She forgot all about Rachel's earlier question until, with the remnants of their food cleared away and two cups of tea steaming on the table between them, Rachel said, 'Right, so now that the *kalamari* crisis is over are you going to talk to me about Peter?'

It sucked the happy out of her in an instant. She pressed her lips together into a hard line. Seconds ticked by. Did she have to? She'd been having such a good time.

'Go on, Cara, you can't avoid it forever.'

'Okay, okay. Just give me a minute.'

She fought to regain control over the weight that had wedged in her chest at the mention of his name. The wind rustled through the vines overhead, bringing with it strands of foreign conversations from all corners of the bistro. Some acoustic trickery made it sound like the sea was breaking onto the sand just a few feet from them instead of way down the beach.

Eventually, in a voice thick with emotion, she replied, 'Honestly? Right now, I am still so angry at him I don't know which way to turn. The only thing I *do* know is that I am done with him. I don't want to talk to him and I definitely don't want to see him. What would be the point? It would only give him the chance to tell me more lies.' Her voice broke.

'Ah, Cara,' Rachel leaned forward squeezed her hand in lieu of a hug. It felt warm and comforting and Cara smiled in appreciation through her tears.

'Don't mind me,' she said. 'I'll be okay. I'm sure the anger will pass and I'll be better able to deal with it all. For now, though, I just need to not think about him, you know?'

Rachel nodded. 'I know. And hey, that's why we're here, remember?'

'Exactly!' Cara sniffed and forced joviality into her voice. 'There's no way a lying, cheating scumbag of a man is going to wreck our holiday.'

'Precisely,' Rachel gave her hand another quick squeeze before letting go.

Cara started to feel better. As long as she kept thoughts of Peter at bay she would be okay. An image of Yiannis materialised in her mind, shirtless on his couch. That was better!

She tilted her chin in defiance. 'And meanwhile I'm free to do whatever I like for a change.'

'Meaning?'

It took courage to challenge Rachel's ice blue stare. 'Well, for once I don't have anyone to answer to. I can have a burger and chips for lunch instead of some posh health food, without hearing his voice in my head telling me how it's going to go straight to my hips.

Okay, so I just ate a bunch of fishy insects but it was *my* choice,' she said in reply to Rachel's grin. 'And I can stay out late if I like. Or sleep in.'

'Or out, with sexy Greek men.'

Cara flushed, but said nothing. A flurry of activity on the promenade behind Rachel caught her eye. Glad of the distraction, she watched and then hooted with laughter and pointed. 'Check out the pelican!'

The bird had moved off the steps and now stood in the middle of the path, blocking it. A boy in his teens stood before it, hands on hips and a look of disbelief on his face. Every time he tried to step past, it stabbed at him with its beak and raised its wings, forcing him back with its imposing size. The creature was almost as tall as he was. A crowd gathered. Some people laughed, others looked perplexed or even frightened. Eventually the boy mustered up all his courage and charged past. The pelican snatched at his shorts but the boy kept running. He made it, but his wallet hit the cement behind him with a thud and the Pelican hopped from foot to foot, as if daring him to come back and get it.

'Can you believe that? Mugged by a pelican!' Cara clapped her hands together in glee. 'This place is unbelievable. I swear I could stay here forever.'

Smiling, Rachel twisted back around in her seat. She picked up a spoon and stirred at her coffee. 'Unfortunately, at some point reality is bound to pull you back.'

'Hey, a girl can dream, right?'

'Don't worry, I'm not going to lecture you.'

'You're not?'

'I think it's a bit late for that, don't you?'

Another image of Yiannis's naked torso popped into her mind and she smothered a grin.

'That's what I thought,' remarked Rachel. 'Look, you have every right to be angry with Peter. I'm sure if I were in your shoes I'd want to skewer the rat bastard.'

Cara fidgeted with the pale green tablecloth in front of her.

'Fine, but I'm here when you're ready to talk about it, okay?'

'Okay,' said Cara. 'And thank you.'

It felt like more needed to be said. 'Rachel, I know you may think that at some point I might end up forgiving him and taking him back and then, if I've gone and had an affair with Yiannis I'll wish I hadn't and I'll carry the guilt with me my whole life.' She held a hand up to stop Rachel interrupting. 'But I really don't believe that's going to happen. I don't think I can ever forgive him for what he's done. Even if I did, though, I don't see how me trying to ease my broken heart would make any difference. I'm so sick of the double standards,' she said, more crossly than she intended. 'Why should I continue to play Little Miss Manners after what Peter has done to me? Why is it okay for a man to screw around but it's not okay for a woman to move on? No,' she shook her head vigorously. 'I refuse to accept that.'

Rachel held up her hands in surrender. 'Easy, tiger, I'm not arguing! I do think you need to sort things out with him though. I'm not saying get back together, but at least sit down and finish it properly, for your own peace of mind, if nothing else. But it's your call.

As for Yiannis, I know I've said it before but . . . be careful. I would hate to see you get hurt any more than you already are. But most of all, Cara I don't want any of this to come between us.'

Cara calmed down instantly. She stirred some sugar into her tea and took a sip. 'Sorry. I didn't mean to get so carried away. I'm not angry at you, please don't think that.'

Rachel offered a reassuring smile. 'It's okay. I get it. I won't say another word. I've said what I wanted to. Whatever you do is your choice and whatever choices you make, I'm still around if you need me.'

They were both silent a while, wrapped up in their own thoughts. It did not take long for Cara's to return to Yiannis. She was saturated by him, could feel his olive skin on hers and smell his musky scent. Last night she had tasted a depth of passion she had not seen for a very, very long time. She and Peter had been together for enough years for their ardour to have cooled as it always did in relationships, although Cara could not remember if Peter had ever shown her that much passion, or she him.

'Do you reckon we can make it past the pelican without being molested?' she asked.

Rachel turned and studied the bird on the pathway. The crowd had thinned but a handful of people still hung around to watch its antics.

'I guess there's only one way to find out,' she said.

They paid the bill, descended onto the promenade and approached with caution. The bird fixed a beady eye on them and they stopped. Now what? Cara noticed a middle-aged man with a bald head and a paunch swaggering towards them from the other direction, oblivious to the avian danger. Rachel obviously had a similar thought for she put a restraining hand on Cara's arm. 'Wait, watch this,' she murmured.

As the man stepped into the pelican's line of sight it rounded on him, swinging its long beak like a sword as it took aim and grabbed at his pockets. He yelped and jumped back and Rachel hissed, 'Now!'

Quick as they could, they dashed past behind it and ran like their lives were at stake. Confused, the pelican grunted and flapped its wings behind them. They ran and ran and did not stop until they rounded a bend in the path. Laughing and gasping for breath they slowed to a walk, jostling each other as they checked over their shoulders to make sure they weren't being chased.

'I think we're safe,' giggled Cara. 'That was a good plan you had there.'

'Why thank you very much,' Rachel made an exaggerated bow. 'I *do* have the odd moment of brilliance. Although I'll admit I never thought I'd need it to outwit a great big bloody pelican.'

They were in high spirits after their little victory but the walk back to their hotel sapped all of Cara's energy. The promenade meandered between manicured hotel lawns littered with empty sun loungers on their right and dark sandy beaches on their left. Strong wind had driven all the people indoors. Cara wished she was among them. It battered her ears and created a knee-high sand storm that stung her legs. She leaned into it with her head down and her eyes streaming. It was hard work to not be blown off-course. It felt like hours before they finally saw the top of their hotel peeking out from behind a wall of trees, although in fact it was only about twenty minutes.

Inside the blissful calm of the hotel Cara called dibs on the bathroom. She left Rachel reading her novel through closed eyelids on her bed, while the bathroom filled with lavender-scented steam. Stripping off her grubby clothes she immersed herself in hot water up to her chin and let her thoughts drift. Talking things through with Rachel had cleared a load from her mind. They might not agree but at least they knew where they stood with each other. A question gnawed at her. What if Rachel was right about Peter? A tantrum in a coffee shop was no way to end a relationship. She hadn't even given his ring back, although not for lack of trying. It wasn't *her* fault the stupid thing wouldn't come off in the heat of the moment. But did that mean he thought they were still engaged? Were they? For the first time, it dawned on Cara that what she was doing with Yiannis might fall somewhere inside a moral grey area. Anger bubbled briefly inside her. It hadn't stopped Peter from screwing around. No. This was not the same thing. Besides, if she really was doing something wrong she would know. A strict Catholic upbringing had ensured she had no shortage of guilt in her life.

So, she put all thoughts of Peter aside and concentrated on the evening ahead instead. A flutter of excitement stirred inside her. Tonight was Yiannis's brother's coming-home party. Was it weird to be meeting his family? What would they think of her, an outsider? She raised a handful of bubbles from the water, blew the foam into the air and chuckled at herself. Talk about over-thinking things! She wasn't meeting his parents, for heaven's sake; he had merely invited her to a party. This was just a bit of fun. It was not like they were in a proper relationship or anything.

Cara told herself she had nothing to worry about.

A few hours later they alighted from a taxi in front of a large hotel in the Tourist Area. It had been dark for some time already. Although the wind had blown itself out, Cara shivered. Her light lavender top looked great with tight jeans and designer boots, but it did little to ward off the cool night air.

She eyed the pub from the curb. A group of people speaking

French sat smoking cigarettes at one of the tables outside, and a welcoming glow and steady beat of music drifted out through open patio doors. A red neon sign over the door pronounced its name in squiggly letters: *Hot Shots!*

'This is the place, is it?' asked Rachel.

Cara checked the piece of paper on which Yiannis had written the address. 'That's what it says here.'

'Are we going in?'

A barrage of doubt ambushed Cara and for a moment she wondered where would she be right now if life had a rewind button. The doubt vanished in an instant. She would be at home in Dublin, that's where, and Peter would probably be 'working late' as usual. *Hah! More likely off shagging Simone somewhere.*

'Yes, we are going in.'

Rachel's blue eyes filled with concern and she held her back. 'Cara, are you sure you want to do this?'

Sure? No. But if she didn't, she would likely never see Yiannis again and Cara knew a thing or two about regrets. If she walked away now she would forever wonder about what might have been, just like she had with Nik. She blinked. Nik, again? She shook him off and grinned at Rachel. 'Hell yes, I'm sure. Let's go have some fun.'

Rachel shrugged. 'Well okay then. I'm right behind you.'

Their heels clacked across the patio. A pretty waitress with honey skin and jet-black hair smiled at them on her way to deliver drinks to the French people. Cara stopped just inside the entrance and Rachel bumped into her a little.

'Oops, sorry.'

But Cara was too busy scanning the room to pay attention. A large bar dominated the pub, which was brightly lit with neon signs and stocked with every kind of booze imaginable. There were a few padded booths along one wall, a heap of tables and chairs scattered throughout and in one corner a pool table, where a handful of pale young men wearing jeans and button-down shirts played a friendly game. Photographs – some in frames, but most not – adorned the pillars and walls and people hung around in clusters at tables and queued for drinks, almost yelling to be heard over the drum of music.

They made their way to the bar where a hunky barman strode straight over and winked at Rachel, completely ignoring half a dozen men who were trying to grab his attention. Rachel smiled back and ordered two glasses of chardonnay.

'Normally I'd happily grumble about sexism and the like, but it sure pays to be blonde in this place,' she observed.

'Yeah, and it doesn't hurt that the locals look the way they do,' laughed Cara. 'I reckon they should send some of them over to Ireland. I know a few lasses who'd be more than happy to show them around.'

She glanced around trying to spot Yiannis in the crowd. Was that him? It was hard to be sure in the smoky light and the man in the black shirt had his back to her. The way he moved seemed familiar, but she lost sight of him as people moved between them.

Rachel thrust a glass of white wine into her hand. 'Here you go.'

'Cheers, thanks.' They clinked glasses.

'Is he here yet?' Rachel asked.

'I don't know. I thought it might have been him in a black shirt over there somewhere,' she indicated with a subtle inclination of her head. 'But I couldn't see his face, so I can't be sure. If he's here, he'll find me.'

Rachel looked over her shoulder towards where Cara had pointed. Neither of them saw Yiannis approach from the opposite direction and they both jumped when he put his hands on their shoulders. 'I am glad you ladies made it.'

Cara spilled her wine in fright. 'You nearly scared the life out of me!'

'I am sorry, I did not intend to surprise you so much.' He leaned in to brush a kiss on her cheek, leaving a trace of his spicy scent in her nostrils. Was it coincidence that the thin cotton shirt stretched over his shoulders matched the olive colour of his eyes exactly? Reigning in her rampant hormones she cleared her throat and asked, 'How's the party going?'

'It is much better now that you are here. You look beautiful tonight – very sexy in those boots.' He winked and she blushed at the memory of him removing those boots last night. It would be really easy to fall for him; almost as easy as it had been with Nik, way back when.

She blinked the thought away in irritation, even as a nagging sense of unease took hold. 'We had quite an interesting lunch today, didn't we Rachel?'

But Rachel was too busy staring intently across the room to respond.

Cara prodded her gently.

'Rachel? I was just saying to Yiannis—'

'Um, Cara,' Rachel fumbled for her hand and said something, but Yiannis spoke at the same time and she heard neither of them. The thumping music did not help.

'What was that?'

They both spoke again. She thought Yiannis said something about his brother but, alarmed by the look on Rachel's face, she turned her focus to her instead. 'What?'

'The guy in the black shirt!' said Rachel.

'What about him?'

As Rachel closed her eyes with the expression of someone trying not to stare at the scene of an accident, Cara became aware of a man approaching from the side. It was the man in the black shirt that she had spotted earlier through the crowd. He stood roughly the same height as Yiannis, but he had more of a wiry build, a narrower face and his black hair was shot with the beginnings of grey. She could see why she had mistaken him for Yiannis, though; the way he moved . . . Cara stopped breathing. *Holy God, no!* Reality fractured and disjointed images flashed through her mind of sweaty limbs entwined on hot Spanish nights.

Yiannis spotted him too. His face crinkled into a smile and he drew the man close. 'Cara and Rachel, meet my brother, Nikolaos.'

Cara opened her mouth and then closed it again. Her world stalled and shrank until nothing existed outside of the three people in front of her, as if the lights had dimmed and a spotlight shone on their little circle. Even the music was drowned out by the rush in her ears. From the look on Nik's face she could only conclude that he was having a similar reaction.

He recovered quickly, though, and the glint of recognition in his eyes was extinguished as he said, '*Yassou.*'

Cara was forced to take breath again to say, 'Hello.'

All at once her instant attraction to Yiannis made sense. No wonder he reminded her of Nik – he was his *brother*! It was not surprising he had been on her mind so much. Hell, it was probably Nik that she had spotted yesterday from the top of Limassol castle, too. Cara felt sick, but Yiannis did not notice the stunned silence in the swirl of noise around them.

'Nikolaos has been away for a very long time,' he said. 'Many years he has travelled around the world. He takes pictures for magazines. Can you believe it? That a man can make a living making photographs!' He threw his head back and laughed.

Cara, Nik and Rachel joined in automatically.

'Really? That must be a great life,' said Rachel and Cara could have hugged her, for she was still unable to form proper words.

Nik continued to play his role. 'There are some good parts and there are some bad parts.' He looked Cara dead in the eye. 'I have met some wonderful people along the way.' Releasing her from his gaze, he shrugged. 'But sometimes I miss my home, my family, my friends – even my little brother.' He punched Yiannis playfully on the shoulder.

Yiannis punched him right back. 'Not so little, anymore.'

Cara's smile felt more like a grimace and she caught Rachel's eye, desperate for help.

'Say, where does a girl go to powder her nose round here?' Rachel asked.

Yiannis looked baffled.

'The toilets. Where are the toilets?' Rachel asked and when Yiannis pointed to a door off to the side of the bar, she continued, 'Cara, are you coming?'

Cara nodded and followed dumbly. Walking felt awkward, almost robotic and it seemed to take forever to cross the room and reach the end of the short, dark passage to the ladies' room. A shaft of light spilled out as Rachel pushed the door open and Cara blinked in the glare of fluorescent lights and white tiles. The moment the door closed behind them she covered her mouth with her hands and squeaked, 'Omigod-what-the-bloody-hell-Rachel-*omigod*!'

Rachel stood and waited for her to calm down. 'Are you finished?'

Cara nodded, not trusting herself to speak.

'Right, so I'm not imagining things – that was Nik, correct?'

Cara nodded again.

'From Spain and France and Italy – *that* Nik? Cara!' Her voice was sharp enough to jolt Cara out of her panic.

She gasped. 'Please tell me that did not just happen. Of all the people in all the world!'

Rachel shook her head helplessly and then started to laugh.

'What's so funny?' Cara demanded, but Rachel seemed unable to stop.

Cara felt tears prick her eyelids. 'Rachel! It's not funny!'

'Really, Cara? This whole thing is ridiculous. You come here to sort out your love life and instead you wind up getting tangled up in some sort of Greek tragedy. All we need now is for Peter to show up and you'd be well screwed.'

'Don't even say that,' cried Cara in horror. She covered her face with her hands and shook her head slowly from side to side. 'I can't believe this is happening to me.' Her voice sounded muffled through her fingers. For a moment, she stayed cocooned in the comforting darkness of her closed eyes behind her hands. She shut everything out and took a deep breath, which she then eased slowly out of her lungs. Wishing for this not to be happening would not make it so.

She lowered her hands and opened her eyes. 'This is your fault, you know.'

'How is it my fault?'

'You were the one who said the chances of bumping into him were a million to one!'

Rachel shrugged, turned to face the mirror and began to fiddle with her hair. 'So, I was a little off. You were the one who said Nik wasn't from Limassol.'

'Well how was I supposed to know the place had two names?' *Limassol – Lemesos – same place*, Yiannis had said last night. She remembered the ping in her brain when he'd said it and wanted to smack herself for not making the connection sooner.

Rachel clucked her tongue impatiently. 'Well, it's immaterial now.'

Cara rubbed at the knot of tension behind her neck, leaning against the hand basin for support. The muted throb of music reached them through the door, along with an eruption of laughter. 'At least *someone* is having fun.'

Rachel rolled her eyes. 'So, what now?'

Cara was tempted to burst into tears but she swallowed them back, trying to break the habit. 'I don't know. Do you have any suggestions?'

Rachel looked incredulous.

'Look, I know this is not your problem, Rachel but I need your help here. Please,' she begged. 'I can't think straight.'

She shut her eyes and hid behind her hands again. After a moment, she felt Rachel's arm go around her shoulders and give her a squeeze. It was a comforting sensation and it helped her relax a little.

'Look, it might feel like it, but it's not the end of the world,' said Rachel.

Cara turned and looked up at her friend, desperate for reassurance. 'It isn't?'

'No. Here, hasn't Nik already taken the first step by pretending he didn't know you?'

'Yeah, I suppose so,' acknowledged Cara with a sniff. 'Hey, what was that about anyway? Talk about disowning me!'

'Hush now, calm down,' Rachel chuckled. 'Think about it. His brother has obviously mentioned this girl he's crazy about. How would he feel to know that Nik—'

'It's Nikolaos now, remember?'

Rachel threw her a look. 'Whatever. How would he feel knowing Nikolaos had, um, history with her – you – whatever. Maybe he didn't want to spoil things between you and Yiannis. After all, it was a long time ago. You were a different person back then – fresh out of college, your first taste of freedom. He's probably changed too. Besides, it didn't go on for that long between you two, did it?'

'A couple of months, although it felt like longer.' Cara sighed nostalgically. Her heart still ached a little when she remembered how he had left to follow a story to South America. 'It took me a long time to get over him.'

'But you did.' Rachel's voice was sharp.

'Sure,' she said. 'And then I met Peter and we fell in love and look how well that worked out.' Surprisingly, Peter's name evoked no emotion now whatsoever. Cara put it down to the stress of her current predicament. She smoothed out her lavender top in a nervous gesture. 'I mean, it's not like I've been carrying a torch for him ever since, or anything.'

'Right, so then there is nothing to worry about. If you think about it he is basically giving you permission to go ahead and date his brother. Oh my God, I can't believe I just said that.'

'Rachel—'

'Never mind, just pull yourself together. Go out there and if it makes things easier then pretend you've never met him. I'm here if you need me but this is up to you. One thing, though; do yourself a favour and think all of this through very carefully before you jump into anything. If you think it's complicated now . . .'

Cara studied her, weighing her words. Behind her the door opened and the honey-skinned waitress walked in. She smiled at the two girls and went into one of the cubicles.

'Yeah, okay. Thanks,' said Cara and turned around to wash her hands.

They did a quick hair-and-makeup check. Cara applied some lip gloss and smoothed the waves of auburn hair that touched on her shoulders. She checked three times that there were no smudges of mascara to betray her. When they were done, Rachel looked at her in the mirror.

'Are you ready?'

Cara nodded.

'You sure?'

She nodded again, this time with conviction.

'Good. You can do this, Cara.'

She nodded at her reflection and squared her shoulders. 'Yes. I can do this.'

They returned to the bar to find that Ari had joined the gang. Cara's bravery deserted her at the sight of Yiannis and Nik together, and she stopped short a few feet shy of them. *Idiot!* How did she not pick up on the resemblance before? The barman deposited three bottles of beer in front of Yiannis, who handed him some money and passed one each to his brother and his friend. They raised them in salutation – three old friends, together again. Rachel nudged Cara from behind at the same time as Yiannis looked up and spotted her. Holding out his hand, he drew her closer. She nearly choked on the effort it took not to freak out at the sight of Nik right there beside him, his eyes dark and unreadable.

Ari greeted the girls with enthusiasm and Cara made a fuss of him to cover her discomfort. He was a willing, if oblivious accomplice. With an impish grin, he enquired if they would like to join him in drinking some Zivania. Rachel groaned at the memory of Sunday's hangover and Ari roared with laughter.

'Zivania? Really?' Nik shook his head in despair. 'You boys have no idea about women.'

'And you know so much better, eh?' Yiannis turned to Cara. 'In all the years my brother is away, he never once brings home a woman.'

Nik shrugged. 'Just because I do not bring one home, it does not mean I do not have someone special.'

'So, where is she?' said Yiannis and Cara squirmed.

'I did not say I have one *now*, my nosy little brother.' Nik sneaked a glance at Cara and she glared at him while Yiannis and Ari roared again with laughter. He met her gaze and for a brief moment she saw him: Nik, the man she had loved, now daring her to challenge him. *God, she had missed him!*

But then she blinked and he was gone and in his place stood Nikolaos, the stranger who talked and joked with Yiannis and Ari as if he had never met Cara, let alone shared her bed.

Rachel thrust a glass into her hand and she drank without even looking at it. The bitter taste of gin grabbed the back of her throat. 'Holy hell, that's strong! What happened to the wine?'

'I thought you could use a double,' said Rachel.

The music changed to a slow and sexy Justin Timberlake song. Yiannis drew her close, hooking his thumb into the front pocket of her jeans. His thigh bumped against the curve of her behind as he moved with the beat. Cara felt trapped and irritated. It took all of her willpower not to yank herself free. Not wanting to make a scene, she slung back some more gin instead. At this rate, she'd be attending AA meetings by the time she got back to Dublin.

'Is everything okay?' Yiannis's voice was hot in her ear.

You mean aside from the fact that I used to bang your brother?

Cara drank again. Rescue came in the form of the honey-skinned waitress who sidled up to Nik, whispered something in his ear and then stalked off, her hips swaying in a tantalizing fashion before she was swallowed up by the crowd. The rest of the group stared at him in inquisitive silence and even Yiannis stopped moving, leaving Mr Timberlake to rock someone else's body.

'It seems I must go,' said Nik and followed her without a backward glance.

The sharp stab of jealousy caught Cara completely off-guard. Eight years later, standing there with his brother's hand in her pocket, she was hardly in a position to get possessive. She drained her glass and the gin kicked in just as the music picked up again. She gave her booty a little shake. 'Well now, did someone say something about this being a party?' Rachel looked like she was about to respond with something sensible so she held up a finger to silence her. 'The next one's on me, pet.'

Ari stared after Nik. 'I have been coming here for years and I never even get a second look from Eleni. Your brother is here one night, Yiannis, and she is whispering in his ear. What does he have that I do not?' asked Ari.

'You mean besides Eleni?'

Ari pulled a face and they all laughed except Cara, who turned away instead to order more drinks. She was going to need more than a little help from her good friends G and T to survive *this* night.

With Nik gone, Ari manoeuvred himself into conversation with Rachel, leaving Yiannis and Cara more-or-less on their own. Cara wondered briefly if it was the sneaky trick of a good wing-man, before her attention switched to more pressing matters, such as the fact that Yiannis looked decidedly like he wanted to kiss her. But instead of leaning in he dropped his weight back against the bar counter, circled her with his arms and studied her face.

'You look afraid,' he said.

Close up, he smelled of beer and cologne. He must have shaved that morning, for his jaw was rough with the shadow of stubble. 'Not afraid,' she said, unsurprised to feel a slight tremor in her voice. 'Just a little nervous.'

'Of me?'

'Maybe.'

'Even after last night?'

She smiled and dropped her gaze. She couldn't very well say it was because of his brother.

'Is it because of my brother?'

A moment of blind panic knocked the breath from her.

'You do not need to worry about meeting my family, Cara. Nikolaos, he will not bite.'

That's what you think. 'How long is he staying?'

'Tonight?'

'In Cyprus.'

Yiannis shrugged. 'I do not know. With Nikolaos, we never know. It could be a week. It could be a month.' He shrugged again and Cara thought bitterly, *I know what you mean.*

'But enough talk about my brother.' He smiled his slow, crinkly smile and the flame of desire ignited in his eyes.

'I would much rather talk about picking up where we left off last night, wouldn't you?'

Cara gulped. Despite the insanity of her situation that look still made her insides quiver. But instead of moving closer she pulled away with a shy smile.

'Not here,' she said because in all honesty, kissing Yiannis while Nik was around did not feel a whole lot different to what Peter had done with Simone.

'Later, then,' said Yiannis, releasing her and drawing their friends once more into the circle.

On the far side of the room an unmarked door was set into the wall. Those familiar with the place knew that it led to the manager's office. Nikolaos Georgiou stood beside this door talking with his friend, Theofanis, whose office was the one behind the door. The waitress had gone back to ferrying drinks to customers, after showing Nikolaos to where Theofanis waited.

A dozen or so old friends had turned up on Yiannis's invitation. They were all enjoying his party but Nikolaos felt at odds, as he always did on coming home. Life in Cyprus continued while he travelled the globe as a photo-journalist, yet it also seemed that time stood still in his absence. People followed the same routines and had the same conversations year in, year out. It would take a few more days before he would feel normal. At least, it would have if he had not stumbled into this parallel universe where his brother had hooked up with Cara. How in the world had that happened?

Theofanis was the only one with whom he always felt at ease. The two men had known each other since childhood when they had played football together in the street outside their houses. Nikolaos was glad that Yiannis had decided on this place to gather everyone together for his homecoming. Theofanis worked late hours and slept through some of the day, so this was the best time to see him. But now, Nikolaos found it hard to concentrate on their conversation.

Theofanis was bringing him up to date on the latest news. This one was getting married, that one was expecting another child. 'And when last did you see Christina?'

Christina was the only thing that had almost come between them, a pretty girl they had both dated in high school. Nikolaos shrugged. 'I do not remember – years ago.'

Theofanis puffed out his cheeks and held his arms out to the side, enjoying the gossip. 'She has grown so fat she needs two chairs to sit on now. Maybe it is a good thing none of us won her heart in the end, eh?' He jabbed Nikolaos with his elbow.

Nikolaos laughed knowingly in the required manner, but his heart wasn't in it. He looked past Theofanis in the direction of the bar. Yiannis and Cara stood close together, deep in conversation. His insides balled into a fist. The shock of finding out that the woman of which his brother had spoken was Cara had not yet worn off. He had reacted instinctively. Yiannis knowing that he had a history with Cara would only complicate things. Chances were that Cara was only here for a short time. It would be better to allow his brother to enjoy his moment in blissful ignorance. All of which was very noble, thought Nikolaos, except that he now had to pay the price and that price was wondering what Cara and Yiannis were doing when they were left alone together. He shook his head. This was terrible.

'Is everything okay, Nikolaos?' Theofanis was watching him with a bemused expression.

'Of course, yes, everything is fine,' he lied with his best attempt at a smile.

'I have known you a long time, my friend. I am sure if you are lying to me there is a good reason.'

Nikolaos folded his arms and rocked back on his heels. 'You are a wise man, Theofanis.'

'And you are full of crap, Nikolaos, but that is okay because I am your friend anyway.' He glanced over his shoulder to see what Nikolaos was looking at. 'Your brother has found himself a nice little English girl to screw, yes?'

'She is Irish, and don't be such a pig.'

Theofanis raised one eyebrow, a talent that had made him popular with the girls as a youngster, but Nikolaos ignored the unspoken question. He knew he had been too defensive in his reply.

'I think that maybe I should give the beautiful Eleni the rest of the night off, eh?'

'Eleni?'

Theofanis shook his head in amazement. 'For a man who has spent so long travelling the world you are quite stupid sometimes. Yes, Eleni, the pretty waitress whose arse you followed to find me.' He jerked his head in her direction.

She was taking an order for drinks from the youngsters at the pool table. He had to admit she had a good body, although she was a bit skinnier and her breasts were smaller than he liked. But the white cropped shirt she wore with a pair of tight jeans showed off her honey-coloured skin to good effect. The young men could hardly keep their eyes off her. She pretended not to notice.

'Do I know her?' he asked.

'You met her the last time you were home. When was that, about two years ago?'

'Three.'

Theofanis nodded thoughtfully, pursing his lips. 'Three years, it is a long time, eh? Eleni had just started working here for me. You must have made an impression on her because she remembers you well. I have not seen her spend so much time in the bathroom fixing her hair before.'

Nikolaos studied her. One of the pool players blocked her path in an obvious attempt to chat her up. She smiled and pinched his cheek like a doting aunt would and he clutched at his heart dramatically as she walked away, leaving a wake of hilarity amongst his friends.

'I cannot see what is so special about her hair,' said Nikolaos. 'It is long and it is loose. What could take so long with that?'

Theofanis laughed and clapped him on the back. 'It is not for us to understand the workings of the female head – on the inside or the outside.'

'This is true,' chuckled Nikolaos. His gaze drifted back to Yiannis and Cara. Rachel was still there, talking to Ari, but where had Yiannis gone with Cara? The music pounded at his head and his eyes darted left and right trying to spot them in the constantly shifting crowd.

'So? Would you like that?' Theofanis grabbed his attention.

'What?'

'Do you want me to tell Eleni she can have the rest of the night off?'

Nikolaos was frantically trying to spot his brother or Cara. He clapped his hand on his friend's shoulder and looked him in the face. 'You are the boss. You do whatever you think is right. Now, I have to go. I will see you later, okay?'

Theofanis let him go with a shake of his head. 'You are still a little bit crazy, Nikolaos. But enjoy yourself tonight. I will tell the barman your next drink is on the house, eh?'

Nikolaos gave him one final pat on the shoulder before he stepped away and started to thread his way through the people. The later it got, the busier the pub became. He had not gone more than a few feet when he spied Yiannis and Cara in front of a collection of photographs around the far side of the bar. Yiannis pointed at one of the pictures and Cara laughed at something he said. Nikolaos flushed. It gutted him to see her looking so happy with another man, let alone his own brother.

'Hey there, Nik, how are you?' The last three words ran together in that peculiar Irish manner so that they sounded like one. *Howareya.*

He turned to face Rachel, who had sidled up to his elbow. Her eyes were also on Cara and Yiannis.

'It is a long time since somebody called me 'Nik',' he said.

'That's right, it's 'Nikolaos' now, isn't it?'

'It always was,' he said. 'Only Cara called me Nik.'

'Yes, it seems she has trouble with names sometimes,' said Rachel.

He had no idea what she was talking about so he waited for an explanation.

'Never mind,' she said. 'Go on then, what's the story?'

'Story?'

'Yeah. What's up with you? Why the charade? Why did you pretend not to know us, back there?'

Nikolaos dropped his gaze and stuffed his hands in the front pockets of his black jeans. 'I was not thinking,' he mumbled.

'What's that? I can't hear you,' she said and as if to illustrate the point the music suddenly blared a trumpet solo just as the young men at the pool table erupted in a roar of laughter.

He clenched his jaw. Why was Rachel being so hard on him? He had done nothing to her. He raised his chin and looked her straight in the eye when he spoke.

'It was a big shock for me to see Cara with my brother. I do not know why I did this. Maybe I thought it would be better for them, if I pretended Cara and I had never met. What good can come from Yiannis knowing? I did not want to spoil this night for him. I am sorry if I did the wrong thing, but to be honest I do not know how to fix it now.'

Rachel narrowed her eyes and tilted her head, as if debating whether or not to believe him.

Irritated, he looked away. Yiannis and Cara were still standing close together on the other side of the bar. Her hair looked a bit dishevelled, the way it somehow did when she was a little bit drunk. He had a strong urge to march over there and take her home before she did something she might regret in the morning.

Rachel's voice distracted him.

'All right, that makes sense – sort of. And for the record, I'm not entirely sure you did the wrong thing.'

'No?'

'No. Look, I know you guys had a thing but it really was a very long time ago, right?'

Nikolaos glowered. What did it matter how much time had passed?

'Look at her, Nik.'

He looked. He sighed. She was so beautiful, so full of life. He had always loved the way her face lit up when she spoke or laughed.

'Her hair is more red than I remember.'

Rachel poked him in the ribs and he grunted. 'Okay, okay, I am looking! But what am I looking for?'

'Do you see how happy she is?'

He nodded, not trusting himself to speak.

'Well let me tell you, I have not seen Cara like that in a very long time. It took some time for her to get over you but she did. And then she met someone and up until a week ago she was engaged to him.'

'Cara was going to get married?'

'Yes, only the bastard broke her heart and I did not know how long it would take to mend, this time. But then, good or bad, she met your brother and now – well, you can see for yourself.'

He watched Yiannis laugh at something Cara said and then reach out and smooth a stray hair away from her face. She looked up at him shyly and he leaned forward and planted a light, lingering kiss on her lips. The tender scene punched Nikolaos in the gut. With clenched fists and glittering eyes, he turned on Rachel. 'Are they sleeping together?'

She placed a hand on his forearm. 'Nik.'

He shook it off with a harsh laugh. 'I see. Do not worry, Rachel. I will not cause trouble. But do not expect me to stand around and watch them together, okay?'

Rachel stepped back. 'Fair enough.'

Nikolaos saw Ari making his way towards them. 'Ari,' he said, pasting a big smile on his face. 'I thought maybe you ran away to leave this beautiful lady for me, no?'

Ari wagged his finger at him. 'Ah, Nikolaos, I cannot turn my back for one minute and there you are, charming all the ladies. Here, the barman tells me to give you this.' He handed over a bottle of beer.

Nikolaos held it up as if to admire it in the light, puckered his lips and nodded with approval. 'This is a fine beer,' he said. This was his party and damn it, he would to make the most of it. He spotted the waitress giving him a sultry look from her station beside the bar. What was her name, Eleni? Nikolaos chugged back a third of the beer, nodded to Rachel and Ari and straightened out his shirt. Perhaps it was time to see if Theofanis had given her the rest of the night off, after all.

Chapter 9

For a brief moment, as Cara emerged from the dregs of sleep the next morning, she thought she had had a terrible dream. But as consciousness returned so did reality and she showered, dressed and ate breakfast on autopilot. Rachel announced that she wanted to spend the morning sunbathing. Unable to think straight, Cara followed suit and by mid-morning she was as comfortable as one could be, propped up in a plastic sun-lounger beside the hotel swimming pool.

Rachel stretched out on the lounger beside hers. Her hair was tied up in a ponytail on the top of her head, sunglasses the only concession to the dangers of the sun. Cara envied her ability to tan a lustrous bronze colour in no time at all. Bleached by the long Irish winter, her own skin showed a tinge of pink that held the promise of a healthy sun-kissed glow if treated gently or a painful shade of lobster if not. A tiny breeze tickled her belly. It smelled of coconuts. Unlike Rachel, Cara needed the sunscreen.

On the other side of the pool two young mothers mirrored them while their three children splashed about in the water. A boy of around ten cannonballed into the pool yet again and two little girls shrieked in excitement. Cara flinched as droplets of ice cold water splattered her legs.

'What?' Only the slightest movement of her lips betrayed the fact that Rachel was even conscious.

'Nothing,' said Cara

'Why are you eyeballing me?'

'I'm not.'

Rachel raised her sunglasses and squinted at her. 'I saw you.'

'I was just wondering how you could sleep with these kids making so much noise.'

Rachel shrugged. 'They're kids. It's a pool. What do you expect?' She lowered her sunglasses and settled her head back again.

Other than watch the kids trying to drown each other in the pool, Cara's mind now had nothing to do but contemplate last night. She was both proud and ashamed of how she had managed to carry on with Yiannis as if nothing was amiss, and not entirely convinced she had pulled it off.

There had been no question of going home with him after finding out he was Nik's brother, but had Yiannis seen through her excuses? It might be only pure lust between them but still she would hate to hurt his feelings. It was not his fault that the universe had decided to play a massive prank on her. As the absurdity of it hit her all over again, Cara folded her arms over the top of her head, squishing her straw hat and pushing her sunglasses askew.

As if it weren't all bad enough, of course, that one honest look from Nik had seen to it that her own feelings were now all tied up in knots, and the lust that had sparked her interest in Yiannis was no longer unadulterated. *Thanks a lot, Nik!* Inside, she wanted to stomp her foot and throw a tantrum just like one of the little girls was doing over at the side of the pool.

'B-but he threw my towel in the water and he won't fetch it out,' the little one cried with huge crocodile tears rolling down her blotchy face.

Her mother's ministrations did nothing to help and neither did the merciless laughter of the ten-year-old boy who was the cause of her consternation.

Boys! You can always count on them to bring you tears, thought Cara. Bloody hell, you couldn't even enjoy a swim without one spoiling it.

God, she felt stupid! How could she not have realised that the reason she was so drawn to Yiannis was because he was so much like Nik? Even Rachel had mentioned it more than once.

A shriek and a splash jolted her back to the moment. 'Little bastards,' she muttered. Squinting, she took off her sunglasses to dry them off on the corner of the towel that peeped out of the purple tote bag beside her. She heard Rachel laugh.

'What's so funny?'

'Are you watching these kids? The little one has the big ones in the water and she won't let them come out. She's found herself a stick and every time they get to the edge she runs over and whacks them with it.'

'Feckin' little devil.'

'Ah, for goodness' sake, Cara. What is your problem with the kids?' Rachel sat up and swung her legs off the sun lounger to face her with exasperation.

'What do you mean? I've no problem with them.' She glanced over to the mothers. They did not appear to be within earshot but she lowered her voice anyway. 'I just wish that the bloody parents would get some control over them in public, that's all.'

'They're not animals, you know. They're children. They need to play and make a noise. That's what children do. If they can't do it at a swimming pool on their holidays, then where can they do it?'

'What are you getting so defensive about? It's not like they're *your* children.'

She stopped at the pained look that had flitted across her friend's face.

'What? What did I say?'

'Nothing. Just give them a break. They're only kids,' said Rachel. She lay down again and gestured towards the mothers. 'Besides, for all you know that could be us a few years from now.'

'Not bloody likely.'

Cara slumped back and plonked her hat over her face. The sun pricked through in bright warm speckles. There was another shriek and a splash, which she ignored.

After a few minutes, the sun baked the sulks right out of her and she flipped over, perched her hat on her head and fished out the novel she had brought along for the trip. Rachel was already dozing again. Even the sounds of the children ceased to bother Cara as she retreated into the entertaining if somewhat unbelievable life of a woman who found herself in the role of The

Other Woman.

Morning turned to afternoon, and at some point the mothers gathered up their noisy children and went in search of lunch. Food seemed like a good idea, so Rachel volunteered to fetch a small pizza from the place across the road. They ate it beside the pool accompanied by sweet freshly-squeezed orange juice provided by Zoran and his dragon-slaying smile.

One of the advantages of holidaying so early in the season was that Cara and Rachel got to enjoy the luxury of having the pool to themselves for hours. The posse of older guests must have gone out. It grew ever hotter as the day wore on and Cara finally plucked up the courage to take a dip in the icy water, circling lazily on her back until her skin pruned. Rachel positioned an umbrella for shade and was snoring lightly when Cara emerged from the water. She towelled herself off and returned to her book, but found it increasingly difficult to find sympathy for the heroine of the story. In her opinion, if the silly bitch wanted to get involved with a married man then she deserved all the heartache she got.

The soft mechanical click of a camera shutter brought her back to consciousness.

'Wake up, Cara,' a man's voice crooned gently in her ear, followed by another soft click.

She knew that voice. A smile crept over her lips and she stretched and turned towards it, opening her eyes. Nik's face swam into focus. She gasped and sat up, sending her paperback thudding to the ground. What was Nik doing here? And why was he holding his camera?

She pointed an accusatory finger at the empty sun lounger beside her. 'Where is Rachel?'

Pushing himself up off his haunches, Nik plonked himself down in the spot she had occupied and busied himself with the buttons and knobs on his camera. 'She went for a walk.'

Cara frowned and he looked up at her silence.

'Okay, yes, I told her I wanted to talk to you in private. She understands things of the heart, your friend.'

Cara reached for her book, dusted it off and stuffed it into her tote bag, buying time while trying to rid herself of the cobwebs of sleep. Aware of Nik's eyes on her she adjusted her bikini so that it offered maximum cover and pulled her towel up around her like a sarong. Finally, she squared up and faced him. 'What do you want, Nik? And how did you find me?'

His mouth twitched as she said his name. 'It was not hard and like I said, I want to talk.'

'Were you taking pictures of me?'

He shrugged as he set the camera down. 'You always look so peaceful when you are asleep, Cara. I wanted to capture this before you wake up and start yelling at me.' He ducked and laughed as she whipped her hat off her head and threw it at him.

It was hard to stay cross with him when he was laughing at her. 'What did you want to talk to me about?'

His laughter faded to a smile and he placed a hand on her knee, speaking gently. 'Cara, I have not seen you in eight years. Last night it did not seem like the right time, but want to say hello and see how you are doing.'

She removed the hand from her knee as if it were a dirty rag, ignoring her body's response to his touch. 'I'm just fine,' she said haughtily. 'Or at least, I was until last night.'

'That is not what I have heard.'

'Oh really, and just what have you heard?'

He shrugged in that maddeningly nonchalant way he had. 'Not much. Enough. Cara, why do you fight with me?'

The question jarred. 'Why did you pretend not to know me?'

She could already read the apology in his eyes, and something more.

He ran a hand through his hair in a gesture that was a carbon copy of the way Yiannis did sometimes. 'It seemed the right thing to do at the time,' he said. 'I am sorry if it was not. There was not time to think. I go to meet the woman my brother is crazy about and there she is, the woman I loved. What was I supposed to do? If I say something, maybe I break his heart and she gets angry. If I do not, I make a lie that she must follow and she gets angry. A man cannot win in this situation.'

'Oh. Well when you put it like that.' The sarcasm died on her lips as his words registered. *The woman he loved?*

'Wait, Yiannis is crazy about me?'

Nik turned a dirty look on her. 'What do you think?'

A few moments passed, in which the only sound was a clink of glasses from across the patio where Zoran pretended to be invisible behind the bar. Even the seagulls had vanished.

'Are you in love with him?'

'Nik, I am not doing this with you.'

He glowered and even as her own anger sparked her body prickled with the memory of him. She swallowed, searching for a safer subject. 'You wanted to talk, so let's talk. Where have you been since I last saw you? How was South America?'

A change came over him. His eyes softened and his face broke into a smile. 'You should have come with me, Cara. You would have liked it there. Although maybe not in the jungles – if I remember, you do not like insects very much.'

Cara grinned. 'I might have surprised you. I ate *kalamari* yesterday, you know. It was surprisingly tasty.'

Nik burst out laughing. 'That is very brave of you! Perhaps you would have enjoyed the adventure more than I thought.'

'Perhaps I would. We'll never know, will we?'

Their laughter faded. He leaned forward and took her hands in his. 'Ah, Cara, it is good to see you again. I have missed you.'

Sarcasm covered the unexpected sadness she felt. 'Sure you have. You probably didn't give me a second thought after you got on that plane.'

He held her gaze and shook his head slowly. 'Saying goodbye to you was the worst mistake I ever made.'

The last eight years dissolved and in an instant, they were right back where they'd left off. Her hands tingled where he touched them. 'I missed you too.'

He leaned forward, his knee brushing hers as he closed the distance between them. The touch of his lips was soft and sweet, his kiss both new and familiar at the same time. Cara floated in a moment of nostalgia. So many nights she had lain awake, missing him and dreaming of exactly this sort of reunion. Only, in her dreams there were no complications, no lies and no Yiannis. Oh hell, what was she doing? She tore herself away.

Nik drew back immediately, rubbing his hands back and forth along his denim-clad thighs in an anxious gesture. 'Cara—'

'Don't 'Cara' me.' Touching her lips with her fingertips she sprang to her feet. She took a few paces towards the pool, stopped and turned.

Nik sat still, watching her, waiting.

Tears threatened again. Damn them. And damn him! There he was, right there in front of her – her dream come true, except that she had no idea what to do with him.

'My God, you have terrible timing.'

He registered surprise but she gave him no chance to speak.

'You have to go, Nik.'

'But—'

She silenced him with her hand. 'Nikolaos, you have to go now,' she said, using his full name for the first time. It tasted foreign on her tongue. 'This isn't right. What we had was years ago, and what about Yiannis? I know how it feels to be betrayed. I can't do that to someone else! No, this is not real. You know as well as I do that there is no way you and I can be together now.'

His eyes flashed. 'I see. You cannot be with me but it is okay for you to sleep with my brother.'

This time her temper flared to match his.

'That's not fair! How was I to know he was your brother, or that you would be here? It's not like I came to Cyprus to see you. I can't believe the ego on you!'

'Okay, yes, you are right,' he replied angrily, 'But you know now, Cara. Must you go on tearing at my heart by going on with Yiannis in front of me now?'

'Now you're telling me I can't see him anymore? Who the hell do you think you are?'

'No, I am not telling,' He took a breath, lowered his voice and spoke more calmly, although his face was still flushed. 'I am asking.'

'You're mad! You get screw every pretty girl you see but I'm not allowed to spend time with the man who is helping to heal my broken heart?'

'What are you talking about? What girl?'

'Do you think I didn't see you with that waitress last night? Although I must say I'm surprised you could manage it with the amount of drink you had.'

He looked as if she had slapped him. He stood.

'It seems I made a mistake coming here. I was hoping we could talk like grown-ups, but no, you are right Cara. I should go.'

'Oh sure, that's your answer. Walk away, just like you did eight years ago.'

He fixed a steady gaze on her. 'Is that how you remember it? Because that is not how I remember it. Do whatever you like, Cara. You are a free woman, after all.'

She felt the heat of his anger as he brushed past her and her gut twisted more with each step he took, until he disappeared from view. Free? What a joke! Cara had never felt more trapped in her life.

It was the suppressed energy in his walk, rather than the movement itself that caught Rachel's eye. From the sanctuary of her seat nestled among the pillars and plants of the hotel lobby she watched Nik leave with angry strides and a thunderous look on his face. Things had obviously not gone well with Cara.

She waited until he was gone before closing her book and slipping downstairs into the late afternoon sunshine. Though its warmth still lingered the day had faded to a soft glow. The few wispy clouds that decorated the sky were bright and dusted with pink.

Cara sat sideways on her sun lounger, slumped forward with her head in her hands. Was she crying? Rachel *really* hoped she was not. Crossing the terrace, she glanced over to the bar shack. Zoran sent her a sympathetic wink before discreetly turning his attention elsewhere.

She touched Cara lightly on the shoulder and reclaimed her seat. 'Hey, you.'

Cara peeped at her through spread fingers. 'Hey, yourself. Where did you get to?'

'Reading. I found a cosy little spot inside behind a giant fern.'

'That's nice,' said Cara and retreated behind her fingers again.

'Are you okay? I saw Nik leave. He looked like he wanted to murder someone.'

At this Cara raised her head and dropped her hands onto her knees. 'He did?'

Rachel nodded. 'Do you want to tell me what happened?' Instantly she regretted asking, for it evoked a wail of despair.

'Oh Rachel, it was horrible! He only came to talk – and to apologise, I guess. And it made sense – why he lied last night – I mean, who could blame him, right? And for a minute there it was all good, like we were all okay. I mean, it's *Nik*, you know? And it felt so normal and then he went and spoiled it all and I s-s-sent him away and now he's g-g-gone and I don't know if I'll ever see him again.' And just like that Cara was sobbing for breath, tears tumbling unchecked down her cheeks.

'Cara, calm down, for heaven's sake. What do you mean he spoiled it all?'

'He told me to stop seeing Yiannis.'

Rachel rolled her eyes. 'Well what did you expect?'

With a big, noisy sniff the tears subsided a bit. 'Are you serious?'

'Are you?'

'Geez, thanks for the support, friend.'

It was like talking to a child. 'They *are* brothers, after all. Damn it, Cara, if you had just listened to me in the first place and not gotten involved with Yiannis, you would not even be in this situation.'

She watched the anger rise on Cara's face and glanced over at Zoran in search of an ally, but he was busy with other things behind the bar counter.

'I cannot believe you're giving me the I-told-you-so speech,' said Cara. 'There was no way on earth either of us could have known he was Nik's brother or anyone other than some random man I could have a little fun with. And what the hell happened to you being there for me? In case you missed it, this would be an appropriate time to live up to your promise!'

She looked really angry. Rachel back-pedalled in alarm. 'Okay, I'm sorry, just calm down, will you? Put away the crazy eyes.'

'Don't tell me to calm down,' yelled Cara, her eyes blazing.

'All right, take it easy!' Rachel held up her hands in surrender. What on earth had sparked this off? She had never seen Cara so upset before. 'You're freaking me out.'

'*I'm* freaking *you* out? Well excuse me, your royal bleedin' highness! Do you honestly think I give a damn how my life is making *you* feel? Do you have any idea what *I'm* going through here? My God, Rachel, I thought you were the one person I could count on in this crazy messed-up world, but now it turns out you're as bad as the rest of them!'

'What rest of them? Of course you can count on me. I said I'm sorry. Can you please calm down? I promise I'll do a better job of listening.'

But Cara had sprung up and was already stuffing her towel and book into her purple tote bag, the one with the big happy flower on the outside. But Cara was not at all happy right now. Her hands were shaking and the look on her face was even worse than Nik's had been.

'Cara, stop it. Where are you going?' Trying to keep the irritation from her voice, Rachel grasped at Cara's arm.

'Why should you care?' Cara shook her off and swore as her bag thudded to the ground, sending her book slithering across the paving.

'I care because I'm your friend. You know I do.'

In stormy silence Cara retrieved the offending book and jammed it back into her bag.

This was bad.

'Come on, Cara. I thought we said we weren't going to fight about this stuff.'

But Cara was already stomping off toward the hotel. A small seagull abandoned its search for crumbs with a squawk and scuttled out the way.

'Great,' called Rachel after her. 'Run away again. You know, at some point you're going to have to stand and face things. You can't run forever, Cara!'

But Cara did not even pause for a moment before vanishing through the doorway.

Rachel rubbed her hand across her face in frustration. She did not understand the intensity of Cara's reaction. Peter, Yiannis and now Nik – was it all simply too much for her? She sighed. Some holiday this was turning out to be.

She looked up to find Zoran watching her.

'Why thank you, Zoran. I'd love a drink. Wait, I'll come over.' She bent to pick up Cara's hat, which for some reason lay on Rachel's lounger, and was surprised to find a camera underneath. Where had that come from? She crossed her arms in a thoughtful pose as she realised Nik must have left it behind. No doubt he would want it back. Rachel knew little about cameras but this was obviously an expensive one. She wrapped it in her towel inside her beach bag and schlepped over to the bar. Maybe he would come back for it when he had cooled off. The thought made her roll her eyes again. With their dramatic exits, Nik and Cara made a fine pair.

The bar stool scraped on the paving as she shifted it closer to the counter. Zoran popped the lid off a beer bottle and looked around for a glass.

'Never mind, it's fine as it is.'

Zoran continued searching anyway while he talked. 'That man, he was your friend's fiancé?'

'Nope. That was the third side of the triangle.'

'I do not understand. From the way they talked it looked like they know each other very well.'

'I suppose you could say that.'

Seeing the look of incomprehension on his face, she brought him up to date on Cara's love life. While she spoke, Zoran finally located a beer glass, gave it a wipe and set it down in front of her.

'It sounds to me like your friend is in some little bit of trouble. I am not an expert, but perhaps it would be good for her to spend some time away from the men?'

Now there was an understatement, if she had ever heard one. As she swigged another mouthful of cold, bitter bubbles, Rachel only hoped that Cara was out somewhere reaching the same conclusion.

Rachel drank her second beer slowly from the glass that Zoran had so diligently procured for her. She wanted to give Cara some time to cool off before she tried talking to her again. But when she returned to the room, Cara was nowhere to be seen. Clearly, she had come back here after leaving Rachel at the pool, because her bag lay carelessly tossed on her bed, the flower on the side looking a little tragic in its happiness. Her towel spilled out and left a damp patch on the bed when Rachel picked it up. She draped it over the chair in the corner and took stock. Cara's suitcase was open, the clothes inside a jumbled mess and her tasselled shoulder bag was missing. So much for making peace – it was difficult to apologise to someone who was not there. Should she be concerned? Probably not. Cara just needed some breathing room. But she dug in her friend's suitcase and found her phone charger anyway. Who cared if it bordered on snooping? She wanted Cara to be able to contact her if need be. Luckily, they both owned Nokias. Who didn't, these days?

To pass the time she took a long, hot shower, the water stinging her skin after her day in the sun. Afterwards, Rachel slathered apricot-scented moisturiser all over her body and sat quietly on the balcony, watching daylight fade out over the ocean. Half a dozen container ships twinkled on the horizon, and a handful of stars pricked through the darkening sky to shimmer on the sea below. Over the rim of her balcony she saw staff in white shirts hurrying about at the hotel next door, straightening furniture and collecting empty glasses now that the sun-worshippers had turned in for the evening. A handful of seagulls made a light smudge in the shadows as they squabbled over some scraps on the small road that ran between the two hotels to the beach. Only they and mild concern about Cara, disturbed her peace.

But twenty minutes passed and there was still no sign of her friend. Where would she have gone? It was now pitch dark outside. Should she go looking for her? What if she was lost, or in trouble? Surely, she would have rung—

What an idiot! Rachel slapped herself on the forehead, abandoned her seat on the balcony and nearly tripped over herself getting to her phone. It was all very well charging the battery, but you had to switch the thing on if you wanted it to work. She settled onto her bed and watched it power up. Moments later the notifications started dropping in, one on top of the other. *Beep-beep! Beep-beep! Beep-beep!*

In all, there were ten new messages. She scrolled through them quickly, scanning for Cara's number and not finding it. For a change, there was only one from her mother: *Where are you?* Rachel felt the claws of suffocation take hold and skipped to the next one. *You have voicemail. Please dial . . .* Her mother again, no doubt.

However, the other eight messages were from Jesse. She frowned. In light of their last conversation, she might have expected one and been pleased with two, but eight? And instead of the expected (or rather, hoped for) I'm-sorry-and-I-can't-wait-to-see-you sentiments, all eight messages were nearly identical: *Call me*, they ordered.

The first one was from Monday. He must have sent it not long after they spoke, but of course her battery had expired and she had not checked the phone since.

Stalling, Rachel dialled the number for her voicemail. Her heart leapt when she heard Jesse's voice instead of her mother's, but her smile faded at his words.

Rachel, I really need to talk to you. I think I might have made a mistake. Please call me as soon as you get this.

No pleasantries, no sweet talk. His normally even tone was urgent and filled with anxiety.

Her concern about Cara momentarily forgotten, Rachel dialled his number. Had Jesse changed his mind about her? Had he decided she were already too much work and he wanted nothing more to do with her? She squeezed her eyes shut and forced away the prick of tears. No, no crying. He had not been in her life long enough to deserve her tears. Hell, he would be doing her a favour. Maybe this was her way out – no more complications. A stubborn tear plopped into her lap and she stared dumbly at the little wet blotch. God, she hoped she was wrong.

He answered the call with a curt hello. She froze, panicked and hung up.

What was she supposed to say? She fixed an accusing stare on the phone and jumped when it rang, answering it immediately to silence its shriek.

'I think we were cut off,' Jesse said.

'Um,' she replied. *Damn caller ID.*

'How's the holiday?'

Now was not the time to dump her worries on him. 'Fine, thanks.'

'Good. So, has anything, um, interesting come up?'

'Interesting?' Her eyes filled and she blinked until her vision cleared. She was not sure she'd call it interesting, exactly.

'Rachel, you sound strange. Is everything okay?'

She hesitated only a moment and her concerns came flooding back. 'Cara and I had an argument.'

'Is that all?'

'You're joking, right?' She should never have switched on her phone.

'No, what I mean is – what happened?'

'Cara has run off, I feel like I let her down and I'm angry as hell because I am sitting here worrying about her instead of enjoying my holiday.' *Not to mention that I'm waiting for you to break my heart,* she refrained from adding as she screwed up her eyes and massaged her temples with her free hand.

'I'm sorry to hear that. Look, hang on a minute, will you? I'm in the office and I just need a moment to find some privacy.'

She had forgotten about the time difference. 'Of course. Sorry, it's been an emotional afternoon.' Why was she apologising? It unnerved her to be on the defensive like this. She wished he would just get it over with.

The background noises on the line faded and she heard a door close. 'Okay, I'm in one of the meeting rooms now. Do you want to tell me what happened?'

Rachel stared glumly into the darkness outside. 'Not really. I'm probably just overreacting about Cara storming out, because I'm worried about her.'

'Why did she storm out?'

'What difference does it make? Like I said, we argued.'

'About what?'

Rachel lost her patience. 'Ah, go on, Jesse, you don't really want to hear about Cara's messed up love-life.'

'You'd be surprised.'

'What the hell does that mean? Would you just come out and tell me what all those messages were about? What is it that couldn't wait a few days until I get home?'

'All right I'll tell you, but please don't be too angry with me.'

She sucked in a noisy breath to steady her nerves.

'Okay, okay! Before you start to yell at me just listen,' he said quickly. 'In my defence, I had no idea they were having problems until I spoke to you on Monday, so really it's not entirely my fault.

And to be fair, he was very good, the sneaky bugger.'

'Who? What are you talking about?'

'Peter. I'm talking about Peter.'

Rachel shook her head, confused. 'Peter who?'

'Cara's fiancé. When you said she had run off I thought that was what you two had argued about. I'm sorry, Rachel, I think I screwed up.'

It dawned on her that this might have nothing to do with Jesse's feelings towards her. Curiosity took over, but with it came a rising sense of foreboding.

'You're making no sense, Jesse. What do you have to do with Peter?'

Rachel listened in silence and her lips pressed together in a grim line as Jesse told her about the phone call he had taken earlier in the week. Why had he been at her desk to answer her phone? How was it possible that he had taken so long to figure out that Peter was playing him? There were so many questions, she had no idea where to start.

'You're saying he knows where we are?'

'More or less. He knows you're in Limassol. I may have told him enough to figure out where you're staying. I'm so sorry, Rachel. I had no idea.'

'You had no idea about what? That you were crossing a line when you went snooping at my desk? That you were passing on private information to a man who, for all intents and purposes, is a complete stranger to you? Or that I would find out you lied about it?' She smacked her hand onto the bed she was sitting on but it made only a disappointingly dull thunk. 'I would have thought you were smarter than that, Jesse. And why didn't you say something when we spoke on Monday?'

His voice was strained. 'At the time, my concern was about us, rather than Peter and Cara. I tried calling you back afterwards but I couldn't get through – hence all the messages on your phone.'

'Oh.'

'I'm sorry,' he said again. 'Um, I assume that Peter has not made contact?'

Rachel sucked in a breath. 'I have to warn Cara.'

'If he hasn't done so yet, perhaps it won't be necessary,' Jesse said hopefully.

'From what I know about him, Peter Reilly doesn't do anything without a reason,' said Rachel. She slumped back on the bed and draped her free arm across her eyes, blocking out the light, blocking out the world. There was comfort in the darkness. 'If he went to that much trouble to find out where Cara is, you can be damn sure he has a plan.'

'Rachel, I don't know what to say. I really am sorry.'

She sighed. 'I know. Damn it, this is just not what I expected, Jesse.'

'I'm sorry.'

'Stop saying that.'

'But I mean it.'

She pulled herself upright again, squinting to readjust to the light. 'I know you do. Look, I'm too wound up to do this now. I need to figure out what I'm going to tell Cara.'

'You're still going to tell her then?'

'How can I not?'

'Will you tell her how sorry I am?'

'Sure.' Of course, first she'd have to inform her of his existence.

There was a brief silence and then he said, 'If there's anything I can do, call me.'

'I think you've done enough.'

'I deserved that.'

'Yeah. Look, I'd better go. I still need to find her, too.'

'I'm sure she'll be back soon.'

'I hope so,' murmured Rachel. Part of her was so mad she wanted to shake him but another part, the part that was tired and hungover and worried about her friend, wished more than anything that Jesse was beside her right now to hug her and comfort her, rather than talking to her from a thousand miles away. And not the gullible, spy-on-you Jesse, but the here-let-me-make-you-a-cup-of-tea-and-ravish-you-while-the-kettle-is-boiling Jesse. What a mess.

'Will I still see you at the weekend?' he asked.

'I'll call you when I get back to London,' she replied and hung up before he could respond.

Rachel stared out of the window into the distance, at a ship that twinkled in the dark horizon. Damn it. Now she had even more to worry about. What the hell was Peter Reilly up to?

Chapter 10

By the time Cara returned to the room, Rachel had stowed her phone, tidied up and was pacing the tiled floor with a half-drunk cup of tea in her hand.

'Thank God you're back. I was so worried about you. Where have you been?'

'Geez, take it easy, Ma.' Cara dropped her bag on her bed and headed straight to the bathroom.

Rachel stopped pacing, took a breath and finished her tea. It was too hot and too sweet but she drank it anyway and set the cup back on the little tray beside the television. She had not meant to sound so frantic. Heaven forbid she should start to sound like her mother.

'I didn't mean to smother you,' she said when Cara emerged. 'I thought you had come up to the room earlier, so when I got here and you were gone—'

'It's okay.' Cara clicked the button to re-boil the kettle. She stared for a moment at the camera that Rachel had unwrapped from her towel and placed beside the television.

'Nik left it behind at the pool.'

'Oh,' was Cara's calm reply.

Rachel eyed her warily. 'Where did you get to?'

'Nowhere.'

'You must have been somewhere.'

162

Cara returned to her bed and for the first time Rachel noticed the blue plastic bag beneath her shoulder bag.

'You went shopping?'

'I went for a walk. I ended up back at that curio shop we were in yesterday so I went in and bought this.' The woody aroma of dried vine leaves filled the air as she slipped the bag off the photo album she had admired, the one she had said would make a great wedding album.

Rachel smiled cautiously, wondering if her friend had lost her mind. 'It's lovely. And you got it for . . ?'

'Twelve Cyprus pounds.'

'That's not what I meant.'

The kettle started to boil. Cara dropped the album on her bed and stepped over to switch it off. She dunked a teabag into a cup and sent Rachel a stinking look. 'I know. I'm just giving you a hard time.'

Rachel relaxed. 'Phew, that's a relief. For a moment, I thought you'd lost your marbles.'

'Not yet. Apparently, I have the capacity to handle even more crap than is currently on my plate.'

Rachel sat down beside the album, opening it up to scan the empty pages. 'Who is it for?'

'It's for me.'

Rachel nodded.

'Just because I'm not getting married, doesn't mean I don't deserve to get myself a gift. I'll use it for the pictures I've taken here.'

'I'm surprised you want any reminders of this trip.'

Cara squeezed out the teabag and dropped it in the bin. 'There have been some good points.'

'Positive thinking. I like it.'

'Don't push it.'

Rachel sighed. 'Okay look, I owe you an apology. I had no idea how upset you were after Nik left. I'm still not sure I understand where you were coming from but regardless, I had no right to speak to you that way.'

Cara finished stirring milk into her tea, walked over to the glass doors and stared out to sea. 'He hasn't changed much, has he?'

'Who, Nik?' Rachel thought back to her brief conversation with him last night. Would the younger Nik have stepped aside? 'He's grown up some. We all have.'

Cara nodded and sipped her tea. Unlike Rachel, she preferred hers scalding hot. Outside on the balcony a lazy breeze shifted her towel on its chair. 'I think we should go out tonight,' she said.

'Good idea. It's still early, if you want to have a bit of a rest first.'

'No. I'll have a quick shower and then we should go.' She spun around, set her cup down on her bedside table and rummaged in her still-open suitcase for clean clothes.

'What's the hurry?'

Cara shoved a bundle of clothes under one arm and drained her cup, which was still steaming. 'Honestly? I want to get out of here in case Yiannis comes looking for me.'

'You're hiding from him now?'

She stopped just long enough to glare at Rachel. 'I just need a bit of space. We can go to that Irish pub down the road. I'm sure they'll serve food there. I could do with a hearty meal.'

While Cara showered, Rachel picked out a change of clothes, glad that they agreed on something at last. A night without men was exactly what they needed. It was strange, the way Cara seemed to have taken charge all of a sudden. Most of the time it was Rachel who steered their little ship. She wriggled into her jeans and slipped on her sandals. Not that it really bothered her, despite her gripe the other day about always being the one to take care of the details. But if Cara wanted to call the shots for a while Rachel had no problem with that. She was just glad they weren't fighting anymore.

Forty minutes later they were ready to go. Sue appeared like a mirage on their way out past the reception desk, greeting them like old friends. 'How are you girls enjoying your holiday? Having fun? Lovely! Pity it's still a bit cool though, isn't it? Mind you, it's warmer than grimy old London? By the way, did you want a wake-up call tomorrow?'

Rachel gave her a blank look. 'Tomorrow?'

'Aren't you girls off to Cairo in the morning?'

'Cairo, right. How did you know about that?'

Sue twittered a laugh. 'Oh, I'm sure Penelope mentioned it

when she was here the other day.'

The travel rep? Had the whole world given up on privacy? Rachel gave Sue her polite-lawyer smile. 'Sure. Thanks for the reminder.'

'Any time,' she beamed. 'Now, where are you off to tonight?'

Rachel was tempted to tell her it was none of her business. She should never have asked Sue to keep an eye out when they had gone out with Yiannis and Ari for the day. 'We're heading out for some supper and a few drinks. Don't wait up.'

Sue's bubbling laugh followed them out through the sliding doors. 'Don't stay out too late, now. You have to be up early in the morning.'

They flagged down a passing taxi and clambered into the back seat. Cara slammed the door behind her with Rachel grumbling, 'Bloody busybody.'

Cara gave her a quizzical look. 'What's got into you?'

'Does it not irritate you when people stick their nose into your business?'

Cara shrugged. 'I think it's kind of nice knowing someone is looking out for us.'

'I'm perfectly capable of looking out for myself. I don't need the whole world keeping tabs on me.' Rachel knew she sounded unreasonable but she was still annoyed with Jesse for giving up their location to Peter. Of course, Cara still knew nothing about that. She chewed her lip. She had to tell her, and soon.

A sudden note of tension in Cara's voice caught Rachel's attention. 'It's not the whole world, Rachel, and there's nothing wrong with having a little backup.'

As the taxi sped along between traffic lights she spied the young driver's reflection in the rear-view mirror. He flicked his gaze away. Was Cara worried because the driver was checking them out? In this part of the world it was almost expected. She was just being paranoid and no wonder, after the stress and strain of the last twenty-four hours.

In the back seat of the taxi in the artificial light of night-time Limassol, Cara's jaw ached with tension. Had she not suffered enough for one day? She eyed the old grey sedan that pulled up beside them at the traffic lights. It might have been silver once, before the sun stripped it of its sparkle. She could see little through the ugly brown tint but the driver's window was down. He leaned over and called out to the driver of their taxi, who responded enthusiastically in Greek. The other man cast an approving look at the two women in the back seat and both of men laughed.

Holy hell, thought Cara. Should they bolt? But the light turned green and the cars moved off, driving slowly and staying abreast of each other so that the men could continue their conversation.

She had first noticed the other car keeping pace with them while Rachel was sulking about Sue. Some instinct had warned her that something was up, although what it was and what she could do about it from the back seat of a moving taxi, she had no idea. Now, it took all of her self-control not to fall into a blind panic. What if these men were making plans to abduct them? Their driver could simply keep going and nobody would even know they were missing until the next morning, when they failed to show for their trip to Cairo. By comparison, Cara's jitters on the way to Yiannis's place on Monday were a joke. Back then she had not really believed in her heart that she was under threat. This time, the danger felt real.

Gripped by fear, she glanced at Rachel. Her friend's oblivion had not lasted very long and she, too, now wore a worried expression. The sign outside the Irish pub came into view. Cara held her breath. Would he stop? He was travelling too fast; he should have started to slow by now!

Without warning the taxi braked sharply and the tyres squealed as the driver made a U-turn to come to a sudden halt right outside the pub. Cara almost cried with relief when the grey sedan continued on.

Before she could even get the door open the driver swung around with a greasy smile and said, 'My friend and I would like you to join us for some drinks down the road.'

'Uh, no thanks. We're meeting friends so right here will be just fine.'

She scrambled out of the taxi and hauled Rachel with her, pushing the fare at him through his open window. Rachel slammed the door behind her and they hurried up the stairs onto the wooden veranda out front.

'Okay, that was way too weird,' she exclaimed.

'Too right . . . and which friends are we meeting, pray tell?'

Cara's heart rate slowed to its regular speed and she sent Rachel a withering look. 'Don't worry, I have no secret lovers waiting for me inside. But the taxi driver does not need to know that.'

Inside, the pub was all dark wood and green pleather seats, polished mirrors and Guinness paraphernalia, just like at home. They found a table and ordered some food and a bottle of wine to share. Cara devoured every last morsel of her Irish stew, relishing the comfort of soft-cooked vegetables and meat that melted in her mouth. A steady stream of patrons trickled in and the noise level rose steadily. Midway through her second glass of wine a young man in a purple satin shirt set up Karaoke equipment not three feet from where they sat. The tables around them were filling rapidly.

'It must be a popular pastime over here,' remarked Cara.

'I'm thinking we should move, unless we fancy being in the thick of it here,' suggested Rachel and Cara needed no further encouragement. They gathered their bags, glasses and the almost-empty wine bottle and scooted over to a couple of high chairs at the bar.

'That's much better,' said Rachel. 'This way we get to watch all the wannabe-rock-stars making arses of themselves from a safe distance.'

'Doesn't it feel weird, though?' asked Cara.

'Doesn't what feel weird?'

'Carrying on with our evening as if nothing happened.'

'You mean with the taxi? Technically nothing did happen.'

'Yes, but it could have.'

'Sure, but then we also *could have* been struck by lightning, or taken by Arab slave traders last weekend, but we weren't.'

Rachel's pragmatism was really annoying sometimes. 'It's not the same thing.'

'Of course it is.' Rachel toyed with her glass before admitting, 'Okay, it's not the same thing. Here's to narrowly escaping abduction and certain torture!'

They clinked glasses.

'Or at the very least, an evening with two nasty greaseballs.' Cara shivered. 'Ugh, that man gave me the creeps.'

A gravelly voice intruded, laced with a heavy Scottish accent and the sour odour of whiskey. 'Excuse me, ladies. I don't mean to eavesdrop—'

Cara looked up into red-rimmed eyes. 'But you did anyway?'

He inclined his head, showed a half-smile and continued. 'Did I hear you right? Are you girls in some sort of trouble?'

It was hard to tell if it was sun or booze he'd had too much of.

'Ah no, we were just blowing off some steam.'

'It sounded a little more serious than that,' he persisted. 'Abduction and torture?'

With a big, fake laugh Rachel and waved him off, 'Not at all. You know how we girls like to exaggerate.'

'Aye, I do,' he chuckled. 'All right then. I only wanted to make sure you were okay, but if you say it was nothing.'

'Yeah, nothing but a rogue taxi driver,' Cara giggled. The wine was doing its work.

'Your taxi driver gave you trouble?'

'Let's just say he tried to pick us up in more ways than one,' she laughed and looked over to see if Rachel had picked up on her clever pun. Rachel only glared at her. *Oh dear.*

The Scotsman nodded. 'Aye, you have to be careful over here, two lovely ladies all alone. The men in this part of the world have no respect for women. You need to watch yourselves.' A shadow crossed his face.

Ah. So that's what Rachel's glare was about. Damn, Cara had gone from paranoid to obtuse in a mere two glasses of wine. She really had to watch that.

'Thanks for your concern,' Rachel responded, her voice firm. 'As you can see, we are just fine.'

'It's no problem,' he drawled. 'We have to look out for each other out here, you know.'

Following Rachel's lead Cara nodded stiffly and turned away from him. Perhaps if she ignored him he would go away. Something in his eyes unnerved her.

He appeared to take the hint and she soon forgot about him.

Not normally a fan of Karaoke, she had a great time despite herself, even singing along to some of the old favourites. A second bottle of wine followed the first and after a particularly rowdy rendition of *Danny Boy* that had all the Irish in the place bellowing their hearts out, she quickly dashed off to the ladies' room. Her head swam with wine and laughter, and she noted with approval the twinkle in her eye as she checked her reflection in the mirror above the basin. Who needed men to have a good time?

But her euphoria was short-lived. She returned to find the Scotsman had engaged Rachel in conversation again. Damn. How many whiskeys he had slotted since their last encounter?

Rachel greeted her like she had been gone for days. 'Oh hey, where have you been? You're missing all the fun! John here has been telling me all about the time he spends working in Kosovo, isn't that right, John?'

Cara caught the tension in her big, fake smile and groaned inwardly. If it wasn't one loony it was the next.

John turned his bloodshot eyes on Cara. The alcohol had broadened his accent even further. 'Aye, it's true. I haven't been back to Glasgow in years.' He grinned and swayed a little. 'When I get the odd few days off I come here to try and relax a bit, get away from the stress of it, you know – unwind.'

Cara nodded slowly, her smile fixed. Instinct told her they needed to get away from him without provoking anything. So much for a quiet evening!

An unfamiliar voice broke in. 'There you are! Hello girls, we've been looking for you.' The voice, crisp with a British accent, belonged to a hand that gently squeezed her shoulder.

Cara spun around to find two young men she had never seen before grinning back at her. The shorter of the two had a steady grey gaze and short, neat, raven-black hair. He released her shoulder and gestured toward John the Scot.

'Who's your friend? Hello there, mate. I don't believe we've met. I'm Andy, and this strapping blonde lad next to me is Damien.'

He was only just as tall as Rachel was but despite his small stature Andy projected a sense of authority that Cara guessed few people argued with. Beside him, Damien made up for his lack of height. He levelled a cool look at John the Scot.

John narrowed his eyes at Rachel. 'Friends of yours?'

'Yes,' Rachel lied without a moment's hesitation. Turning to Andy and Damien she continued the act seamlessly. 'Hey, lads. Cara and I were beginning to wonder where you were, weren't we Cara?'

'That's right Rachel, we were.' Damn, her sister had always said she'd make a terrible actress. Nonetheless, the lie was corroborated. An awkward silence ensued, during which a bland-looking middle-aged accountant type drew huge applause for his Elvis imitation.

John narrowed his eyes and Cara's heart skipped a beat or two. It resumed its regular beat when after a moment he drained his glass, set it down on the bar counter. Gathering himself up to his rather impressive height he nodded to the girls. 'Well, I can see you lasses are in capable hands.' He threw a murderous look at Andy and Damien. 'Ladies, it's been a pleasure,' he said and left.

Oh thank God, thought Cara but her relief was short-lived for there was still the matter of the two young men who now stood possessively beside them. This was ridiculous. Just how many weirdos could accost them in one evening? Okay, this pair did not look particularly scary but you never knew.

'I don't think he'll be bothering you anymore,' said Andy, the picture of politeness, now that there was no longer a need to pretend.

Cara relaxed.

'No, I believe he got the message,' agreed Damien.

'Thanks lads, but we would have managed fine by ourselves, you know,' said Rachel.

'Oh, we don't doubt it for a second,' replied a gallant Andy. 'But when we saw the bloke was bothering you we thought, what better way to meet you than to come to your aid?' He flashed Rachel a winning smile and this time she smiled back.

'How kind of you. I should probably tell you up front though, that you couldn't have picked a worse pair than us to hang out with this evening. We're a couple of walking disasters at the moment.'

'Well I am, at any rate,' said Cara with a little frown. 'Rachel is playing nursemaid to me this week while I recover from my life falling to tatters.'

'Sounds serious,' said Andy. 'Actually, Damien here is in a similar predicament.'

'Is that so?'

'It's true,' Damien nodded with a woeful smile. 'My wife is divorcing me.'

'So you're also hiding out here this week, are you?' Cara mirrored his expression.

'Not exactly. We're based here.'

Cara noticed Rachel sat just a fraction straighter in her seat. 'You lads are in the military?'

'Air force,' Andy confirmed. 'Damien here fixes aeroplanes.'

'You do?'

'Yes, and Andy flies them.'

'Really? What sort of planes?'

'Red ones,' Damien grinned and Andy laughed.

'That's right, mate. Red ones.'

He was a pilot. Well that explained his immense self-confidence, thought Cara and a moment later she made the connection. 'Wait, Red – you mean the Red Arrows? We saw them a couple of days ago while we were poking around the theatre at Kourion.'

'That was us,' said Andy with a mock bow. 'We were having a bit of a practise.'

'You got awfully low,' said Rachel. 'Damn near scared the life out of us when you flew over.'

A burst of laughter marred Andy's apology and Rachel smiled again. He certainly was a likeable fellow, thought Cara and with a flash of clarity only slightly blurred by the two bottles of wine she saw that there was only one logical outcome for this evening. It was time Rachel had some fun, too. In a gallant and selfless act she immediately engaged Damien in a conversation about their respective broken relationships, leaving Rachel free to enjoy the attentions of the young, attractive pilot called Andy.

Damien proved pleasant company. He was a sweet soul, utterly heart-broken despite the brave face he put on about his divorce. Cara could tell that he was a little relieved to not have to impress her while they conspired to make it as easy as possible for their friends to hook up. It seemed obvious to both of them that they would. It was all going according to plan too, until the Karaoke came to an abrupt end some time later. The lights flickered and people started to trickle out, many singing snatches of their favourite songs and some still carrying drinks in their hands.

'Is that it?' Cara asked, surprised. 'It's only eleven o'clock.'

'No, now we move downstairs,' Damien informed her. 'There is a nightclub in the basement. Anyone in the pub when it opens gets in for free. Would you ladies care to join us?'

Rachel jumped in before Cara could answer. 'You know, I think it's time we called it a night. Another time, perhaps.'

'There's no rush, Rachel. I'm sure we can stay for one more drink.'

'I don't think that's a good idea, Cara. We need to be up early tomorrow, remember?'

Cara frowned and glanced over at Andy. He looked disappointed.

'One more drink won't make that much of a difference.'

'You're welcome to stay if you like, but I'm going back to the hotel. It has been a long day and I'm tired.' Rachel looked from Andy to Damien and back again. 'Thanks for the rescue lads, it's been a blast. But this damsel needs to go beddy-bye.'

A short, uncomfortable silence followed her words. Cara slid off her bar stool. Her feet clunked to the floor in their spindly heels and she wobbled a bit. They all looked at her and she smiled self-consciously. 'Well, lads, you heard the lady. It looks like we're outta here.'

As they said their goodbyes Cara noticed that Andy held Rachel's hand a fraction longer than necessary, regret in his eyes. 'Can I call you?'

She was kind, but firm. 'I don't think so.' His smile, in return, said that he understood.

Cara, on the other hand, did not and as soon as they were out of earshot she tackled her friend, almost running to keep pace with her. 'Rachel, are you mad? Did you not see how hot Andy was?'

'I saw.'

'So, what then – did you not notice the gorgeous puppy-dog eyes he was making at you?'

'I noticed.'

'Rachel, stop!' She screeched to a halt and grabbed her friend's elbow.

Rachel spun round and glared at her. 'What? What is your problem, Cara?'

Cara teetered backwards with the force of her reaction. 'Whoa, easy now, pet. Why so angry?'

Rachel looked up and down the street as if searching for a taxi. 'I am not.'

'Like hell you're not. You nearly bit my head off.'

'Leave it alone, Cara. I'm tired of people sticking their nose in where it's not wanted.'

'I'm not 'people', I am your friend, remember?'

'Well then as my friend, I'm asking you to drop it.'

'Why? What is so wrong with me wanting to see you hook up with a cute guy while we're on holiday? I only want to see you happy.'

'I don't need a man to be happy.'

'Yeah, but it wouldn't hurt,' said Cara with a sloppy grin.

Rachel's eyes grew wide. 'Really? You have a broken engagement. You've spent the last few days playing two other men off against each other – brothers, no less! And now you want to spend the night with somebody else, someone you met just hours ago. You really don't think you have a problem? How the hell did you ever manage to stay faithful to Peter all those years, Cara? The way you're behaving I find it hard to believe you were ever in a relationship at all!'

Cara felt as if she had been slapped. 'That is not what happened here tonight and you know it.'

'Rubbish.'

'No, Rachel, it's not rubbish,' she said, tripping over the r's a bit. 'Are you that blind? It was obvious Andy had his eye on you right from the start. The only reason I was talking to Damien was to give you two a chance to get to know each other. Damien is going through a divorce, for heaven's sake. He wasn't any more interested in me than I was in him. He was doing the same for Andy as I was doing for you. And don't bring Nik and Yiannis into this. It's not my fault—' She took a ragged breath, unable to finish the sentence. 'I just don't want to be alone right now.'

'Nobody wants to be alone, Cara, but sometimes we have to

be so that we can figure out what we want and who we want to be with.' Rachel flapped her hand at a passing taxi but it drove by without even slowing. A group of youngsters all glitzed up alighted from another across the road but it, too, moved off as soon as it had offloaded its passengers.

Cara shivered in the breath of a chilly breeze. Rachel was not going to distract her so easily. 'Is it because Andy is in the military?'

Rachel's face creased in bewilderment. 'Come again?'

'You heard me,' Cara goaded her. It was high time to bring it out in the open. Rachel had surely been dodging this for far too long.

'I have no idea what you're talking about.'

'Yeah you do but fine, if you won't say it, then I will,' said Cara. 'I think the reason you pushed Andy away is that you're afraid history might repeat itself. You lost your husband in combat and so you don't want to get involved with another military man.' She took a deep breath and held it, waiting for the hammer to fall.

Rachel's laugh was strained and bitter. 'Yeah, that's it, Cara. Everything I do that doesn't fit in with your idea of what should happen can be blamed on my dead husband. Would you just get over it? I certainly have.' She stepped sideways and stared down the road. 'Where's a bloody taxi when you need one?'

The group of sparkly clubbers passed in a cloud of perfume and cologne, laughing and talking at the top of their voices as they shimmied up the steps.

Something pinged in Cara's mind. 'What do you mean?'

Rachel glanced at her briefly then scanned the road in the other direction.

'When you said that about getting over Phillip – what did you mean?'

'Nothing.'

'Don't 'nothing' me; I know you too well,' she said sharply. 'What is it you're not telling me?'

'Forget it.'

'Don't tell me to forget it.' In a fit of frustration, Cara grabbed her hands and searched her eyes. Normally bright blue, they looked colourless under the orange glow of the streetlights. 'Rachel, I'm your friend, remember? The one you could always tell everything to. What is going on? What is it that has you so riled up at the mention of Phillip?'

Rachel shook herself free and looked away, her mouth squeezed tightly shut.

Cara reached for her again.

'For heaven's sake!' Rachel exploded. 'It's not what you think, okay.'

'I don't think anything. That's why I'm asking you to talk to me.'

Rachel finally spotted a vacant taxi on the other side of the road and waved it down. It slowed to make a U-turn. 'Are you ready to take a chance on another taxi ride?'

In that moment Cara knew she would get nothing further out of her. She sighed. 'Sure, as long as it's not the same pervy driver who brought us here.'

It was not, and the short drive back to their hotel was uneventful. Cara felt deflated. She had enjoyed her evening tremendously but it had ended on a sour note and even though the argument had ended, things with Rachel still felt unsettled.

Lying in bed in the dark, the taste of toothpaste fresh in her mouth and with the silence of the hotel room broken only by the heavy breathing of her friend in the other bed, thoughts of Nik and Yiannis once again crowded in. She wished now that she had never met Yiannis, or rather that she had not gotten involved with him. It would have made seeing Nik again so much easier. But without Yiannis, chances were she would not have seen Nik again at all.

But why was she so hung up on him, anyway? Shouldn't she be pining for Peter, the man she was supposedly going to marry? The questions chased each other around in her head like a rabble of disorganised footballers and to add to it another, unrelated one watched from the sidelines.

What the hell was going on with Rachel?

Through the fog of hangover the next morning, Cara wondered what would happen if she ditched the trip to Cairo. Rachel was behaving as if their argument had never taken place and overnight Cara had developed an urgent need to find Nik. If anyone had asked she would have told them she only wanted to return his camera. It would have been a lie. She could have left it at the Reception desk back at the hotel, if that were the case. He was bound to go looking for it there at some point. Instead she had made a nest for it in her bag and it now it rested heavily against her foot. The truth was that Cara hated that they had parted angry and she wanted to set things right with him.

Finding him, however, might prove troublesome. The most obvious route was through Yiannis, but as unlikely as it sounded, Cara had no idea how to contact him. Why had she not thought to ask him for his number? There was no way she would be able to find his apartment again. They had driven there in the dark and she had hardly taken note of where they were going at the time. Mind you, even if she *could* find him, how would she go from there to finding Nik? The thought of wheedling the information out of Yiannis by devious means sat uneasily with her. Yiannis had been nothing but kind. Using him to get to his brother would be plain mean. Just the thought of it made her shudder.

Rachel stirred sleepily beside her in the luxury bus ferrying them to the airport at Paphos. Her voice was barely audible above the drone of the engine. 'You alright?'

'Yes, go back to sleep.' Cara closed her eyes too and tried to lose herself to the gentle motion of the coach, but rest eluded her. Perhaps she could go back to the bar that had hosted Nik's party. The manager was a friend of theirs, right? She could always invent some reason for asking him. Cara could think of no reasonable explanation for how Nik's camera could have ended up in her possession, so that cover would not work. Perhaps she could say she needed Nik's help to plan a surprise for Yiannis. That might keep him from saying something to Yiannis, and it felt marginally less sleazy.

She opened her eyes and stared into the murky dawn landscape. The sky was just beginning to blush and the world passed by her window in a hundred shades of grey. It occurred to her that she would have to scope the place out first, to ensure that skanky waitress wasn't around. Imagine running into her! *Excuse me I'm looking for Nikolaos, the man you hooked up with a few nights ago.* Did she even speak English? Cara could just imagine herself trying to explain: *The hot photographer you shagged . . .*

you know . . . banged . . . had sex with. Do you understand? Perhaps with hand signals for emphasis. Ugh, that would be way too weird and besides—

She blinked rapidly as a thought took hold, that she did not actually know with complete certainty that Nik had, in fact, slept with the woman. The last Cara remembered seeing was his hand on her butt while he did his best impression of drunken flirtation. Who knew what had transpired next? What if Cara had it wrong? She frowned. Surely, he would have denied it yesterday when they were arguing?

No, he would not it because Nik was just as hard-headed as she was.

Her need to find him ballooned, as all the hurt from their break-up eight years ago resurfaced. It seared through her chest, making it hard to breathe until the bus jolted over a bump in the road. Gratefully Cara gulped a big lungful of air and her panic abated. She glanced at Rachel dozing beside her, peaceful and oblivious, and closed her eyes against the pain. A small tear squeezed itself out and rolled down her cheek. She could not abandon Rachel today. Not after last night, no matter how much Rachel behaved as nothing had happened. It would be unforgivable and no man was worth sacrificing their friendship over.

Besides, her plan would never work. At some point the friend who owned the bar would ask Yiannis about his mythical surprise. At some point Yiannis would get hurt.

With a shattered heart Cara resigned herself to getting through the day without seeing either of the men who had turned her world upside down. Never mind. It would all still be there when she returned.

By the time they reached the airport she had brought her emotions under control, leaving Rachel none the wiser. Their flight left Paphos on time and about an hour later the world tilted as the plane banked in preparation for landing. Cara caught a distorted glimpse of Cairo through the window and a flutter of excitement finally replaced the lump that had lodged in her belly.

Officials corralled their tour group inside the sleek terminal building for a head count before herding them through Egyptian customs. Outside, five luxury coaches idled in the sunshine. Even at eight o'clock in the morning, the city shimmered with heat, an illusion amplified by the haze of pollution that hung thick and dusky in the air. A short, attractive woman in a silk headscarf introduced herself as Ana. She would be their tour guide for the day and she handed a bright red rose to every woman who stepped aboard Bus Number Five. The sweet fragrance rushed in and tickled every corner of Cara's head when she brought it to her nose. It was a far cry from the sculpted, soulless blooms Peter always sent her for Valentine's Day.

She wriggled into a seat beside Rachel and scanned her fellow passengers with idle interest. Most were middle-aged or older and most looked or sounded British – holiday makers on package deals, she guessed. They were entirely unremarkable . . . until Ms Margaret arrived.

Slim, pale and perhaps a couple of inches taller than the average little old lady, she wore her wispy grey hair pulled back into a bun at the nape of her long, thin neck. Were it not for her hat Cara would probably not have given her a second glance.

'I have just got to get me one of those,' she murmured, unable to not stare.

Faded blue eyes met hers from beneath a lime green straw hat that was decorated with an assortment of glossy artificial fruit and vine tendrils, topped off with a couple of spotted feathers. The eyes narrowed and Cara looked away guiltily, a naughty schoolgirl caught out by a steely headmistress.

Stopping in the aisle to glare at Cara, she was causing a bottleneck at the door and Ana called from the front of the bus, 'Excuse me, Miss?'

Her chin snapped up. 'Pendleton-Smythe,' replied the woman haughtily. Her voice was clear and strong. 'Margaret Pendleton-Smythe and it is Ms, not Miss.'

Cara stifled a laugh. Was she for real?

Ana continued unperturbed. 'My apologies, *Miz* Margaret; there are two seats together about halfway down for you and your companion, if you wouldn't mind taking them so we can keep moving? We have a lot to see today.' Ana's tone, although pleasant held an authority not to be argued with.

Ms Margaret reddened. This was a woman unaccustomed to being chastised. Behind her, her companion – a middle-aged woman with short, mousy hair and glasses – flushed and murmured something, pointing to the row behind Cara and Rachel.

'That must be her lady-in-waiting,' whispered Rachel, sending Cara into a fit of giggles.

Muttering under her breath, Ms Margaret Pendleton-Smythe edged into the seat behind hers, disdain radiating from every pore. Cara ducked her head to hide her smirk. Perhaps this day might turn out to be a bit of fun, after all.

When she finally risked looking up again Ana was standing at the top of the aisle waiting for everyone to take their seats, but it was the man standing beside her that caused the smile on Cara's lips to die. His face was blank, his uniform dark and he held a sub-machine gun in his hands as casually as Ana held her microphone.

She nudged Rachel. 'Should we be worried?'

Before Rachel could reply, Ana's soothing voice reached them through the on-board PA system. 'Good morning ladies and gentlemen and welcome to Cairo. For those of you who missed it, my name is Ana. In case you are wondering about the gentleman standing next to me, the reason is that we will be accompanied by an armed escort today. Tourism is very important to Egypt and so every precaution is taken to ensure your safety.'

Gentleman? In Ireland, not even the *Gardaí* carried firearms. Cara's skin prickled. From behind her Ms Margaret said in a scathing tone, 'That's the trouble with these third-world places, Tilly – a complete lack of order. I only hope that man knows which is the pointy end of that thing. Savages, I tell you.'

This did nothing to dispel her concerns and while Ana continued outlining their itinerary the coach started forward and Cara leaned in to converse with Rachel.

'What exactly do you think they're protecting us from?'

Rachel patted her hand. 'I'm sure it's nothing to worry about. Sure, they wouldn't fly plane-loads of people in here if there was any real danger, would they?'

Cara felt less than reassured but there was not a lot that she could do about it. A shaft of sunlight rolled over her as they turned a corner and she tried to put it out of her mind. It was hard to believe they might be in danger while surrounded by glorious sunshine and delicious red roses.

Cairo passed by in a medley of sprawling government buildings, immaculately maintained mansions surrounded by high walls, and endless blocks of drab-looking high-rises with a tangle of satellite dishes on their roofs.

A lofty voice carried from behind them. 'Honestly, Tilly, look at the state of the place. How do they live like this? Have they never seen a tin of paint? Surely it can't be that hard to make it look nice?'

Rachel nudged her, rolling her eyes. 'Would you listen to Her Royal Hatness back there?'

'Don't you feel a bit like royalty yourself, though?' Cara replied, pointing out the window as they passed through an intersection. Their armed guard's colleagues sat astride motorcycles, halting the traffic so that the five-coach convoy could pass uninterrupted. 'That's a first for me. Now I know how the Queen feels,' she chuckled before growing serious. 'I have to say, though, it's all very well for Ana to tell us that the Egyptians are such a peaceful people and that crime is very low here, but if that's the case I can't help but wonder why we need the guys with the guns.'

Rachel shrugged.

'I'm sure it's just a precaution. We're only an hour away from Israel here. Baghdad is just a hop further along; Nine-Eleven wasn't that long ago and they're all busy shooting each other in the desert. Let's face it, this is not exactly the most stable region on the map right now. Take comfort that the guys with guns are on our side.'

She had a point, although 'comfort' was not a word Cara would have chosen. 'Comfort' would have been if those two from last night were here with them, Andy and Damien – or Nik or even Yiannis. A wicked smile tugged at her mouth at the image of them armed and in uniform but she kept the thought to herself. She and Rachel had their own peace to keep.

Their visit to the Egyptian Museum, though enjoyable, did little to shift her unease. White-uniformed security men carrying automatic rifles swarmed all over the area where dozens of tour buses were already parked. Eyeing them warily, the passengers from Bus Number Five obediently followed the blue umbrella that Ana held aloft as she carved a space among the other tour groups inside. The halls and passages were choked with people and thousands of voices echoed off the walls and thundered painfully in Cara's head. Last night's wine had really done a number on her. She craned her neck to catch sight of ancient sarcophagi and the shiny treasure surrounding King Tut's throne.

'I thought it would be bigger.' She had to shout to be heard and her head throbbed a little harder.

'Sure, he was only a child, wasn't he?' Rachel replied, standing on tiptoes at Cara's elbow.

'Yeah, but you'd think as the king he'd have a bigger chair.'

'Well it *is* made of gold. Maybe that makes up for it.'

They ogled the opulence for a few moments longer.

'I wonder what the Queen of Hat's throne looks like,' said Cara and Rachel grinned.

Cara's spirits lifted suddenly. It was good to be sharing a laugh with her, in spite of the hangovers and the guns. Things were definitely looking up.

At Giza, they continued to improve. The two bottles of water she had consumed by then went some way to easing her clanging head and it was impossible to be anything short of awed by the three great pyramids. Scorching heat reflected off bleached sand and seared the back of her throat. To Cara the whole place felt magical; the desert sand with Cairo sprawled at her feet, the great pyramids towering to the heavens, the colourful Bedouins with their camels – although she remembered Yiannis's warning and kept a respectful distance from those smelly beasts.

It was harder to avoid the flocks of scruffy hawkers that badgered them to buy their wares, shoving T-shirts and key chains at them at every turn. The more the tourists pushed them away, the more the hawkers feigned ignorance. The only English words they uttered were the insistent, 'One Pound! Two Pound!' and an incongruous 'Hello' delivered in precise, clipped English at random moments. Cara found this hilarious, coming as it did from the mouths of grubby little men in Bedouin garb. Even the sight of the Tourist Police, who roamed about dressed in white bearing their automatic rifles in a deceptively casual manner, could not break the spell. Some of them were on camels too, only they had the added benefit of carrying whips – supposedly for the camels, however Cara saw more than one blow land on a tardy hawker.

Snapping photographs at every turn, it wasn't long before Cara reached the end of the roll of film in her camera. Resisting the urge to switch to Nik's expensive one, she stepped into the shade of one of the coaches to load a new spool. Rachel waited with her and they debated joining the queue to go inside the Great Pyramids.

'I have to say, unlike King Tut's throne these are far bigger than I expected.'

'Maybe, but that entrance looks awfully narrow, don't you think?'

They eyed the dark opening from a distance.

'Sure, but we're only little, ourselves.'

'True, plus we probably won't get the opportunity again.'

Cara knocked a stone about in the dust with her foot. 'On the other hand, I'm not mad on small, dark spaces.'

Rachel remained silent as they both contemplated this.

In the end, it was Ms Margaret Pendleton-Smythe who made up their minds. She came shuffling past, leaning heavily on poor Tilly, with her lime green hat perched at a crazy angle on her head.

'They said it would be tight but I had no idea,' she puffed.

'Not to worry, my dear. I'm sure it happens to many people.'

'I feel so silly for panicking like that.'

'Well it really was quite dark in that musty little tunnel.'

'You're telling me! And when they said we'd have to crawl through it, I thought it was just an expression!'

In silent agreement Cara and Rachel turned their backs on the queue and did not broach the subject again. As Cara watched the two ladies wander off – Ms Margaret pale and shaken, Tilly flushed from heat and exertion – it was hard not to feel sympathy for the old bat.

The sentiment was short-lived, however. Only thirty minutes later she stepped into the frame of what would have been a great photograph of the sphinx, ruining the shot and not even bothering to apologise. With so many people milling around someone was always stumbling into someone else's frame, but always with good-humoured apology and tolerance. Not Ms Margaret, though; she merely gave Cara a haughty stare and took her time moving on.

'Great, now it's going to look like it has a big green hat hanging from its poor, broken nose,' grumbled Cara. She wondered if Nik ever had this sort of trouble in his line of work. The thought blind-sided her and she was gripped by a pang of anxiety. *Oh God, please let me have the chance to ask him!* It took a moment to regain her composure and re-take the photograph, this time without the lime green hat.

They re-boarded the coach after what seemed an eternity in dust and sand, having travelled so far and seen so much that Cara felt like she had been on the go for days. Unbelievably, it was only lunch-time and for this they were ferried to the plush Le Meridien hotel with its unobstructed view of the pyramids. They looked close enough to touch, although you'd take your life in your hands crossing a treacherously busy road to get there.

Once inside the hotel, cool luxury soothed away the unrelenting Cairo heat. At the entrance to the lunch room reserved for the tour group, a young man in plain hotel uniform stood bearing a silver tray with what looked like a pile of neatly stacked scrolls. Dipping his head, he offered, 'Hot towel?'

Gratefully, Cara accepted one of the hot, moist facecloths and used it to wipe the desert from her neck, arms and hands. Inside, an army of waiters hovered in attendance over a sumptuous buffet.

'Peter would hate this,' she remarked. How odd that this was the first time he had entered her thoughts all day.

Rachel looked up from her own hot towel wipe-down. 'Really? Why?'

'Because he's a snob. He hates these organised tours and won't eat from a buffet. If I could ever get him to leave bloody Dublin to come here, he would insist on having a travel agent book us a room – probably in a hotel like this one – and hire a taxi or a private car or something to see the sights.'

'Sounds expensive,' Rachel remarked.

'It is, which is why we never go anywhere. *It's an awful lot of money to spend on a few days away, don't you think, Cara?*' She mimicked him. 'He'd rather spend the cash on a new gadget or designer shirts, or in the damn pub with the lads.'

They loaded their plates with meat, rice and vegetables and found two empty seats at a large round table. Their glasses were filled with cool, clear water the moment they sat down. Rachel fiddled with her fork.

'Cara, can I say something without you getting angry with me?'

That sounded ominous. Cara stiffened and folded her hands in her lap. 'Sure.'

Rachel spoke slowly, as if choosing her words carefully and with some surprise Cara realised she was nervous.

'Here's the thing. Sometimes, from the way you speak about Peter, it would seem to me that you might not have been all that happy with him. I mean sure, it's understandable you're upset about what he did but it's starting to sound like more than that, to me, like when you talk about him it's almost as if you're relieved you're not with him anymore.'

Cara blinked rapidly a few times. 'That's it?'

'I'm sorry; I should not have said anything—'

'No, Rachel, it's okay. The way you led up to it, I was expecting something worse.'

Rachel looked puzzled. 'Worse than 'Hey I know your fiancé just broke your heart but I don't think you're all that torn up about it'?'

'Okay I can see why you might have been apprehensive.'

'You're not angry?'

Unfolding her hands, Cara picked up her fork and speared a carrot. She stared at it for a moment and then popped it in her mouth, buying time while she chewed and swallowed. It tasted like cooked carrot, but spicy.

'You know, if you had said something like that to me a few weeks ago, I would have said you were mad – that I loved Peter and we were meant to be together and everything was perfect and exactly as it should be. But then when it all went pear-shaped . . .' She sighed. 'The truth is, Rachel, that you may not be entirely wrong.'

'Really? I'm surprised.'

'At what?'

'I would not have thought you'd have been able to see it with all the stuff you've been dealing with.'

Cara shrugged and ate a piece of chicken. At least, it *looked* like chicken. It was so well disguised by its spicy sauce it could well have been toad and she probably would not have known, although it was highly unlikely in these surroundings. Could toads even survive in the desert?

'Look, I'm not saying I have it all figured out, but in the past few days I've come to realise that life with Peter might not have been all I thought it was. I used to believe that loving him was enough, but now I'm not so sure. Take today, for example. It's been absolutely amazing and if I hadn't caught him with Slutty Simone, there's a good chance I would never have come here. If there's one thing this trip has reminded me it's how much I love to travel. It has been so long since I went anywhere that I had forgotten. Shouldn't I be with someone who loves it too, or at least makes an effort to allow me to do it, even if they don't share my passion? And it's not just the travelling,' She took a deep breath. 'It's a lot of things.'

Rachel reached out and placed a warm, comforting hand on Cara's. 'I know it's hard but you'll figure it out. I have great faith in you.'

She did? Cara had little time to explore that thought, because just then Ms Margaret and the long-suffering Tilly arrived at the table in a flurry of nervous activity. Cara nearly groaned out loud. Why them? Could the woman not find a seat at another table? For the next fifteen minutes, they listened to her complain about the uncouth natives who had forced her to buy a cheap bracelet beside the Sphinx. Cara could only surmise that she had fully recovered from her foray into the horrors of the pyramid, although she noticed the fruity hat was still nowhere to be seen.

Smothering an ironic grin Cara had to concede that when it came to package tours, Peter might have a point. At least with private transport you could pick your companions.

After lunch and a surprisingly entertaining visit to a papyrus factory, their convoy headed deep into the heart of Cairo. They drew up beside the wide, murky waters of the Nile where a heady scent of frangipani, oleander and hibiscus hung in the air. These bright flowers grew everywhere, as if trying to disguise the ugly parts of Cairo – the peeling paint and graffiti that were an inevitable result of inner-city squalor.

A brass band and a red carpet welcomed the tourists on board *Maxim*, a floating restaurant on a large riverboat. It was heading toward late afternoon and once underway they drank sweet hibiscus juice and snacked on exotic nibbles while Egyptian musicians and belly-dancers put on a vibrant show. It was like a private carnival and the tour group was soon caught up in the party spirit.

After a while, though, the swirl of colour and festivity overwhelmed her tired head and Cara slipped outside onto the narrow deck. She pulled the door shut behind her, muting the raucous merriment inside.

She moved up the side of the vessel and leaned against the bulwark, watching the riverbank slide by. They had left the towering high-rises of the city far behind and she watched the water change from green to brown to glittering orange as the sun slipped lower, turning palm trees and minarets into silhouettes against a flaming sky. It was unbelievably beautiful and romantic.

Lulled by the moment, Cara was overcome by an unexpected well of emotion. Damn Nik! She had been coping just fine until he turned up. If it weren't for him she would probably be standing here having an innocuous daydream about the gorgeous Yiannis. Why did he have to turn up and dredge up all these old feelings? And damn Peter for starting her off on this rollercoaster!

Anger turned to a lonely ache. Yesterday's outburst seemed so silly now. She'd had no intention of continuing to see Yiannis past the end of this holiday. He was a fling, a salve for her broken heart. It was pure belligerence that had made her argue with Nik about it. And why not? What right did he have to tell her what to do? She'd had enough of that with Peter. She was done with it. Why could he not just have left it alone? Why did he have to go all alpha male on her?

And why, oh why, had she let him walk away again?

But as tears threatened to take hold once more, the voice of reason that had recently taken up residence inside her head cleared its throat.

That's enough, cry-baby. There is no point in shedding tears over it. What's done is done. There is nothing you can do about it from here, so you may as well enjoy what is left of this amazing day. You can worry about fixing it all tomorrow. Have faith; it will all work out the way it is supposed to.

Wow, the voice sure liked its clichés, she thought, and it definitely bore a remarkable resemblance to her sister. But as she basked in the dying embers of an Egyptian sunset, Cara Sullivan had to admit that she could do a lot worse than heed its advice.

With their heads still brimming with fiesta from their sunset river cruise, the tourists were chaperoned to a posh-looking jewellery store somewhere in the dark maze of the city. Ms Margaret, whose fruit-bedecked lime hat had come home to roost, warned Tilly that this was no more than a shameless attempt to con them into spending their cash on something other than the cheap, mass-produced trinkets that flooded the tourist attractions.

Cara thought Tilly showed remarkable restraint in not pointing out that the bracelet tinkling merrily on the old girl's wrist was exactly that, whether she had been conned into buying it or not. Mind you, she had a point. The jewellery in the store was lovely but expensive and she admired it with only passing interest. Most people seemed to do the same although one counter seemed particularly popular.

She peered through the crowd to see what the fuss was about and caught flashes of gold and silver changing hands between a sea of heads and shoulders.

'Name tags,' said a soft voice close by. She turned to see Tilly hovering behind her.

'Excuse me?'

'They're queuing for the name tags,' Tilly's smile was small, almost apologetic. 'They engrave your name in hieroglyphics onto a disc for you, sort of like the dog-tags they give the soldiers but far nicer, of course – smaller, and quite dainty, the ladies' ones.

There are a few to choose from, in silver or gold. They're really quite pretty.'

'And no doubt as overpriced as the rest of their stock,' lectured Ms Margaret, materialising at her side like some sort of silent demon.

'No doubt,' said Cara.

She flashed Tilly a kind smile as the poor woman turned away, and wondered what terrible sin she had committed, to have to put up with Ms Margaret Pendleton-Smythe as penance. Cara's own travel buddy, although perplexing at times, was a breeze by comparison. She scanned the room for Rachel. There she was, hanging out in a quiet corner, not taking too much notice of anyone. What a relief it was that she and Rachel could resolve their differences without any lasting damage to their friendship.

Preoccupied with the counting of her blessings Cara failed to notice that the crowd around her had shifted until suddenly her hip pressed up against hot glass of the display counter and she found herself at the front of the queue.

A petite Egyptian man looked at her expectantly over the array of pendants glinting on a black velvet cloth.

'Oh no thank you, I . . .' On the other hand, why not? She pointed to a small silver rectangle. 'How much for one of those?'

The answer made her grimace, but could she really put a price on a token of her new-found independence? She fished out her credit card and resisted the urge to pull her tongue at the engagement ring still trapped in the folds of her purse.

An hour later she and Rachel sat in a noisy coffee house in the *Bazar de Khan El-Khalili*, their final stop of the day. Cara tried to draw Rachel into conversation.

'So, what do you think?' she asked, toying with her new necklace. 'Gorgeous, isn't it? You know, not so long ago I would have worried about spending that much. I'm sure Peter would tell me I'm wasting money on kitsch, touristy crap but you know what? I couldn't care less. I deserve this.'

'Hm,' said Rachel, and Cara got the feeling she wasn't really listening.

Mind you, it was hard not to be distracted here. This bazaar was something else. It started at the edge of a grassy square, on the far side of which a large mosque basked in the glow of well-placed spotlights. Night had fallen some time ago and the market was like some mystical nocturnal creature, snaking away from the square and disappearing into the warm night in a brightly lit hubbub of overstuffed shops and stalls. So many people milled about that it was hard to move at times. Music played out from somewhere, exotic and foreign to Cara's ears, but it was almost drowned out by the sound of human voices talking, laughing or calling their sales pitch. From the moment the tourists stepped off their sterile luxury coaches they were assailed by noise, heat and spicy smells, not to mention hawkers whose persistence and numbers made those at the pyramids look like amateurs.

After just a few minutes in a shop the size of an elevator, the constant bump and jostle had become too much for Rachel and she had declared that she was going to sit this one out. Tired and overwhelmed from the day, Cara was happy to do the same and so they squished onto a hard, wooden bench at a coffee house. Although small and crowded, this was a haven after the chaos in the street outside.

Still fiddling with her necklace, Cara waited for a paunchy old Egyptian man to push his way through to take their order. They asked for Nescafé, which was what Ana had told them to ask for if they wanted a plain old cup of coffee in this part of the world. After some time, the man returned with two clear glasses nestled in matching saucers, each the size of a large shot glass and from two delicate little brass decanters he poured a dollop of sludgy Turkish coffee into each.

Cara shrugged. Turkish coffee would be fine, too.

She drank tentatively at first, for the aroma alone was enough to wake a mummy. But the coffee was surprisingly good and her next sip was more enthusiastic.

Ana spotted them through the window and breezed in, pulling up a chair. 'Do you mind if I join you? It is tiring work, this tour guide stuff.' She summonsed a trio of young men and fired a brief set of instructions to them in a language entirely foreign to Cara's ears. Then, while she kept a friendly conversation going with Cara and Rachel, the three lads hovered outside the open shop front with their eyes peeled for tourists with the number five pinned to their chests. Most of the people swarming about the market were locals with dark hair, honey skin and almond eyes, and most of the women wore headscarves. The foreigners were easy to spot. As soon as they found one, Ana's lads alerted her and she would dash off to show her wards where to find her. She took her job as mother hen very seriously.

Cara sat back and soaked it all in. The glare from the market lights bounced off buildings the colour of desert sand, silhouetting tall palm trees against the night sky. Throngs of people moved about and vendors hustled each other for space and custom. Some were brazen enough to sneak into the cafés to tout their wares to the tourists, but were quickly chased away amid much shouting and yelling by eagle-eyed waiters. A strong smell of spices, hot food and coffee pervaded the warm night air and over the din Cara heard someone chanting the call to prayer. It was nearly eight o'clock. It was not long before one of Ana's watchers called her over, a serious look on his face.

'Oh dear. It looks like I might be a while. Enjoy your coffee, ladies,' she said and swished off. Cara followed the watcher's concerned glance.

'Naturally,' muttered Rachel. Ms Margaret stood outside and she looked like she was in an awful state. Tilly stood behind her, head down, shoulders hunched.

'Poor thing,' said Cara. 'Imagine having to put up with that. It'd be almost as bad as being tethered to an overbearing, know-it-all fiancé.'

'Hm,' said Rachel.

Squinting at her, Cara poked her playfully on the arm. 'That's it? Have the faeries got you, pet?' She was surprised when Rachel's expression remained solemn. 'Ah, I'm only messing with you.'

'Cara, there's something I need to tell you.'

Cara replied in a droll voice. 'I thought we were over all that.'

'No, it's not about – it's something else. Well, it's about Peter.'

'You just said it was about something else.'

Rachel went on as if she hadn't even heard her. 'I don't really know how to say it, but you need to know before we get back to Cyprus.'

The way she was fiddling with her hands and the edge in her voice finally made Cara sit up and take notice. 'Well don't keep me in suspense. Just say it.'

Rachel took a deep breath and looked at her for a long moment. Her hands stilled.

Cara realised she was holding her breath and she let it go in a rush. 'Geez, Rachel, you're killing me here.'

'Peter is in Cyprus,' blurted Rachel.

It took a few seconds for the words to sink in. With the din around them she wondered if she had misheard. She shook her head. 'I'm sorry, I thought you said Peter is in Cyprus, but that's just silly. Why would Peter be in Cyprus?' She laughed.

'You heard right, I'm afraid. As for why, well he would be looking for you, I imagine.'

Cara pushed a stray auburn lock off her face. 'That's crazy. How would he even know I was here? I mean there. I mean – oh, you know.'

A hawker strayed into the coffee house and the paunchy old man who had brought them the wrong coffee let loose a torrent of abuse and chased him out, his arms flapping about like he was shooing an errant chicken. Cara watched with detachment. She fingered her new silver necklace, her talisman.

Okay, so what if Peter *was* in Cyprus? It wouldn't change anything. She frowned. 'Seriously, how would he know where to find me? Declan is the only person who knows where I went and he would never have said anything. Besides, how do you know this?'

Rachel's hands resumed their own fiddling. 'He rang my work. Must've figured out you were with me. One of my colleagues, Jesse, was at my desk when the phone rang. Peter worked his magic and conned him into telling him what he knew.'

'I thought you didn't tell anyone at work where we were going.'

'I didn't, but I'd jotted down the flight numbers at my desk and he – Jesse – figured it out from there.'

Cara frowned. Something was off. 'Back up there a minute. Who is this Jesse person and what was he doing snooping at your desk? I thought you guys had a whole respect-your-colleague's-privacy thing going at work.'

To her surprise, Rachel blushed. 'He's a new paralegal who started recently. He came in to replace Mad Marion – remember I told you about her? Well she finally did have that breakdown I said was coming. She sent us a postcard from Spain a few weeks back, actually.'

'You're avoiding. I asked you about this bloke Jesse and what he was doing at your desk.'

'I told you, he's new. We have become friends.' Rachel looked down at her fidgeting hands as if they held something of huge interest.

Cara gasped. 'Rachel Jones, you lying fiend! Do you have a boyfriend you haven't told me about?'

'No, of course not,' Rachel protested. 'He's not my boyfriend. At least, not yet. And that's not the point, anyway. We're supposed to be talking about you and Peter.'

'To hell with Peter! So, he knows where I am. That doesn't mean he's gone looking for me. He hates to travel. No, you'll not get out of this so easily. I want to know more about your man, Jesse.'

She folded her arms, sat back and fixed an accusing stare on her friend. It felt good to be in the role of accuser instead of accused for a change.

'But Cara, what if Peter—'

'What if he, what? What's the worst that can happen? It hardly makes sense that he'd come all the way out here to find me. At worst, he might be at the airport when I get back. So, he makes scene there – big deal. It wouldn't even be the first time this month that we've shouted at each other in public. No, forget Peter. I want to know about Jesse and I'll not stop nagging until you tell me everything.'

'You're a real piece of work, you know that?'

'Yeah, yeah,' Cara smiled. 'Come on, speak up.'

Rachel gave up. 'Fine, I'll tell you about Jesse.'

The way her face softened when she said his name told Cara all she needed to know but she listened as Rachel spoke about the friendship that had blossomed between them and how sparks flew whenever he drew near, until things had finally ignited the weekend they had found themselves alone together at work.

She lowered her voice a little when she got to that part and

Cara strained to hear her over the hubbub in the coffee house. She heard the important bits, though, and gaped, 'In the office? You wicked woman! Tell me more,' she ordered, gleefully absorbed in the tale.

'There is not much more to tell,' said Rachel. 'I went straight home and called you.'

Cara frowned, confused again. 'I think I would remember if you had. When was this?'

Rachel smiled thinly and dropped her gaze. 'Two Saturdays ago; the night I rang and found you on Declan's couch and you drank all his wine.'

'I didn't drink *all* his wine,' said Cara. It was starting to make sense now. 'Damn, I wish you had told me, Rachel.'

Rachel shrugged. 'How could I? You were in such a state over Peter, it just didn't seem right for me to barge in on that with my happy little love story.'

'I'm sorry,' said Cara and meant it.

'What for? It was not your fault Peter is a lying, cheating bastard, as you so eloquently put it,' she teased.

'Scumbag. I believe the phrase I used was 'lying, cheating scumbag'', grinned Cara. 'But bastard works too.'

'You're really getting over him, aren't you?'

Cara nodded. 'I think I am.'

'And Yiannis and Nik?'

'I'll figure it out,' she said as evenly as possible. 'But we're talking about you now, not me.' She held up her hand to quiet Rachel's protests. 'No arguments. Now, where were we? Ah, yes. You were telling me about your happy little love story.' She cocked her head. 'Is that what this is? Are you in love with this guy, Jesse?'

It would certainly explain a lot of her behaviour, especially where a certain handsome pilot was concerned. She was surprised to see Rachel's eyes suddenly fill with tears, but before she could say anything a little brown man shoved an armful of fake Rolex's between them, his beady black eyes glinting with sincerity as he practised his version of the English language on them.

'Ten pound, ten pound!'

A quick cuff on the ear from the eagle-eyed waiter saw him off but by the time Cara looked back, Rachel's eyes had cleared.

Cara took a final sip from her coffee glass, careful not to swallow any of the sludge that remained. Setting it gently back in its saucer she said, 'You know, this whole week has been a succession of one Cara crisis after another, yet I've had the vague impression that something's been eating you, too. How about we forget about me and instead, you tell me what's really going on with you?'

'I thought I just did.'

'You just confessed you did the naked tango with a guy in the office. I get the feeling there's more to it than that. What is it you're not telling me?'

But Rachel ignored her, nodding instead towards the street outside. 'It looks like it's time to go.'

Indeed, there stood Ana. She pointed at her watch and gestured back towards the square where the buses were waiting. Rachel was already out of her seat and Cara watched her for a moment before following. She was holding something back, for sure.

Unfortunately, the frantic pace of their itinerary prevented her finding out more. Bus Number Five already had its engine running as they clambered back on board. Cara saw relief on many of the faces around her as the door hissed closed and the world shrank back to an air-conditioned hum.

By contrast, she wished they could stay longer. Sure, it had been a bit overwhelming at first, but something had happened to her in the midst of the noise and craziness of the bazaar, as if the essence of life that permeated the air had touched her with a magic finger, bringing her back to life after a long slumber.

From the seat behind hers Ms Margaret Pendleton-Smythe aired a very different opinion. Cara could almost hear her wrinkling her nose as she spoke.

'Well thank goodness that's over,' she declared. 'I don't think I could bear another moment in that nasty, smelly place. Thieves and beggars, the lot of them.'

'It must be a shame to miss out on the joys of life because you're too busy looking down your nose at it,' Cara snapped.

Rachel dug her in the ribs. 'Don't be causing trouble,' she hissed and darted a glance over her shoulder. 'Do you want to get us thrown off the bus? You're lucky she didn't hear you.'

'Lucky, my arse. She's done nothing but bitch and moan all

day. Why did she even bother coming if all she wanted to do is complain? She should just stay in her cosy little house in the Shires and play Bridge on Thursdays and judge people from the safety of her wingback chairs.' She paused for a breath, warming to her rant. 'What did she expect to find here anyway? It's Cairo, for feck's sake! If she wanted silence and high tea in genteel surroundings she should have gone to bloody London. What? What is so funny?'

Rachel had gone pink in the face, she was laughing so hard. 'You really don't like her, do you?'

Cara pursed her lips and folded her arms across her chest. She hated being laughed at.

'Come now Cara. Don't take it so personally. This is not for everyone and I'm sure the locals don't care if one old biddy doesn't like their digs.'

Cara picked at an imaginary piece of fluff on her shirt. Rachel was right, of course. Cara had taken it personally. She had taken the whole day personally. How could she explain that she was cranky because the trip was drawing to a close? Talk about childish tantrums! But coming to Cairo had awakened something in her and the thought that it might not stay past the day's end terrified her. 'She's a snobby, opinionated bitch,' she sulked. 'And she ruined one of my photos.'

Rachel only laughed harder and Cara gave a grudging smile. By this time, they were on the move again and there were things to see. With a microphone in her hand Ana pointed out sights of interest as they sped through the city. There was the City of the Dead, where the living and the dead shared the streets, and the imposing hulk of the Citadel. And then they were back in modern Cairo where upmarket shopping strips boasted designer names in neon lights. Cara sighed. The magic was gone. But when her hand slipped up to finger the silver disk that now hung from her neck she smiled to herself in the rushing shadows of the night. The magic might be gone, but her resolve remained.

Chapter 11

Bathed in the soft light of a new day Peter Reilly stood naked at the window of his hotel room. He yawned loudly, stretched and planted his hands on his hips as he stared out to sea. A sound night's sleep in the five-star hotel had left him refreshed and eager to resume his mission. By this time tomorrow Cara would be back in his bed and his world would once again be in order.

Movement from the swimming pool several storeys below caught his attention and he watched the hotel staff set up sun-loungers and umbrellas beneath the palm trees. It occurred to him that it looked quite pleasant down there amid the flaming bougainvillea. He might even suggest to Cara that they go to a place like this some time for a holiday. There was no shortage of resorts dotted around the Mediterranean. He was certain he could put up with it for a week, as long as she did not expect him to go traipsing around caves or tombs or eat in any of those tacky local places that had never heard of health and safety regulations. Peter did not fancy dying of dysentery in some foreign hospital.

At the thought of Cara his stomach tightened and he turned away from the tranquil scenery. It annoyed him that he had not found her the previous day. He knew she was staying in the little hotel next door. That irritating blonde receptionist had given it away despite her insistence that she could not give out such information. She must be terrible at poker. The barman, however was a different story. Peter had waited until the receptionist stepped away from her desk before sneaking back inside to look around. But the only people down at the pool were an older couple who looked at him blankly when he tried to talk to them. Bloody foreigners.

When the barman had turned up to open the pool bar, Peter thought he had hit the jackpot. Barmen always knew everything. But getting him to talk proved challenging. Peter had set to work to gain his trust, or at the very least win his sympathy. He was a broken man, desperate to find the woman he loved. No-one could resist a little romance, right? A young, good-looking chap like that was bound to understand. It should have been no problem.

But the man was a fortress. Peter had employed every trick he knew but the bloke gave away nothing. In the end, he had given up and left, frustrated as hell and none the wiser.

He had spent the afternoon at a table outside a pizzeria across the road where he could keep an eye on the entrance to the Lionheart Hotel but that, too, had been a waste of time. Plus, the pizza was terrible. Had they not heard of Dominos in this dusty, godforsaken place?

Peter shook himself and stretched again. Today was another day. Armed with a cup of coffee ordered from room service he sat down and went through his plan for the umpteenth time. It had taken him days to perfect what he wanted to say. Presentation was crucial. Peter needed this to succeed more than he had needed anything in a long time. Starting over was not an option. His parents would throw a fit if they found out what had happened.

So, he ran through his key points again and nodded with satisfaction. The guileless Cara would not stand a chance once he started to apply his charm. It had always worked before. There was no reason for it not to work now.

Peter nodded in satisfaction. He was ready.

Even after a solid nine hours of sleep Cara felt sluggish, as if someone had flipped on one light bulb in her head instead of four. Rachel, too, looked like she was sleepwalking as they followed the smell of bacon downstairs.

It was their last day in Cyprus. They wanted to make the most of it so they took their breakfast outside. Sunshine, blue skies and twittering birds made for a beautiful day. She screwed up her eyes against the glare off the white plastic chairs and fumbled to shift her sunglasses from the top of her head while holding her plate in one hand. Her knife clattered to the floor.

'Drat,' she muttered.

'Here,' said Rachel, taking her plate from her and setting it on a nearby table. 'Go get another one.'

While Cara dutifully ducked back inside to fetch a clean knife, it occurred to her that she had almost forgotten her intention to quiz Rachel about the whole Jesse business again. It still rankled that she had kept it from her, regardless of Cara's own troubles. Re-joining her friend at the table she devoured a juicy pork sausage and mulled over the best way to start the conversation.

'So, Jesse, huh?'

Rachel paused with her glass of juice halfway to her mouth. 'What about him?'

'What's he like?'

Rachel shrugged and sipped her juice, playing it cool until a devilish grin split her face. 'Hot. Really hot.'

'Naturally. Nothing but the best for you, Ms Jones. Go on, tell me more.'

Unfortunately for her curiosity the waiter, Stevan, chose that moment to interrupt, scurrying over with flailing arms as if in some distress.

'Mees Sullivan,' he called out.

Cara gritted her teeth. He really knew how to pick his timing. His black eyes sparkled, his swarthy face was flushed and he shifted from one foot to another in agitation beside their table as he spoke. 'I have message for Mees Sullivan.'

'I am Miss Sullivan,' said Cara. Her mind kicked into gear. A message? The only people who knew she was here were Rachel, Declan, Yiannis and Nik. Her heart skipped at the thought. Perhaps she would not need to go in search of them, after all. Wait, what if it wasn't them? What if it was Declan, and something had happened at home? All these thoughts flashed through her mind in an instant and erupted in a mild panic. 'What is it, Stevan?'

'Yes, okay, one moment please.' He dug in his pockets and Cara waited with growing impatience until he finally pulled out a scrap of paper in triumph. 'Yes,' he said. 'I tell you now.' Clearing his throat, he announced, 'You have a phone call yesterday.'

'From who?'

'It says here to telephone this number.' He frowned at the piece of paper and muttered something under his breath.

'Yes, and who is it?' she cried, ready to throttle him.

His face flushed even redder. 'I cannot see what it says. I think Mees Sue she wrote too quickly.' Mortified, he handed her the note.

She snatched it from his fingers and scoured it for clues but it bore only an illegible scribble and a series of numbers. 'Is this a local number?'

Stevan nodded.

Seeing how distraught he looked, Cara softened. 'Thank you, Stevan, thank you very much.'

He brightened at her smile and flashed one back at her before vanishing back inside the dining room. She checked her watch. It was nine-thirty in the morning. 'Rachel, I'm sorry but—.'

'You have to make a phone call? It's okay. Go. I'll be here when you get back.'

It took a few moments for her eyes to adjust after the brightness outside. The lobby appeared more gloomy than usual, with more shadowed corners, and those shadows seemed darker. The slap of her flip-flops echoed as she crossed the gleaming tiled floor towards the reception desk. She was certain that she remembered seeing a telephone on a table near the entrance. Sure enough, there it was, a big blue one beside piles of tourist brochures. With not a soul around to ask, she lifted the receiver and crossed her fingers, hoping it was an open line and thus saving her the trip up to her room. Her breath quickened at the sound of the dial tone. With quivering hands Cara smoothed out the note and punched the numbers. It started to ring and she sucked in a quick breath to quell the tide of nerves that rose in her belly.

A slow, sexy voice came on the line. 'Yiannis Georgiou.'

'It's Cara,' she croaked, her heart thudding.

'Cara. You got my message,' he crooned and she could almost hear his lazy smile. Cara's nerves abated in response. He sounded really happy to hear from her.

Out of the corner of her eye she observed Sue come out of her office and fuss with the papers on the desk while pretending not to eavesdrop. Cara turned her back on her.

Yiannis told her he wanted to hear all about her trip to Cairo. 'But now is not such a good time,' he said.

He must be at work. It was Friday, after all.

'For me too,' she replied, acutely aware of being watched.

Yiannis suggested they meet for lunch. He knew a place in Old Town, not far from the castle. 'You will find it alright?'

Cara smiled and recited the directions he had given her. 'I'm a big girl – I'll find it. I'll see you at one.'

After hanging up she stared at the phone for a moment, trying to marshal her emotions. Yiannis really was lovely and easy to talk to, and he had a way of making her feel like the most beautiful woman on the planet. She wondered what might have happened if circumstances were different.

The feeling of being watched intruded on her thoughts and she swung around but to her surprise, Sue had gone. Cara chuckled, shaking her head at her own paranoia, and turned to go.

'You got your message then, did you?'

She jumped. The woman was like a ninja. She must have been hovering in the back room, just out of sight.

'Most of it,' she replied and headed back towards the staircase with the wrought-iron railing. Preoccupied with thoughts of her impending lunch date she paid no attention to the man reading a newspaper in the shadows of a giant fern.

True to her word Rachel was right where she had left her, staring into a cup of coffee in bright sunshine. She looked up as Cara sat.

'They cleared the plates already. I wasn't sure how long you'd be gone.'

'That's okay. I'm not mad about cold eggs.' Her appetite had vanished anyway.

'I got you some coffee,' Rachel offered.

'Thanks.' It was just the right temperature and she savoured a long sip. They were sitting close enough to the open doors to the dining room to hear the clatter of cutlery inside, sprinkled with snatches of conversation and occasional laughter. The German contingent must be enjoying their stay. A small finch-like bird hopped around on the ground near their table, pecking hopefully at the ground.

'Did you get to make your phone call?' Rachel asked.

'I did, thanks.'

'Is everything okay?'

The bird hopped a little closer, cocked its head and fixed a beady eye on her as if it, too, was waiting for an answer.

'It was Yiannis,' said Cara, with a nonchalance she did not feel. 'I said I'd meet him for lunch.'

'Oh?'

Cara watched her for any sign that would betray judgement or disapproval, but found none. Rachel displayed little more than conversational interest. In fact, she was paying more attention to the little bird than to Cara. 'Yes. At a place in Old Town. You don't mind, do you?'

'Why would I mind?'

'Well, I know it's our last day here and I wasn't sure if you wanted to do something special.'

Rachel shrugged. 'Not really. Yesterday was pretty full-on. A nice quiet day here by the pool sounds about right to me. I may go onto the beach later, but that's about it.' She brushed a couple of crumbs off the table into the palm of her hand and threw them towards the bird. It darted forward greedily and cleaned them up in no time.

'That sounds good. I might join you when I get back,' said Cara. She had no intention of staying out all day, but there were things she needed to take care of. It was a relief to her that Rachel appeared to understand this and was giving her the space to do it.

Rachel looked up, just a trace of concern on her face. 'Will you be alright? With Yiannis, I mean – have you figured things out?'

'Pretty much.'

'And Nik? Not to be pedantic, but don't we still have his camera?'

'I can always leave it at Reception. He's a bright boy. He'll figure it out.' She managed to keep her voice steady as she said this but was glad her sunglasses hid her eyes. It was one thing to make decisions when you were away in the desert, far removed from the situation, but it was another to speak of it out loud. Right now, even with her new silver talisman around her neck she did not trust herself to say more.

The little bird stopped pecking at the ground, watched her for a moment and then fluttered up onto the back of a chair before flying away. Cara thought that in her next life, she might like to come back as a bird. It must be awfully handy to be able to just fly away whenever you wanted to.

Back in their room, she washed her hair and dried it as best she could, with the hairdryer attached to the bathroom wall. Eyeing herself critically in the mirror, she turned her head this way and that. The spotlights above picked out her auburn highlights and when she nodded with satisfaction her shoulder-length tresses bounced agreeably. Not quite straight-from-the-salon good, but not just-stepped-off-the-ferry bad, either. She donned a light floral sundress and sandals, both of which showed off her legs, which had magically turned from lily-white to creamy latté over the course of the week. After adding silver earrings to match her necklace from Cairo, she left the hotel with half an hour to spare, waiting just a few minutes at the kerb for the bus that took her to Old Town. Yiannis had given good directions and she even had time to browse linens and pottery in a small shop along the way, before arriving at the restaurant at four minutes past the appointed time of one o'clock.

The bistro doubled as an art gallery. It had a dark stone floor and white walls adorned with dozens of framed photographs, each with an inconspicuous price card attached. The place was tightly packed and busy. Cara only spotted him when he rose and waved from a table tucked away in the corner, through an archway. A number of female heads turned as he did so. He certainly was a handsome man, she thought a tad wistfully as she threaded her way to him.

He drew her into a warm embrace, his lips brushing her cheek. 'I was afraid you would leave without saying goodbye.'

Cara laughed softly, hoping she did not sound as nervous as she felt. 'Now why would I do that?'

The heavy wooden chair scraped on the floor as he pulled

it out. She sat and he reached across the table for her hand. 'I thought maybe your friend would talk you out of coming.'

'Rachel? Why should she?'

'I think she does not like me.'

Cara shook her head and her hair bounced on cue. 'Don't take it to heart. She thought I had gone off the rails, but we've had a little chat since I last saw you. She understands now.'

'Tell her she is a good friend, but she need not worry. I also will look out for you.'

'For crying out loud, what is it with the pair of you? I am perfectly capable of taking care of myself.'

He shrugged and in his slow, nonchalant manner replied, 'I am sure this is true, but what can I say? You make me want to take care of you.'

Rendered speechless for a moment, Cara was grateful for the arrival of a waiter bearing a carafe of sparkling water and a plate of bruschetta. 'You have already ordered?'

Yiannis's face split into an exuberant smile. 'I hope you do not mind too much, Cara, but the food here is excellent, a real experience. Before you came I spoke with the manager. He will make certain they serve us the best things on the menu today. It is part of the special service they can give here.' As if suddenly concerned that he might have overstepped, his smile faded a little. 'This is okay with you?'

It was a little weird, but it seemed unnecessary to ruin his moment so Cara nodded. Who was she to complain about getting special service?

His smile returned. 'Good. Would you like some wine?'

She nodded again and he spoke a few words to the waiter, who melted away.

Cara looked around in wonder. Yiannis had obviously put a lot of thought and effort into this lunch, far more than she had expected. Frankly, she would have been happy with a pub lunch but here they were in a classy bistro with personalised service and food that was art. She couldn't wait to tell Declan about it. Did her brother have a place like this in Dublin – somewhere fancy to bring a girl he wanted to impress? It was just the sort of thing she could imagine him doing when he wanted to soften one up to get into her knickers.

She blinked and mentally slapped herself. Yiannis looked happy and enthusiastic, kind of like a Labrador in drop-dead gorgeous sort of way. Man, was he going to be disappointed.

He broke off a small piece of bruschetta, made sure not to leave any topping behind and leaned forward to offer her a taste.

'Try this, Cara. I promise, you will love it.'

She caught a whiff of fresh garlic and herbs as his fingers gently touched her lips. She parted them to accept the entrée and her eyes widened at the flavours that followed. He wasn't kidding – it was sublime. Chewing slowly to savour the mouthful, Cara reasoned that there was little harm in appreciating a superb meal that was already on its way. She would let him down gently later.

The wine arrived, followed by servings of Carpaccio, hot brie parcels and a delicious chicken and mango salad. Yiannis had a great love of food and he told her that it filled him with delight to see her experience the same pleasure. Lubricated by wine, their conversation flowed easily. Cara reported on her day in Cairo in glowing terms, her hands working overtime to assist in her explanations. He laughed at her description of Margaret Pendleton-Smythe and her ridiculous hat, and made all the right noises when she showed him her necklace. If this was how he got girls into bed, thought Cara, then he must have a very successful sex life.

At last, just when she thought she could eat not another morsel, the waiter returned with the *pièce de résistance*.

'Death By Chocolate,' he announced, unable to conceal a smile. 'The best you will ever eat.'

It was no exaggeration. 'Oh wow,' groaned Cara, closing her eyes to fully savour the taste.

'That must be some dessert you have there. That's the same face you make in bed.'

Her eyes flew open to confirm what her ears already knew. Aye, there he stood: tall, blonde and with a face like a winter storm. *Peter!*

'The difference is I'm not faking this,' she said with an acid smile. 'What the hell are you doing here?'

'Those are fighting words coming from someone in your

position.'

Cara could barely contain her anger. 'And what position is that, exactly?'

Normally a mask of pleasantry, Peter's features twisted in an ugly sneer of accusation. 'One where your fiancé finds you enjoying a romantic meal with an oversexed boy-toy.'

That galvanised Yiannis into action and he sprang to his feet, eyes flashing. He faced Peter with clenched fists. 'Friend, I do not know who you are or what this is about but you should go now.'

'Friend? Oh, I'm no friend to you, Romeo,' said Peter, poking him in the chest. 'I'm the guy whose girl you're messing with here.'

Nearly four inches taller than Yiannis, he glared down at him. Nevertheless, when Yiannis puffed out his chest and moved towards him, Peter took a step backwards.

'That's enough,' hissed Cara. 'I will not have you two fighting in here. Yiannis, sit down. Peter, you have no right to be here.'

His smirk faded, as Cara rose to her feet and stood trembling with rage before the man who had shattered her life.

'How dare you barge in here and harass me? I am not yours to claim. You gave up that privilege when you decided to screw other women. As far as I'm concerned, we are over. Do you understand? We are finished, Peter, now get out of here and stay the hell out of my life.'

Drawn by the commotion the manager came and stood beside Peter.

'Excuse me, is there a problem?'

'Yeah, there's a problem,' he said. 'I have come to fetch my fiancée home, but she seems intent on toying with lover-boy here instead.'

Before she knew what was happening Cara had slapped him, a sharp, stinging slap that made him stumble sideways. It was the second time in as many weeks and Cara wondered at her sudden propensity for violence.

All eyes were on them and before the situation could escalate any further, the manager took firm hold of Peter's elbow.

'It is time for you to leave, sir.'

Peter rubbed his cheek in disbelief. 'No, wait. Cara, this is ridiculous! You're angry, I understand and you have made your point but it's time to come home now. This was not how it was supposed to go!'

Cara stood firm, saying nothing and the manager tugged at his arm, 'Sir, I believe the lady has made herself quite clear. Please come with me.'

'But—'

'Yes, thank you, this way please,' the manager insisted. Very calmly, holding Peter's arm in a vice grip, he escorted him out of his bistro. Peter's protests could be heard all the way out into the street. The manager went out with him and Cara finally sank to her seat, mortified, while around them the other diners resumed their lunch.

'Oh God, they're all talking about me now.'

Yiannis had calmed down remarkably quickly. One sip of wine and he reverted to his amiable self.

'Who cares? You do not know them. Good shot, by the way.'

Cara experienced a pang of regret and buried her face in her hands. 'Oh hell, I am so sorry.'

He reached over and touched her gently. 'Hey. It is okay now. It is over.'

She groaned, unable to meet his eyes.

'Cara, are you going to tell me what that was about?'

She sighed. He deserved a proper explanation. Raising her head, she smoothed her hair and composed herself. 'That was Peter – the man I was supposed to marry up until a couple of weeks ago. He cheated on me and I left. I came here to try and figure out what to do next.' She sighed again and picked at an imaginary crumb on the white damask tablecloth. 'Rachel warned me yesterday that he found out I was in Cyprus. But I never thought he'd actually come over here to find me, never mind pull something like this!' Her blood boiled again and she banged a fist on her thigh. 'Ouch, that actually hurt.'

Yiannis laughed at her surprise. 'Be careful, Cara. Cheating fiancés I can protect you from, but I cannot save you from yourself.'

'I thought it would be less noisy than if I hit the table. I've caused enough trouble for one meal, don't you think?'

As if summonsed, the manager returned, his face a portrait of supreme control. 'Is everything alright now?'

'Yes, thank you so much. I am so terribly sorry about that.'

Cara did not think she could ever apologise enough.

Yiannis exchanged a few words with him in Greek. They shook hands and the manager bowed his head to her with a look that conveyed understanding and sympathy, whilst still remaining aloof. He blinked to show that all was forgiven and moved on to the next table. No doubt there were some feathers that needed soothing. This was not the sort of establishment given to dramatic outbursts.

'It is okay,' Yiannis told her, patting her hand again. 'There is no problem. Let us enjoy our dessert, okay?'

Cara stared at the little piece of chocolate-flavoured heaven before her. She had no appetite for it now. It was time they talked about more serious things than camels and food. 'Yiannis, you do know that I leave tomorrow, right?'

He took his time swallowing a mouthful, raised his gaze to meet hers and sighed. 'Sadly, yes.'

She gave a small smile. 'You are too kind.'

He shrugged. 'I like you, Cara and if you do not mind me saying so, you do not have to go.'

'Don't be silly, of course I do.'

'Why?'

'I have a life to go back to, Yiannis. There's my job—'

'You told me the other night you hate your job. Why are you in so much hurry to go back to it? You could stay another week, or you could find work here. There are many people looking for someone who speaks English to work for them. I will help you find a place to stay.'

'Wait, are you saying I should stay here permanently?'

'I am saying that it will make me very sad when you go, Cara. You are not like the girls I normally meet, and I would like to have more time with you.' He smiled his dazzling smile. 'I cannot make you fall in love with me in only one week.'

'Love?' she squeaked, her mouth suddenly dry as the desert at Giza. Holy crap, this was not at all how she had pictured this going. Her head was spinning. He was saying all the right things and it tore at her because she wished with all her heart that it was his brother saying them instead.

'Oh, Yiannis. You couldn't possibly understand, but I can't.'

'So make me understand.' His beautiful olive eyes pleaded with her.

She hid the guilt behind fluster. 'Look, my life is really complicated right now – you just saw that for yourself. I have just come out of a long relationship and while you are really lovely,' A little sigh escaped as her gaze wandered over his muscular frame, 'You must know that what we have is not serious. You understand that, right?'

He laughed. 'I do not suggest that we should get married, Cara but if you stay a little longer I can show you the real Cyprus. There is so much more here than what you have seen and I think you would like it. We could have a lot of fun together, you and me. Think about it.'

'Oh Yiannis, you cannot be serious.' Her throat ached with tension.

'Why not?'

'Because that's not what this is! This was supposed to be a bit of fun. It's not supposed to go anywhere – it's not how these things work.' As soon as she heard herself say them, she knew it was a poor choice of words.

'Fun. Yes. You come to the islands, play with the local men and then go away again.' Bitterness crept into his voice. 'I understand this is how it works for you English girls.'

'For God's sake, I am Irish,' Cara protested. 'And are you serious? It is the other way around, you dope! All you gorgeous men have to do is flex your muscles and you can have your pick of all the girls who come here on holidays. Now you're telling me you want to build a relationship? You must be joking! Do you really expect me to believe that this lovely lunch was not about you trying to get me into bed before I go?'

Yiannis raised his eyebrows. 'Is it working?'

Cara blinked, then chuckled. 'We would need a lot more wine. Also, the crazy ex-fiancé sort of ruined the mood.'

He reached for her hand across the table, planted a kiss on it and then held it gently. 'My lovely Cara, I think I have lost you,' he said sadly.

'Oh Yiannis,' replied Cara softly. 'I think maybe you never really had me.'

When Yiannis walked her to the bus stop Cara fought the urge to pat him on the shoulder and say, 'Ah, you'll be grand, so!' He seemed reluctant to part ways. His excuse was that he was concerned Peter might still be hanging about.

'I doubt it,' Cara reassured him. 'He's probably off somewhere licking his wounds. Besides, he might be an arsehole but he would never do me any physical harm.'

Still, he kept up his vigil until Cara was safely seated on the bus, cutting a forlorn figure on the side of the road as it pulled away. She waved goodbye through the window and he raised his hand in response. If they were in the movies, thought Cara, this would be the part where she jumped up and demanded the driver stop the bus so she could run back into his arms. They would then live happily ever after. She rolled her eyes at the melodramatics playing out in her head. Cara Sullivan was the kind of girl who married a respectable man, raised three chubby kids and spent her golden years reading Maeve Binchy novels in the conservatory in dear old Ireland. She was not the sort of girl to go haring down the street on a Mediterranean island after a man who looked like a Calvin Klein model . . . and honestly if she ever did such a thing it would not be for Yiannis.

The thought sobered her. Lovely as he was, Cara was relieved she had ended things with him. He was a holiday fling, not a relationship. His brother, on the other hand . . .

Cara slumped in her seat and stared unseeingly at the passing palm trees that swayed gently in the ocean breeze in front of the shops, bars and apartment blocks along the foreshore. Thoughts of Nik had been banished while Cara dealt with Yiannis, but now those thoughts returned to haunt her. Nik had never been just a fling. But what could she do about it now? In less than twenty-four hours she would be back in Ireland. There was simply not enough time to track him down before she left. She straightened up, smoothed the delicate floral fabric of her dress in her lap and got her head straight, reminding herself that she had made her decisions already.

In fact, she had made them two days ago after storming out on

Rachel. Somewhere between a random walk along the beach and the purchase of her photo album Cara had reached the realisation that if she was ever to be happy with someone else, she first needed to be on her own to figure out who she was. Her day in Cairo had reinforced that and given her a renewed energy and determination to follow it through. The silver necklace she now wore was there to remind her of this. Cara had finished with Nik years ago and now that she had cut ties with his brother the best thing to do was forget them both.

All she had to do was get her heart to agree with her head.

As the bus neared the stop outside the Lionheart Hotel she scanned the area carefully. Peter showing up like that in the middle of her lunch was completely out of character, and despite what she had told Yiannis, his behaviour made her nervous. He had never done a spontaneous thing in his life.

How had he even known she was there? Had he been following her? Remembering the man behind the newspaper in the lobby earlier and knowing now that it was probably Peter, eavesdropping before following her, she shuddered. Cara did not know him to be unpredictable and she did not like it one bit. What else did he have up his sleeve? After coming all this way to find her, he surely would not give up after one little scene in a bistro. He must have a plan. Peter always had a plan.

But if he was around he was staying out of sight. She scooted inside the hotel as fast as she could, feeling like a fugitive. For once she wished it was busier this early in the season. The place felt deserted and it creeped her out.

Rachel was not in the room, and her sun hat and beach towel were gone. Quickly swapping her sandals for flip-flops and her sundress for a light sarong over her bikini, Cara went in search of her friend. She found her on the small public beach beside the larger private one belonging to the Hotel Somptueux next door.

'Oh, hey,' Rachel greeted her with a lazy smile. 'How was your lunch?'

To her own horror, Cara burst into tears.

'Whoa! What happened?' Rachel immediately jumped up to console her.

'I-I'm sorry,' snivelled Cara. 'I d-d-didn't mean to do that.' She sucked in a ragged breath and wiped away her tears. 'Oh my, I don't know where that came from. It's nothing, I'm okay now.'

'Something must have happened to set you off. What on earth has you so upset?'

Cara flung herself onto a sun-lounger and it creaked in protest. For a moment, she thought it might collapse and send her sprawling in the sand but it did not and she mustered her thoughts while Rachel sank back into her own seat. Embarrassed and shaken at her unexpected outburst, she had every intention of keeping the dramatics to a minimum, but her words had other ideas.

'Well first of all, you were right. Peter is here and there's a good chance he's stalking me. Also, Yiannis has gone all hearts-and-flowers, wanting me to stay and fall in love with him. Yeah, I know, I couldn't believe it either,' she replied to Rachel's look of surprise. 'Oh, and of course in the meantime I can't stop thinking about Nik—'

Rachel stopped her. 'Wait, you need to back up a moment. Peter is here? How do you know? Did you see him?'

'He crashed our lunch,' snivelled Cara. 'He made a huge scene. I slapped him again, right before the manager threw him out.'

'You did not!'

She grinned morosely. 'I'm afraid I did. Classy, huh?'

Rachel merely shook her head in amazement, or perhaps dismay. It was hard to tell.

'After that, Yiannis got all mushy, which was awful because the reason I was there was to break up with him.'

'Oh.' The word was loaded with unasked questions.

'Yes, I did in the end. He was not happy but he understood.'

'And Nik?'

'I didn't tell him about Nik.'

Rachel nodded thoughtfully. 'It's probably best, all things considered.'

Cara pondered this for a moment. Warmth from the afternoon sun soaked into her exposed skin and the steady splash of tiny waves rolling onto the dark sand beside them soothed her overwrought nerves. 'It's probably best for them, sure,' she said at length. 'I don't know about me, though.'

'Yeah, well, this was never going to end with a happily-ever-after.'

Know-it-all, thought Cara, pouting.

'What, did you think it would go differently? Did you think that you could shag one guy while deceiving him at the same time about dating his brother? I hate to tell you this, Cara, but there is no way all three of you were going to come through this unscathed. You cannot lie to someone about something so important and get away with it. You, of all people, should understand that. The truth about lying is that someone always gets hurt. In this case, it's you. But don't you think that is better than tearing two brothers apart, especially since you were never really serious about either of them?'

Cara could no longer contain herself. 'But that's the problem, Rachel. I am!'

'You are what?' Rachel looked confused.

Cara snivelled. 'I am serious about one of them.'

'I thought you said you broke up with Yiannis.'

'I did,' she said, exasperated. 'I'm not talking about Yiannis, I'm talking about Nik.'

Comprehension dawned in Rachel's bright blue eyes at last. 'Ah, so *that's* why you were so upset after he came to see you the other day.'

Cara sniffed again and Rachel fished a tissue out of the bag at her feet. 'Here.'

'Thanks,' said Cara, dabbing at her watery eyes and nose. Why did crying have to be so gross? 'You know, for someone smart enough to work in a law firm, you sure can be slow on the uptake.'

'Yeah, well, I've had other things on my mind besides your messed-up love-life,' grumbled Rachel, then, upon seeing the hurt expression on Cara's face, 'Sorry.'

Cara fiddled with the tissue. The breeze stirred and a strand of hair blew across her eyes. She pushed it behind her ear as best she could. Since her haircut it was just too short to stay put. 'I guess I'm sorry, too.'

'What for?'

'I've been totally self-absorbed. I wanted to talk to you about

Jesse this morning, you know, but then I got that phone call and after that it just slipped my mind. I should have paid more attention to you instead of letting my own stuff get in the way yet again.'

'Why did you want to talk about Jesse?'

Had Rachel finally reached a point where she might open up? The breeze gathered strength and the stray lock of hair whipped across Cara's face, stinging her eyeball. She swiped it away and glanced around. A small sandstorm was gathering around their feet, and the sea, which a few minutes before had sparkled invitingly, now splashed angrily. Seagulls circled low over the water just off shore, their cries nearly lost in the wind.

'How about we continue this on the way back to the hotel,' she suggested and Rachel looked only too happy to agree. She folded her towel and pushed it neatly into her beach bag along with her sun hat, which wouldn't last more than a few seconds on her head. They trudged through the soft sand to the road, where a tall hedge offered some protection. It was quieter there and Cara was determined this time not to be distracted from the conversation.

'So, you were going to tell me all about Jesse.'

'Why are you so interested in Jesse? I told you: he's hot, and we had an encounter. End of story.'

Cara glared sideways at her. 'Do I look like I was born yesterday?'

'Okay, yes, I like him. But it can't go anywhere.'

'Why not?'

'It's complicated.'

'Don't give me that.'

'Well it is! We work together.'

'So?'

They reached the gate that led to the back of the Lionheart Hotel and Rachel pushed it open. It creaked on its hinges. 'Someone should oil those,' she said.

'Don't change the subject.' Cara peeked in to survey the pool area before following her across the patio. She had not forgotten that Peter was on the loose, although to her relief he was not hanging out at the Lionheart Hotel's pool bar at that particular moment. 'Tell me, what is so complicated?'

She could see Rachel was wrestling with something so she

waited patiently as they climbed the stairs to the lobby level, rode the elevator to the fourth floor and crossed the hallway to their room in silence. Cara used her key to let them in, closed the door behind her and tossed her beach towel onto the chair. Rachel went over to the windows and stood with her back to the room.

Sitting on the corner of her bed, Cara used her gentlest voice. 'Rachel, talk to me.'

'I don't want to end up like Lady Margaret.'

It took her a moment to figure out who Rachel was talking about. 'The Bat In The Hat, from Cairo?'

What did *she* have to do with anything?

'When you were off buying your necklace in the jewellers, Tilly came over and stood with me for a bit. Lady Muck was giving Ana an earful and Tilly suddenly said to me 'She wasn't always like that, you know', as if she wanted to explain it to someone.'

Cara was intrigued. 'What else did she say?'

'She called her Aunt Margaret and told me that when Tilly was a youngster, she was the most fun and interesting adult that she knew, always glamming up for parties and living life to the max.'

This was so far from the nasty old hag Cara remembered that she could not even picture this.

'What happened?'

'That's what I said, too!' Rachel paused and a shadow passed over her face. 'Tilly didn't tell me the details. All she said was that she let her one great love get away and was never the same after that. For a time, she went on as normal but as the years passed her regrets caught up with her and turned her into the bitter old woman we met on the bus. Of course, those are my words, not hers. She still remembers Margaret as she was, and that is the reason she sticks around.'

Cara nodded slowly. 'Wow.'

'You think you know something, right?'

'Well I can tell you one thing right now. If you ever get like *that*, you can forget about me going on holidays with you.'

Rachel snorted a laugh. 'Thanks, friend.'

Cara chuckled, then frowned. 'I still don't understand – are you worried that Phillip was your one true love, and you'll never be happy again?'

'Phillip?' Rachel's voice hardened. 'No. Phillip was not my one true love.'

'I'm confused.'

Rachel swung around and the light filtering in through the window behind her seemed to shimmer like a halo around her body.

'I told you, it's complicated.'

'Why don't you try me?'

It was as if someone had suddenly sucked all the strength right out of her. Rachel sank down into the chair beside her, not even bothering to move Cara's bundled up towel first. Her face crumpled. 'Oh God, Cara. I can't keep on pretending that Phillip and I were the happy couple anymore. It's all such a mess.'

Cara remained silent while she composed herself.

'When Phillip died we were already on the verge of getting divorced.'

Cara's jaw dropped. 'How did I not know this?'

Rachel slumped in her seat. 'I didn't know how to tell anyone. We had been having problems – big problems – for some time. We got married so young and he was away so much. I missed him, but then I got lonely and bored and eventually the time he *did* spend at home, we did nothing but argue. There was an incident,' her voice dropped so low Cara had to strain to hear her next words. 'I fell pregnant but I had it terminated. It was the hardest decision of my life, but Phillip would not leave the army and I did not want to raise a child on my own. He could not find it in his heart to forgive me.

'We had been separated a few months. I had already filed the papers for divorce when he was killed. We just had not told anyone yet. He didn't want to say anything until he came back from his next deployment.'

Her eyes filled with tears and Cara ached for her.

'But he never did, and what was I supposed to say to everyone then?' She sniffed and looked Cara in the eye. 'So, there you go. Now you know my dirty little secret.'

'My God, you poor thing,' said Cara and her heart ached for her friend. 'You should have told me.'

'I couldn't. Not until now. I felt so guilty and I wasn't sure how you would react.'

'I would react as your friend, like I'm doing now.' She covered the few feet between them in an instant and knelt on the floor beside Rachel, covering her hands with her own. 'You should not have to go through these things alone, Rachel.'

Rachel sniffed, obviously fighting to regain control of her emotions.

Cara waited a few moments before asking, 'So the reason you're holding back with Jesse is guilt?'

'I told you it's complicated,' she muttered.

'Except that it isn't.'

Rachel's eyes narrowed.

'Think about it,' said Cara. 'If Phillip had not died – if you had gone through with the divorce instead – would you be hesitating about Jesse now?'

'Probably not, but that's not the point.'

'What *is* the point?'

'The point is I can't. We work together and – oh hell, I don't know! It still seems too soon to start dating again. I am supposed to be the grieving widow, remember?'

'It sounds to me like you've been listening to your mother too much,' Cara interjected. 'You should know better than that.'

Rachel responded with a wry chuckle. 'You might have a point there.'

'A year is plenty long enough for a respectable mourning period,' pronounced Cara. 'So that cannot be an excuse anymore.'

'Maybe, but I just don't know how to get past this. How can I carry on like nothing happened?'

'You do not have to pretend nothing happened. Something *did* happen. Your husband died. Regardless of how separated you were, that will be part of your history forever. But allowing it to prevent you having a future would just be a tragedy.'

Rachel sat silent for a while and Cara watched her work through her emotions as she thought about it all.

'Do you love him?'

With a shy smile she confessed, 'Jesse? He makes me feel all warm and fuzzy inside.'

Cara chuckled. 'Is that so.'

Rachel emitted a dreamy sigh. 'He's gorgeous, you know, very Italian-looking with his black hair and dark eyes. He has this way of looking at me,' her eyes glazed over for a moment as she drifted off into la-la land. 'But it's more than that – more than the way he turns my legs to jelly and my head to mush. He's smart, and funny. Thoughtful, too. I don't know about love, but I really like him.'

Cara nodded. 'I can see that. And how does he feel about you?'

Rachel paused to contemplate. 'He tried to make plans with me last Friday, but I blew him off and then just disappeared on him. I suppose he wouldn't have gone snooping at my desk to find out where I was if he didn't care. Oh dear. I haven't treated him very well, have I?'

'Yet he is still around,' Cara pointed out gently.

'Well, he *was*. After the way I spoke to him last, he may not be anymore.' Rachel lowered her head, filled with remorse.

'From what you've told me it sounds like you need to give him a little more credit than that. I'm sure it's nothing that can't be fixed with a bit of grovelling and some sexy lingerie.'

Rachel looked at her friend and laughed. 'You know something, Cara? Sometimes you're a real piece of work.'

Cara grinned. 'So you keep telling me.'

'Okay, it's your turn. What about Nik?' Rachel asked with an abrupt change of direction.

Cara's grin faded. 'What about Nik?'

'We've solved my problem, now what about yours? I had no idea you were still into him.'

Cara turned her head and stared out of the window, unable to meet her friend's eyes.

'I'm afraid it might be too late for me and Nik,' she said quietly. 'You were right. There is no way this could have worked out well for us. We lied to Yiannis. This is the consequence. Besides, I was so mean to him the other day. I chased him away. I doubt he'll ever want to talk to me again. It's probably for the best, anyway. I need to learn how to be without a man.'

Rachel leaned forward and rubbed her shoulder in consolation. 'Maybe, but I know it doesn't stop it from hurting.'

Cara simply nodded. Really, what more was there to say?

Chapter 12

Nikolaos Georgiou took a couple of steps into the bar and waited for his eyes to grow accustomed to the gloom. It was hard to forget that the last time he'd been in Hot Shots was the night he had unexpectedly become reacquainted with Cara, after so many years.

The place was quiet now. There were a few tourists scattered about enjoying a relaxing drink, but the rush had not yet started. Later, he knew, it would be packed.

The smell of stale beer and fries reached him, mingled with a trace of cigarette smoke, which he followed to its source. Yiannis sat alone in a booth in the darkest corner of the bar. Nik frowned. His brother only smoked when he was seriously upset.

He clapped his hand on Yiannis's back before flopping down opposite him. 'Hello, little brother. What has you drinking alone on a Friday evening?'

'What, a man cannot have a drink if he wants to?' replied Yiannis.

'Certainly he can.' He pointed at the handful of empty beer bottles on the table. 'But when he drinks alone like that, there is normally a reason for it.'

Yiannis stubbed his cigarette out in a metal ashtray already overflowing and looked around. His eyes settled on the waitress over by the bar. She was shuffling sachets of salt and pepper for the tables, a task that apparently required intense concentration for she kept her head down, studiously oblivious to him. He cursed the poor service and Nik laughed.

'Do not blame the service,' he said. 'You have a face like a thunderstorm. Poor Eleni is afraid to come too close in case she gets rained on.'

'Eleni?'

'The waitress, dumb-ass. She's the one who told our good friend Theofanis to call me.'

'Are you two going out now?'

'Me and Theofanis? No, he is not my type,' Nik grinned.

'Do not be an idiot. You know I meant the waitress, Eleni.'

Nik toyed with an empty beer bottle. The idea was not that far-fetched. She was pretty enough. But a pair of blue-green eyes flashed in his mind and he shook his head. 'No. We are not together.'

'That is not how it looked the other night.'

'The other night it was I who was very drunk, and you know me . . .'

Yiannis's resentment toward the world spilled out in his words. 'Not really, no.'

Nik prodded at him with his foot under the table. 'What is wrong with you?'

'Nothing. I am just saying that if you were home more I would know you better.'

Nik shrugged. 'You may be right. I regret sometimes that my work takes me away so much. Maybe I should have chosen a different life, eh? One that would keep me close to home so that I can keep an eye on my little brother.'

Yiannis eyed him with suspicion. 'You are messing with my head.'

'Maybe a little,' laughed Nik. 'Now, do you want to tell me why you look as if your best friend has stolen your fortune and run off with your daughter?'

'She is leaving,' he said and a morose expression settled on his face.

Nik spread his hands in a gesture of confusion. 'Who is leaving? And where is she going?'

'Cara,' said Yiannis. 'The pretty Irish girl I was with the other night. She is going home tomorrow. I tried to change her mind but she says she does not want to be with me.'

Nik grew very still. 'She broke your heart.' He knew how *that* felt.

Yiannis finally caught Eleni's eye and signalled her to bring him another beer. 'Why do you think I drink all this beer today?'

Nik wanted to hide the relief that flooded him, but all-out sympathy would only seem fake. 'Let me understand: in less than one week you fell in love with this woman?'

'I do not know if I would call it love, exactly.'

'No? What, then?'

Eleni set two beers on the table with a clunk. Yiannis looked away and she gave Nik a sharp look while she gathered up the five empty bottles in front of him. Her message was clear: *No trouble in here.*

He nodded to indicate that it was under control. It was, for now anyway. Yiannis seemed pretty emotional, because as soon as she was gone he burst out, 'She did not even give me a chance!'

'Who, Eleni?'

'Cara, you imbecile! I just wanted someone who was mine, someone to come home to. Bah! She is as bad as Alexia,' he stopped suddenly.

'Who is Alexia?'

'Nobody. Just a girl.'

'Why do I not believe you?'

Yiannis just sat and glowered.

'Yiannis Georgiou, you stubborn ass, what is going on with you?'

Yiannis took a fresh cigarette from the box on the table. It took four matches to get it lit and each time the flame flickered out Nik expected his brother to explode in frustration. Thankfully, he did not and finally the tip glowed with a bright orange coal as he sucked in a deep lungful of smoke, then blew it out in a long stream.

His voice rasped when he finally replied. 'Alexia is a girl I was seeing last year. Sadly for me, it seemed I was more serious about her than she was about me, because she broke it off with me. Last week I heard she is marrying someone else next month.'

'And Cara?' Saying her name to Yiannis was like a knife to the stomach.

Yiannis shrugged and pulled on his cigarette. 'She is a sweet girl, the beautiful Cara, and a lot of fun. I thought that if she stayed a bit longer it would take my mind off Alexia, and maybe if Alexia saw me with a pretty foreign girl she would get jealous,' he took a glum swig of beer. 'Now that I say it out loud I can see how stupid it sounds.'

Nik's temples began to throb. He could hardly believe what he was hearing. 'That is what you are upset about? You wanted to use Cara to try and get this woman Alexia back?'

'Do not be mistaken – I like Cara, although to be honest she is having some issues. Do you know she would not even sleep with me? At least Alexia . . . but why do I tell you all of this? You do not understand!' Yiannis's eyes blazed again. 'You would not know anything about being in love, you with your playboy life of fun and adventure.'

'Yes, of course that is what you believe,' muttered Nik but the fight had gone out of him. This was crazy. Cara had *not* slept with Yiannis? Why had she not denied it the other day? The woman would be the end of him!

He stared at his brother across the table. 'You know what, little brother? You are right. I think we do not know each other at all, you and I. Because I would not have expected this from the Yiannis I know. Perhaps it is time to pull your head out of your arse and grow up a little, eh?'

With a shake of his head he stood to leave.

'That is it? You are going?'

'Enjoy your beers, Yiannis. I hope you find someone to have some fun and adventure with tonight. Maybe they can help you play your childish game.'

He strode to the exit without a backwards glance. Yiannis would be fine and Nik was too perplexed to deal with him right now. After all he had done to spare his brother's feelings, and for what? He pushed open the door and headed for his car. The air was thick with salty moisture from the ocean and daylight had faded to soft pink. But Nikolaos Georgiou hardly even noticed.

He had more important matters on his mind than photogenic sunsets.

Through the windows that overlooked the pool below Cara watched darkness descend and settle in for the night. Soft lighting from the recessed spotlights over the bar reflected in the polished counter at her elbow. A handful of older guests passed by, their spirited conversation echoing amongst the potted palms and pillars in the vast marble expanse of the Lionheart Hotel's ground floor. The two English mothers and their bratty children from the pool had settled in near the television some time ago. They all preferred the comfort of the lounge area rather than the high bar stools on which Cara and Rachel were perched.

The pair had already eaten dinner. Having skipped lunch, Rachel had made sure they were the first to arrive at the dining-room when it opened for supper at seven. Cara was still full from her gourmet lunch and had picked at a plate of salad and a fresh white roll, while her friend dug into a generous serving of pasta.

She wondered what sort of entertainment they might expect that night. Singing? Dancing? Drinking games? Okay, the last was just wishful thinking, much like slipping on her best jeans – the ones with the sparkles on the pockets – just in case Nik turned up. The plain black V-neck tee she wore with them accentuated her curves but there was no need to dress up tonight. Still, she could not resist adding her strappy heels. Staying in was no reason to look like a slob.

Rachel looked great in black jeans and a startling lime green blouse that complimented her tanned skin and bright blue eyes. Despite all the drama, the week away had been good for her and she looked healthy and relaxed.

'Are you sure you're okay with staying in tonight?' Cara asked.

Rachel nodded. 'We have to be up early tomorrow and I still have to finish packing.'

Cara wondered if she, too was feeling a touch of the end-of-holiday deflation. She would be sad to part ways with Rachel again in London, and it hardly seemed wise to stay out late when they were leaving first thing in the morning. 'We sound like a couple of old ladies,' she said. 'Is this what happens when you turn thirty?'

Laughing, Rachel replied, 'In our defence, our expedition to Cairo yesterday was pretty epic and have you forgotten about the night before? I knocked back a good bit of wine while that poor pilot was trying to charm the pants off me in the pub. What was his name, again?'

'Andy. He did pull out all the stops, didn't he?'

'Poor guy. I suppose I should have been more honest with him. I don't know if he would have bothered had he known my affections lay elsewhere.'

By the way her face softened Cara could see she was thinking about seeing Jesse again. Her own heart sank. At least Rachel had something to look forward to when she went home. All Cara could think of was a mundane job, a pile of wedding invitations to cancel and an address book full of people demanding explanations. She groaned.

'You know, Yiannis's suggestion that I stay on in Cyprus is starting to seem like quite a good one.'

'In what way, exactly?'

'Don't panic. I'm not thinking of staying with him. There will be no more of that for a while. But I do need to look for a new place to stay anyway so why not here, instead of Dublin?'

'When you mentioned it a few days ago I thought you were joking. Are you seriously thinking about this?'

Cara swivelled in her seat and picked up her drink. Condensation dribbled down the outside of the glass and into a little puddle on the bar counter. She pushed her little paper umbrella to one side, so it would not poke her in the eye when she took a sip. A moment later, a bitter mouthful of gin zapped her in the back of the throat on its way down. Zoran grinned at her from behind the bar. He must be feeling generous again this evening. Meanwhile, Cara contemplated the question.

Was she serious?

'Maybe I am. I don't know. I just can't think of a single good reason to go back.'

Rachel raised her eyebrows. 'Really?'

'I know I have responsibilities, but I feel like I need a plan and I still don't have one, not really.' She sighed. 'Don't worry, pet. I am not going to run away from things this time. I shall go back and cancel the wedding, clear my stuff out of the apartment, reassure my mother I have not lost my mind – but I'm warning you, if Bridget starts on at me I will not stay quiet. I am done with being bullied and treated like a child. What are you laughing at?'

'Look at you, getting all feisty and fighting with your sister and she's not even here to defend herself.'

Cara released a grudging chuckle. 'I am only saying I will not be pushed around anymore. I need to take control of my life and make my own decisions.'

'Hear, hear,' Rachel raised her glass. 'To strong, independent women.'

Cara clinked the toast while Zoran, who up until now had maintained a discreet distance from them, sidled closer.

She winked at him. 'I don't think we're ready for another round just yet, thanks.'

'That is not why I came over.' Casually wiping a rag over the puddle from Cara's drink, he flicked a surreptitious glance over her shoulder. 'I think you have a visitor.'

Cara turned to look and her stomach lurched. She knew it! 'Rachel, whatever you do, don't leave me.'

'Cara!' Peter barked her name like it was an order.

With his long legs, he covered the distance between them in no time. Anger replaced Cara's unease, bubbling up inside her and erupting in a throaty, 'What!'

Rachel jumped a little and behind the bar, Zoran backed away. The ferocity in her voice surprised even Cara, but she had no intention of letting Peter see that. She swivelled on her stool to face him head-on and he stopped a few feet in front of her.

Just beyond arm's reach, she thought in a private moment of amusement.

He cleared his throat and despite a heavy frown his tone was far more conciliatory when he asked, 'Can we talk?'

'Talk away.'

'Somewhere private?'

'I am quite comfortable here, thank you.'

He looked pointedly at Rachel and Zoran but neither of them moved.

'Cara, I know you're angry with me and I can't say I blame you but we really need to talk. I came all this way to find you. Can you at least hear me out?'

Her heart hammered in her chest and a dull roar throbbed in her ears. She looked at Rachel, whose response was a miniscule shrug. Cara swallowed. What harm could it do to listen?

'Fine, if it will get you out of my hair, then go ahead.'

'Is there a quiet corner somewhere?'

'Right here is just fine.'

When he made to sit on an adjacent bar stool she stopped him, taking perverse pleasure in his discomfort. 'Don't bother, Peter. You won't be staying.'

He threw his hands up in frustration. 'For crying out loud, this is so childish!'

'If you are going to shout at me, then you may as well leave.'

She turned away with her nose in the air, impressed by how calm her voice sounded even though she trembled inside. To steady her nerves, she focussed on the sound of a guitar that someone had started to play over in the lounge area. The evening's entertainment had begun.

'Okay. We'll do it your way.'

She turned back to fix an icy stare on him. 'Alright then. What is it that was so urgent you came all this way to say?'

Later that night Cara and Rachel would agree that he gave a sterling performance on Why They Should Not Break Up, although the beginning was a bit predictable. He loved her, he said, and hadn't they had a wonderful life together so far? They shared a beautiful apartment, friends, a busy social life – hell, even his parents liked her. He went on to tell her he missed her, and that his life was meaningless and their bed so empty at night without her there. That was followed by a less-than-subtle attempt at manipulation: the invitations had already been sent out for the wedding. Had she not been looking forward to it for so long? In a masterful stroke, he drew attention to her age: She was nearly thirty. If she intended to settle down and raise a family she would want to do it soon. How long would it take for her to find a new man? She would have to go through all the hassle of dating and waiting a respectable time to move in together, just to reach the point again that she had already reached with him. Plus, in all seriousness, Peter really was quite a catch. He could buy her anything her heart desired, and was heir to a company that would ensure that Cara and their as-yet unborn children would never have to worry about money a day in their lives.

Finally, he swore upon all that he held holy that he would never cheat again (an interesting choice of words, thought Cara, since Peter had not seen the inside of a church since his Confirmation). Was it really worth throwing away all their years together over one silly mistake? He understood that she was angry, but now that she'd had time to think about things, she surely must agree that it was time she got past all that and came home? He was quite willing to forgive her indiscretion here in Cyprus. After all, was the love they had for each other not strong enough to overcome all of that?

When he reached the end, Cara stared at him. Across the way the guitar fell silent and applause followed.

Peter squirmed as Cara looked him over from head to toe. 'What?'

'I'm just checking to see where you hid your crib notes,' she said. 'Nobody gives a presentation that polished without crib notes.'

Rachel spluttered as she choked on her drink.

Peter's face flushed with anger and disbelief, but he held his tongue.

'No notes? Hm.' She drummed her fingers on the bar counter beside her in slow deliberation. The guitar started playing again. Peter stuffed his hands in the pockets of his expensive tan trousers and waited, showing far more self-control than she expected.

'All right Peter, I heard you out. Now it's my turn. That wonderful life we have? It's yours, not mine. Those are your friends. You chose the apartment and everything in it. Your parents don't like me – they tolerate me because I haven't caused any scandal for the family until now, but you and I both know they look down their noses at me. And do you honestly think that I am stupid enough to believe that the slut I caught you with that day was the first?'

'Cara, I swear—'

'Be careful what you say, Peter. The day may come where you'll be held accountable for what you have said.'

'For heaven's sake, Cara, don't you understand that I love you? And you know you love me too.'

Drawn by the commotion, Sue poked her head around the corner. Her eyes widened as she took in the scene. She opened her mouth to speak but Cara sent her a hard, challenging stare that sent her away without a word.

'You know, you might well believe you do love me, Peter but here's the thing,' Cara stopped, took a sip of her drink and replaced the glass on the bar counter. But she never got to finish her sentence, for at that moment another voice rang out across the lobby.

'Cara!'

She squinted towards it with a sense of déjà vu and her heart stopped. 'Nik?'

When her heart started to beat again it was twice as fast as before. Looking tousled and breathless, wearing faded blue jeans and a black shirt that hung on him in a manner that took her breath away, he spoke as he crossed the floor, the soles of his shoes squeaking with each step. 'Cara, I need to talk to you.'

'Stand in line, pal,' growled Peter and stepped between them. 'Cara, who is this? He is not the playboy I met earlier. '

Nik stepped around him as if he were invisible and placed a hand on Cara's arm. 'You cannot leave without at least saying goodbye.'

Whoever was playing the guitar must have had a sense of the dramatic because he immediately switched to a sweet ballad. Nik's gaze was intense and Cara was drawn into it, mesmerised.

Peter's words sucked her back out, however. 'And here comes Romeo. Perfect.'

Guiltily Cara snatched her arm away. Nik turned to see why and Cara caught the bewildered expression on Yiannis's face as he took in the scene.

You have got to be joking, she thought and there was a moment of pure silence, akin to that which follows a car crash.

Nik broke it. 'Yiannis, what are you doing here? How did you get here – surely you did not drive?'

Yiannis slurred when he spoke. 'Do I look crazy to you? I can hardly walk, let alone drive. No, I took a taxi and followed you.

What are you doing here, Nikolaos?'

As he came abreast of Peter, Cara saw that his eyes were bloodshot and he swayed slightly where he stood. Even from a distance of a few feet she could smell the beer and cigarette smoke that clung to him.

She looked back to Nik. 'Actually, that is a good question. Why *are* you here, Nik?'

Yiannis peered at him. 'Nik?'

'Wait, Nik?' Peter echoed. He frowned, turning to Cara. 'Why does that name sound familiar?' He snapped his fingers. 'I remember now. This is the guy in that photograph I found buried in your bedside drawer. Yeah, that's it. He the one you screwed around Europe during your gap year, right?'

Cara groaned and squeezed her eyes shut. A small gasp escaped Rachel and when she looked up, her friend's eyes leaked sympathy for her.

In the silence that followed the only person to move was Zoran. Unasked, he poured a fresh drink for each of the girls and set them down with a small clunk. Not knowing what else to do Cara sucked a big gulp, wincing as the bitter coldness headed south.

Nik spoke again. 'Yiannis, what are you doing here?'

Yiannis swayed and looked him the eye the way a bull sizes up a matador – a confused bull, mind you, for he still had not quite figured it out. 'We did not finish our conversation earlier so I followed you. Why did you come here?'

'Oh my,' smirked Peter. 'Cara my dear, what have you been up to this week?'

'Shut up, Peter,' snapped Cara.

'Yes, shut up Peterrr,' Yiannis slurred his name. 'Was it not enough that she had you thrown out of the restaurant today? Why are you even here? Do you not realise she is no longer your woman?'

'Nor is she yours, Yiannis,' said Nik, a note of warning in his voice. 'You told me this yourself. That is why you are drunk, little brother, don't you remember?'

Nik had taken up a subtly protective stance in front of Cara during the exchange. Leaning a fraction closer, she murmured, 'Just how drunk is he? Should I be worried?' He gave a subtle shake of his head and despite the explosiveness of the situation Cara felt reassured.

Peter missed nothing. His face displayed a rainbow of emotions starting with jealousy and finally settling on pure spite. 'Brother? Romeo here is your ex's brother? Oh, nicely done, Cara. Bravo.'

After studying him for a moment Yiannis appealed to Cara, his confusion still obvious. 'What is this asshole talking about?'

Peter finally dropped every shred of decorum. His face drew into a nasty sneer. 'Go on Cara, why don't you tell him?'

'Peter, shut up!' Cara and Rachel hissed, in sync.

The sound echoed louder than expected. It seemed even the musician and the guests in the lounge next door had stopped to listen. Silence hung heavily around them and Peter rolled his eyes theatrically and folded his arms. The bastard actually looked like he was enjoying this.

It was then that Cara realised there was only one thing to do. This was not a bad dream from which she could wake at a crucial moment and there could certainly be no more running away. Her only option was to be truthful and hope that the fallout would not leave scars too deep to heal.

But Nik got there first. 'Cara and I knew each other many years ago, Yiannis,' he said. 'It was in Spain when I was just starting out as a journalist. I was there to do a story on the crazy people who run with the bulls. Afterwards, I had some free time and we travelled around Europe together.'

'You and Cara.'

'Yes,' confirmed Cara. 'Rachel was there, too. We took some time off after college to travel.'

Yiannis threw an accusing look at Rachel, who offered an apologetic smile. 'Hey, don't look at me. I'm an innocent bystander in all of this. Like Switzerland, you know?'

Yiannis looked even more puzzled for a moment, then shook his head and turned back to Cara.

Nik stood firm, still half-shielding her with his body. Though not touching, he was close enough for her to sense his warmth and smell his familiar scent. It was silly, she knew, but his protectiveness appealed to some base instinct that filled her heart and she wanted to slap herself for the inappropriate rush of hormones.

Hurt finally replaced confusion on Yiannis's face as he processed Nik's words. 'You and Cara were lovers? You both did not think to tell me this before?'

'I am sorry,' said Cara. 'I would give anything to change this and to save you from being hurt. You have been so good to me this week. But by the time I realised you were Nik's brother it was too late. I got such a shock when I saw him, and then—'

'It is my fault,' said Nik. 'I thought it would be better for you if you did not know. How would you feel if you knew this about your brother and your girlfriend?' He shrugged. 'I did not know what you would do, and I did not want to spoil it for you, so I said nothing.'

'You lied. Both of you, you lied. You are liars.'

That made Peter laugh.

'What is so damn funny?' Cara demanded, furious. 'And what the hell are you still doing here anyway?'

He appeared unfazed. 'Oh, Cara darling, you are what is so damn funny. You were so bloody high-and-mighty when you found out about my little slip-up and yet here you are. Not only have you been two-timing your fiancé but you have also screwed around with Romeo's brother. Nice going!'

He laughed again, a malicious sound that drove Cara into a rage. She jumped off her seat, pushed past Nik and stormed over to him. Yiannis also took a step back but Cara hardly noticed. Her focus was entirely on Peter.

It did not matter that he towered over her in height. She jabbed her finger at his chest as she spoke and with each poke he backed away.

'Don't you dare compare me to yourself! I don't know what I ever saw in you, Peter Reilly. You are self-centred, egotistical and selfish. You care about nothing and no-one other than yourself, and while I may have made a mess of things here this week, I have realised one truth: I don't love you, and it has been a very long time since I did. You have become nothing but a bad habit for me and I deserve better. So take your smug little attitude and your stupid justifications and get out!'

He rolled his eyes. 'Come on Cara, you're just upset.'

'Of course I'm upset,' she cried, throwing her hands in the air. 'But this is not heat-of-the-moment, Peter. I've had two weeks to think about it and I mean it. I don't want to be with you. Not now. Not ever. I don't care about the apartment and the money and the bloody wedding invitations. I do not love you. You are going to have to find a way to deal with that. But for heaven's sake do it somewhere else because I am done talking to you and I'm done listening to you.'

'But Cara—'

'Go!' She roared, vaguely aware that Sue had poked her head out of her office again to watch.

Over in the lounge area the guitar was still silent and the other guests were staring, yet Care cared not one bit.

Peter gaped at her. 'This wasn't how it was supposed to go.'

'Actually, this is exactly how it's supposed to go. In fact . . .' She stepped back and snatched her purse off the bar counter, reached inside with trembling fingers and fished out the diamond ring that had lain there the last two weeks.

'Cara, I'm warning you, do not do something you'll regret.'

'The only thing I regret is that I didn't do this sooner,' she said and shoved the ring at him. His fingers closed around it in reflex.

There was a stunned silence as everyone waited to see what he would do next.

Peter stared first at the ring, then at Cara. His eyes blue eyes hardened. 'I would have given you everything, you know. You have no idea what you're giving up.'

'Oh, but I think I do. I'll be in touch to get my things back when I get back to Dublin.'

Recognizing his dismissal at last Peter took one last look at the small gathering in front of him, turned on his heel and walked out of Cara's life, shaking his head all the way.

Nik, Yiannis, Rachel and Zoran watched him leave. Cara had no need to. Instead, she took a few deep breaths to calm herself. The noise in her head subsided, the trembling stopped and finally the angry fist released its vice grip on her chest. Her knees turned to jelly and she stayed put for fear they would give way at the first step. A few gossipy murmurs sounded from some of the more inquisitive guests in the lounge and she thought she heard one or two quiet claps, which later struck her as extremely funny.

Rachel reached out and touched her lightly on the arm. 'You okay?'

Cara shot her a grateful smile. She would be. Slowly she turned around to face the two handsome Cypriot brothers, who were staring at her with surprised admiration.

'I see you were right. You do not need somebody to take care of you,' said Yiannis. He looked like he was sobering up.

'I'm tougher than I look,' she said. 'Yiannis, I am truly sorry if I hurt you.'

He contemplated this for a few seconds. 'You know what? It is okay.'

'It is?'

He shrugged. 'Think about it. I have only known you for one week and already look at all the things that have happened around you. You are a beautiful woman Cara, but I do not need all this craziness in my life.'

He clapped Nik on the shoulder. 'As for you, my brother, perhaps one day we will know each other better.'

Nik and Cara were both rendered speechless as he raised his hand in farewell and walked away. At the exit, he turned and called out something in Greek.

Nik burst out laughing.

'What did he say?' asked Cara.

Nik shook his head, smiling. 'He said I must not forget about lunch on Sunday at our mother's house. I am to bring the wine.'

Cara threw up her hands. 'Men! I give up.'

An instant later Nik had her wrapped in a tight hug. She smelled his familiar scent and melted into his warmth, her head pressed to his shoulder.

'Men are simple creatures,' he murmured huskily into her hair. 'All we need is the love of a good woman.'

She sighed into his chest and extricated herself from his arms. 'I need to apologise to you too, Nik. I said some pretty mean things to you this week.'

'Cara, it is okay.' He tilted her chin up and met her gaze. 'I understand. I also was shocked to see you again. But it is okay now. We are together again and that is all that matters.'

Cara shook her head. 'Well, no, Nik. That is not really how it is.'

His face crumpled as he realised where this was leading. 'Look me in the eye and tell me you do not still love me at least a little.'

It was impossible to look anywhere else. 'You know I do, but look at me! My life is a mess. I am a wreck. I have no idea who I am anymore.'

'I think you know more than you realise. But never mind, I can help you.'

He pushed her stray auburn lock from her face and his hand came to rest behind her neck. He was standing very, very close.

Cara leaned in and dropped a tender kiss on his cheek before stepping back, out of his embrace. She needed the physical distance to keep her head clear – her knees were only just holding up.

'No. I need to do this alone. Oh man, I sound like one big cliché,' she said with a self-deprecating laugh.

A pained expression crossed Nik's face. 'I only just found you again. All these years nobody else even came close. I know it is strange. After all we were not together very long, but—'

'I know,' she interrupted. 'It is the same for me, but like I said, your timing sucks. I need to work out how to live my life alone, before I can think about sharing it with someone else again. Do you understand?'

'I hate to say it, but yes.' He sighed and put on a brave face. 'So that is it, eh? This is goodbye.'

'I'm afraid so.' Cara's voice dropped to a whisper and her eyes filled with tears.

He planted a lingering kiss on her forehead and squeezed her shoulder.

'Goodbye, Cara. I will see you next time.'

He followed the same path his brother had taken, but with his shoulders slumped and his head down.

'It's not every day you have three men walk away from you in less than an hour,' said Cara, attempting a joke even as she wiped the tears from her face. She dropped back onto the barstool beside Rachel's and her friend patted her on one shaky knee.

'You did good, Cara. I'm proud of you.'

Cara snivelled and nodded. 'I know. And you know something? I will be fine. I really will.' She drained her glass, set it down and cast her eyes up at her other, unexpected ally.

'Keep 'em coming, Zoran. I think this might be a long night.'

The next morning Cara vowed that she would never drink again – or at least not for another week, and definitely not gin and tonic, nor any of the weird blue cocktails Zoran had invented around one o'clock in the morning. But despite her pounding head, fuzzy mouth and near inability to form a coherent thought, she was smiling as she dragged her luggage over to the reception desk.

'Checking out?' Sue asked brightly.

She and Rachel mumbled a yes and Sue busied herself with the process of collecting their key-cards and preparing their final bill.

While Rachel checked it briefly before signing it off, Cara looked around with nostalgia. The bar and lounge were empty and bright sunlight spilled in through the windows so that the lobby, with its shiny marble floors, pillars and plants, resembled something out of ancient Greece. She expected to see Zoran or the little waiter, Stevan, or even the nameless mop lady appear at any moment, but they did not.

'Right, that's all done now,' said Sue.

Rachel nudged her and started to gather her bags. 'Are you ready to go?'

The coach to take them back to the airport waited outside at the kerb.

'Yes,' said Cara with a sigh.

It was a pity, really. She could do with a week's holiday.

The glass door slid open and Rachel stepped outside.

Cara turned back. 'Sue, I almost forgot. Can I leave this with you? My, uh, friend left it behind, but I'm sure he'll be back for it.' She held out Nik's camera.

'Goodness, I almost forgot too! Would that be the same friend who left this for you?' Sue held out a business card with one hand while taking the camera with the other. 'Of course, I'll hold on to this for you, love. You take care now.'

Cara took a few steps and then paused to examine the card.

The watermark on the textured paper was a close-up of a camera lens and on it was printed his name: Nikolaos Georgiou, and below this was an email address and telephone number. She flipped it over and her eyes misted up, for on the back, in bold black handwriting, was written:

Cara,
When you have found yourself, find me.
Nik xx

With a smile in her heart Cara slipped the card into her shoulder bag and stepped out into the sunshine. Now *that* sounded like a plan.

For more about the author go to
www.theresewelch.com